AHGOTTAHANDLEONIT

AHGOTTAHANDLEONIT

DONOVAN MIXON

Cinco Puntos Press
EL PASO, TEXAS

Printed in the U.S.

First Edition
10 9 8 7 6 5 4 3 2 1

Library of Congress Cataloging-in-Publication Data

Names: Mixon, Donovan, author.
Title: Ahgottahandleonit / by Donovan Mixon.
Other titles: I got a handle on it
Description: First edition. | El Paso, TX : Cinco Puntos Press, [2017] | Summary: "Tim's a dyslexic black kid from the streets of Newark. He wants to do what is right, but anger boils deep inside him. Despite everything, Tim wants his life to matter"—Provided by publisher.
Identifiers: LCCN 2016023652| ISBN 978-1-941026-47-2 (paperback) | ISBN 978-1-941026-46-5 (cloth) | ISBN 978-1-941026-48-9 (e-book)
Subjects: | CYAC: Anger—Fiction. | Dyslexia—Fiction. | African Americans—Fiction. | BISAC: JUVENILE FICTION / Boys & Men. | JUVENILE FICTION / Family / Multigenerational. | JUVENILE FICTION / Social Issues / Bullying. | JUVENILE FICTION / Social Issues / Special Needs. Classification: LCC PZ7.1.M634 Ah 2017 | DDC [Fic]—dc23
LC record available at https://lccn.loc.gov/2016023652

Book & cover design by Anne M. Giangiulio

I dedicate this work to my son
Ozan Barrie Mixon

"We are all capable of evil, son. Don't be fooled. All of us! But almost always the opportunity to own up to our mistakes comes around. With your kin especially, you should take advantage when it does, to do and say the right thing, take your part without any double talk. Your family'll forgive you. Because when you forgive a family member, more than with people unrelated, you be forgiving yourself for your own misdeeds."

—Gentrale Thornton

IT WAS A SIGN

It was the next-to-last day of school. From a block away, Tim could see his best friend Les hanging with Lucy and some others. It had become a sort of a ritual—a group of buds would gather for an early morning smoke to catch up on the latest gossip. But he wasn't in the mood, having just remembered that today might be his last chance to catch up with Maria. He slipped under a fence that bordered Branchbrook Park, one of the few green spots left in Newark.

It was remarkable that this place even existed. Only a couple feet in from the sidewalk, Tim forgot the sweat and grime of the street as his body surrendered to the cool and hush of tall oaks, ferns and birches. Birds chattered away and mosquitoes rallied at the scent of fresh human blood—his.

Happy to be alone, Tim felt better as he moved deeper into the woods. He would never admit it, but he loved the scent of the flowers that seemed to be everywhere. The fragrance of wild jasmine kept tickling his nose, mysteriously bringing to mind his ex-girlfriend, Rene.

A strange growth of wild mushrooms jutting from the base of a tree trunk distracted him from the nagging heartbreak of losing her and stopped him in his tracks—he wondered if it would feel as strange as it looked. Squatting, resisting the urge to touch it, he stared at the asymmetrical shape and rubbery appearance but after a couple minutes his attention began to wander. *Too much nature*, he thought, and then something in the bushes moved. He started, loose earth rolled from under his heels to send him flying backwards into the mud. He jumped up and ran towards his usual shortcut, a shallow spot of the stream where it was possible to cross. A few more minutes of roughing it through the brush over the familiar uneven terrain of moist grass and mud patches brought him to a giant fallen tree trunk. It forced him to make his way back up to the paved road.

At the top of the hill, there was a large orange and white construction barrier. A sign read:

DANGER HOT AS HALT

He squatted, catching his breath, and stared at the sign. The first and second words were clear. His heart descended into a familiar despondency as it dawned on him that he was, once again, simply stuck. Shame gave way to anger when the laugh of a crow cut through the whispering trees overhead. Anger gave way to carelessness when he stood up to throw something at the bird. Carelessness must have given way to blindness, for he never saw the patch of black tar at the edge of the new road. His left sneaker found it though.

That's when Maurice Rice caught up with him.

"Yo, look who we got here!" said Maurice, pointing a fat index finger like a gun held sideways. "Tim, right?" He grinned, a gold front tooth reflecting light in all directions.

Tim struggled to free his sneaker from the goop. "Yeah, that's right." He didn't have to turn his head to know who it was, but he did anyway. And yes, it was that fool Maurice with the out-sized tattoos and the huge gold ear stud. Tim had never liked him. The bad dude took a step in.

"Yo man, I heard you be looking for me," the thug said, shooting spit into the air.

Focusing his attention on his sneaker, Tim thought about how he could outrun them if he were to get loose. "Nah man, I-I ain't been lo-looking for nobody. I don't even kn-know you," he said slowly, trying to decide whether to abandon his sneaker or hang in. He was pissed that his stutter was kicking in too.

Tim watched as Maurice took a step back to talk with his boys, to justify what was about to happen. He had on some seriously low-hung jeans—on top, only a leather vest, dark shades, a gold neck chain in the style of a dog collar and several rings. The other three boys wore over-sized white tee-shirts and jeans. One guy, hanging on the side, silently watching, had a single fingerless leather glove on his right hand.

"Ha! You know me all right," Maurice sneered as he took account of Tim's disappearing sneaker and muddy pants. "Yo' sister said"—pausing, smirking—"that you was gonna kick my ass for messin' with her the other day."

Tim's foot was almost completely outside of his shoe as he tried to free himself. He didn't want to use his hands because he would have to bend over and take his eyes off the boy. "Nah, Mau-Maurice. I don't remember saying nothing li-like that to nobod—"

Before he could even finish his sentence, Maurice slapped him hard across the mouth. The metal from his rings drew blood immediately. Tim lost his balance but instead of falling back into the barrier and the tar, he lurched forward like a drunk, straight into Maurice's arms, leaving his shoe behind. The bully pushed him away into the arms of his friends. They caught him, pulled him up straight and held his arms behind his back so that their leader could have his way with him.

And he did.

Tim caught a short, hard jab a hair above his right eye. Maurice grinned and moved in close. Tim brought both feet up and kicked the thug in the forehead. Fear hit him like a brick in the chest when he heard the dude say, "Now Tim, or whatever the fuck your name is, you done really pissed me off!" As if on cue, they dead-dropped him to the ground. Tim rolled over to run, but there was no escape. Surrounded, he heard Maurice yell, "Pick his ass up!" When they reached for him, Tim grabbed the smaller dude by the neck, kicking at the other with his sneaker-less foot. His struggle was useless. Soon enough, he again faced his nemesis, arms held behind his back. Maurice, grinning like a shark, said nothing this time as he punched him once, hard in the gut. Tim gasped and they let him collapse to the ground. Someone kicked him. Someone else mocked him in a whisper. "Hey…psst, taking a nap, Timmy boy?" Eyes still closed, he lay there listening to their laughter as if in a bad dream.

Soon it was quiet again. If you had been the blackbird sitting on a branch of the hundred-year-old oak overhead, you would have seen the gang of four leave a crumpled, dirty heap—in the form of a teenager—on the ground next to a orange and white construction barrier. You would have watched the halo of mosquitoes—levitating an inch above his head—work in shifts. You would have probably contemplated flying down for the bright orange and black ladybug crawling along his pant-leg. To you, the almost skinny kid would appear to be sleeping. You couldn't have known that he was faking it, waiting for his assaulters to get bored and leave. You would have been completely oblivious to the fact that in spite of everything, Tim wondered if, on this next-to-last day of school, he would make it to school on time. He also wondered what his teacher Mr. Jones would say about all of this.

The sudden squeal of the phone in his pocket would have frightened you, sending you away in a flutter of indifference.

MARIA

Miraculously, Tim arrived to first period just one minute after the bell. The teacher took a curious look at him but said nothing. With one more day before summer break, Tim imagined she wasn't up for another confrontation with a student.

It took seven periods of classes for the hurt in his side to become a dull throb—a painful reminder of the ass-kicking Maurice and his boys gave him that morning. Tim sat alone in the back of his eighth-period class trying to ignore people as he had done all day: "Hey…what-up, Tim? What happened, bro? What's that shit on yo' sneaker?" Instead of reading the English evaluation on his desk, he opted to just sit and stare out the window. He knew what it said: he would have to repeat sophomore English if he were unable to pass the last-chance proficiency in September. Everybody warned him, even Mr. Jones, his self-appointed tutor, but he wouldn't listen. He'd been cutting Jones' study hall lately. However, this morning he awakened with a strong feeling to see him and had planned to attend the next period, just to touch base before the term was up. Besides, he thought, Maria would be there. The sly smile that crept across his lips caused him to wince with pain as he watched a wasp dumbly inch its way over the surface of the glass.

Maria was from Guatemala. And though he had no idea where exactly that was, he knew that it was warm. He'd thought many times about going there one day—with her, of course. Curiously it never occurred to him to look up Guatemala on the net. For him, it didn't matter. As long as she was speaking to him, nothing else seemed important. *It's seriously dope, man, the way she says my name—like she puts a bunch of 'e's' in the middle of it…Teeeeiiim.*

The girl was fucking gorgeous, beautiful in a completely different way from his so-called former girlfriend Rene or Boo, his nickname for her. Also the Guatemalan, unlike Rene, was no athlete, but, ohhh, she could really move on the dance floor.

Tim leaned his cheek hard into the palm of his hand and imagined the touch of her hair. While he still loved Rene's short curly cut, the flow and shine of Maria's captivated him as well. He wondered how it would feel to his hands. She had very wide-set eyes similar to his, but her skin, unlike his, had a pecan brown tint to it. He was quite the chocolate boy as Rene used to call him.

Just the thought of Rene made his heart sag heavily in his chest.

Since he'd been cutting study hall, he had been seeing Maria only in passing the last couple weeks. He wondered what her large expressive eyes would say to him next period. At the bell, he skipped over to the stairwell that let out to the parking lot exit for a quick smoke before heading to see Jones. The hard surfaces of the empty stairway sang with a soft echo from his footsteps. Opening the heavy door, he paused—one foot outside, the other inside—fished a butt from his back pocket and smiled at the stark light of summer. The door squeaked softly as he leaned his weight into it.

He thought of the long hazy days to come and how after tomorrow, there would be plenty of time to kick it with Spank and Les. Tim closed his eyes with each pull on the cigarette, enjoying the shade and cool of the corner area.

That morning, he had argued with his uncle Gentrale. In spite of himself, he was impressed at the old man's determination to help him and his sister and his mom. His mom had recently been 'born again.' It made him sigh just thinking about it. He blew air through his lips. *How could she be so sure about what's going to happen when we die? Why is everybody getting so worked up about things, worried about getting an education, passing tests, getting a job and shit, if one day we all will end up hard and brittle like one of those dead street cats? And what's all this positive hopey-dopey shit Jones is always talking about? How can he be so sure that everything will be all right?*

Tim wondered again, as he'd done every day for the past year—if life, school, everything, anything was even worth the trouble.

At the sound of the warning bell, he took a long last drag and looked for Jones' old Ford. It wasn't in its regular space or in anyone else's spot. He must not be here today. *Shit, I might as well go home. The chump probably had to play a gig or something. I'll see him tomorrow.*

A text beeped in from his dad:

> *Sorry son, I can't make it today,*
> *gotta work late.*

Damn! I figured he'd pull some bullshit like this.

The metal door banged shut like a missile silo. Fighting a pain in his hip, Tim ran through the parking lot towards the street.

ON THE HOME FRONT

The six steps from the sidewalk to the front porch of the three-flat where Tim lived felt like a mountain with a handrail. Pausing midway, he leaned onto the metal bar and peered up and down the block. With still plenty of time before sunset, sweaty kids played in the street ignoring the waves of heat rising from the black top. People on the night shift were leaving for work, jaws set with determination. A bus rumbled by, followed by a car with darkened windows and a thousand-watt stereo vomiting the lyrics of the latest slap-a-bitch hit.

As he climbed the stairs, Tim felt nothing of his usual urge to complain about the noise. Or about the fact that the outside door of their apartment opened directly into their tiny living room like a FEMA trailer. Not even the whine and bang of the screen bothered him. He even cracked a smile when Scruffy, their old parrot, jumped in surprise as if it was the first time she'd ever heard the creaky thing. His weary eyes ignored the dirty coffee cups and circular stains that decorated almost every horizontal surface in the room. He almost nodded at the pencils, pens and Post-its that were everywhere–a consequence of his mom's habit of writing to-do lists and then forgetting about them. Tim found himself strangely pleased to see the pictureless walls of the drab room that shunned natural light from the bay windows as if it were a nosey neighbor.

He didn't even have to turn his head to take in the entire room. In his mind's eye, he could see the two upholstered chairs, well past their prime, nursing huge dust balls like fat grey hens. The sofa struggled to hold up Gentrale, who sat too close to the TV because he could barely hear—or see for that matter, his coke-bottle specs being of little use.

Seeing this older and skinnier version of his dad rendered him speechless and reminded him of the pitiful details, the suffocating hopelessness of their situation—his mom and dad had split for good this time. Gentrale watched him as he skulked through the room like a wounded animal, hoping that for once the old codger would let him pass by in peace.

"Damn, boy. What happened to you?" exclaimed the crusty wise-ass, waving a wrinkled hand and holding his nose. "Whew, get your butt in the bathroom, quick! I told you to take a shower this morning. You be funkier than a James Brown record! Julia! Hey, Julia! Get in here, somethin' done happened to Tim."

Tim picked up his pace through the room but was again unable to resist a smile, breaking open a fresh seal of dried blood on his lower lip. He had to get away from the old man. If his uncle got a good look at him, he would surely guess all that had happened, all that he wasn't ready to talk about.

Finally alone in the bathroom, the crescendo of his mother's footsteps running up to the door told him that peace was not his just yet. The pounding began.

"Tim, Tim! Are you okay? Open this door. Now!" she screamed, slapping the thin wood with her palm.

Instead, Tim opened the spigot. "I'm okay, Mom. I'll be out after my shower," he said as casually as he could. Even with the water running, he could follow the conversation on the other side of the door.

"JULIA, DID YOU SEE HIM? WHAT HAPPENED?" yelled Gentrale. His voice sounded alarmed, but Tim knew that he wasn't, not really. From the sound of her voice, Tim could tell that his mom had turned towards the front room and imagined her hands resting on her hips. "Turn that darn TV down, Gentrale! And you in there,"— slapping the door again—"open up this minute. You hear me, boy?"

A burn just over his eye, the spot that collided with Maurice's fist, told him there was some skin missing. Staring blankly at the toothpaste on the sink, he remembered when the thug cocked his arm and how he'd moved his head just in time, making it only a glancing blow. In the foggy mirror, he looked exactly how he felt—like shit. He wanted to be hugged by his mom more than he could admit, but a simple embrace was not waiting for him on the other side of that door. If she saw him like this, he would have to listen to her fuss for hours.

He pulled aside the shower curtain, stepped into the tub, torn basketball jersey, saggy-baggy jeans, sneakers and all.

Ten minutes later it was his sister Sheila yelling outside the door, shaking the knob. "Tim! Do you know how long I've been waiting for you to come out of there? Open this door! Now! I have to go bad!"

"Shh! Ok, just keep your yo-your voice down. I don't fe-feel like dealing with Mom right now," he whispered through the plywood.

"Well, open up and let me in—please!" she whined through the small opening.

Tim popped through the door like a cuckoo from its clock to find himself nose to nose with his sister—something hit the floor with a thud and a fizz. He leaned in even closer and screamed at her as softly as he could, "Besides, you got some serious explaining to do!"

"Wha? Watch what you're doing, boy! Now I have to get me another soda. And you are going to clean up this mess," she exclaimed, left hand resting on her hip. "And, what are you talking about? Humph. Looks like you got yourself beat up." Tim squeezed the bath towel in his hand and wondered if it were literally possible to wipe the smirk off her face with it.

"Me? I did wha—? No, it was you and your big mou—"

"—Talk to the hand, man," she cut in, elbowing him aside with a meaty limb, pointing towards the floor with the other. "And you better clean up that soda," she said and slammed the door behind her.

Tim moved close to the doorjamb and pushed the words from his lips as if they could pry their way through the narrow space. "Fat cow!"

Tim's body sank heavily into his mattress. Staring at the ceiling, he breathed deeply, feeling the events of the day weigh upon him. Through the window, he watched a fine drizzle hit the side of the building next door. He hated rain. But at that moment, as he pondered his sneaker covered in black tar, rain was exactly what he needed. The shoe lay next to the bureau on top of which sat the old Nikomat SLR his dad gave him when he was in fifth grade. He sighed hard at the thought of his dad being interested in something other than the bottle. Mostly, he remembered his laugh and how his dad's voice went up and down as he explained the functions of the camera and how he'd guided his hands along the sliding rings on the lens. In spite of its bulk and weight, Tim loved the machine quality of it. All manual, it took great shots if you set the shutter speed, ASA, F-stop and focus right. It wasn't long before finding film for the thing became near impossible.

Next to the SLR sat a Barringer High School mug full of pens and markers. In the middle towering above them all, stood Mr. Jones' old baton. Once, at the end of a reading session, Tim picked it up and waved his hands in the air, doing what he thought was a good impersonation of his teacher. The way they both laughed told him that his teacher must have recognized himself.

Do you want it?
What? This stick? What's the cork for anyway?
It's a baton, Tim. The cork is there to provide grip. Sometimes a conductor has to hold onto it for quite a long time during a performance. They use it to keep the musicians together. You can have it if you like. I recently bought a new one anyway.

On the floor, next to the tarred sneaker, sat his baseball mitt. Tim couldn't have been more than seven-eight years old when his dad bought it for him. Both his mom and dad got a big kick out of watching him try to use the over-sized outfielder's glove that fell off with every movement. Tim loved baseball. But it had been years since his last game—the final game of his junior high team. They'd ranked number four in the city.

Groaning wearily, Tim rolled over onto his stomach. His entire body ached, especially his legs. Maurice and his friends had kicked him a couple times before losing interest. Thinking how he'd gotten himself into such a mess, it occurred to him this reading thing had become a real problem. *If I hadn't been so busy—like a dummy stuck on that stupid sign, whatever it said—Maurice wouldn't have caught up with my ass.*

How he would pass the proficiency in September, Tim didn't know, but he had to figure this thing out. As he thought about it, he began to riff on an idea in his head.

I'm staring at a sign I should have taken as a sign, to get on
with my life before I really fall on my behind. Not
sure of what I'm seeing
I take a guess at its meaning, I mean
what can it be saying so important now I'm laying in a
pool of my own blood this ain't the way things should be playing.

Danger is the first thing I see on that stupid notice.
From the look on my face you'd think it was a note from POTUS.
Easy work for Maurice am I—and his two homeboys.
In the end I had to choose to leave my shoe or face that fool.

What's the word?
To know the word.
Yeah, I took a chance,
On ignorance.

When they grab me from the rear I can't think
I'm so blind,
The rage in me breaks open like a
cheap bottle of wine.
My nemesis calls out my sis before he tried to break my face it
must have been a stroke of luck just
in time I move out the way.
I'm losing chances, I need answers

It's not a rehearsal nor controversial.
I'm getting hung up on *such*—a simple phrase
like a bat in a tree, I look but can't even see.
In a daze I write it down for all to see not sympathy my sister's
face was full of glee my mom looks
like she has to pee.

It's yo fault—*Ass_halt*
    What's the word?
It's yo fault—*Ass_halt*
    To know the word,
It's yo fault—*Ass_halt*
    Yeah, I took a chance
It's yo fault—*Ass_halt*
    On ig-no-rance.
It's yo fault—*Ass_halt*
    What's the word?
It's yo fault—*Ass_halt*
    To know the word.
It's yo fault—*Ass_halt*
    If I can't read?
It's yo fault—*Ass_halt*
    Yeah—it's on me.

Eventually his thoughts gave way to a dreamless sleep, so deep that
his mother's voice, when she called him to dinner, seemed to come from
miles away. A full meal waited for him in the kitchen: stewed oxtails,
string beans, baked macaroni and cheese, beets, cornbread and iced tea.

DANGER, HOT...

Sheila didn't say anything at the sight of the nasty scar over her brother's eye. Yes, he had gotten the stuffing kicked out of him. Even though she wondered what had happened this time, she didn't say anything as he slipped silently into his chair. Mom was in the middle of saying grace.

By contrast, Uncle Gentrale felt no such mercy for Tim. When Mom was done, he quipped, "I bet Funk-Bones is hungry!" His blue and yellow bowtie matched the grin on his face.

Unable to resist, Sheila let go on him too. "Aahh, Funk-Bones!" she screamed, spewing bits of cornbread into the air, double chin and belly shaking in opposite directions. "You'll never live that one down!" she cried, then immediately felt sorry for saying it.

"That's ahrite, Uncle Gentrale. Cold-blooded, but ahrite," Tim said into his plate.

"ALL right!" Mom chided quickly, correcting Tim.

Yeah, Sheila thought, *he's hiding something.* But even with his cut-up face and mouth already down to business, it impressed her that he'd managed to laugh it off so easily. Something inside of her hoped that they would give him a break. Whatever it was would eventually come out. But her mom looked real tired. Those double shifts were taking a toll on her.

"Now, Tim, tell me. What happened to you? Lord, this place is getting too wild for me." She raised her right hand up as if giving testimony.

"And dangerous too," Gentrale grunted, gnawing on a chicken wing.

Watching him chew, Julia nodded and said through a sigh, "Maybe

I *should* take that job in Chicago like my brother said and get us out of here once and for all."

Sheila didn't like the way things were going. "Mom, what about our friends? And Daddy? Are we going to just *leave* him here?" She really dialed up the whine in her voice for that last part. It must have done the trick. Julia cleared her throat, sat back in her chair and took a swig of her tea. "I suppose that now is not the time for such a conversation. Eh-hem, Tim! Did you get into a fight? Your face looks like it has been bleeding."

Sheila could see that the concern in their mom's voice pained her brother. She hoped that he would be able to take his time, perhaps start from the beginning, spill his guts and tell them everything, as he saw fit. Then they could all say to him that it would be okay and that would be that. So he got in a fight? Boys, silly as they often are, do that kind of thing. Don't they? She imagined him trying to figure out how to tell it without getting preached to by her mom and uncle. Which was practically impossible. He probably was worried about what she would say too. But she couldn't—not after their uncle's wisecrack—say anything now. She could only wait.

Finally, Tim spoke. "It happened at the park," he said dryly. He watched them as they took in his words. Sheila could feel the shadow of a smirk on her face, but there was nothing she could do to get rid of it—nothing apart from leaving the table, and it was way too late for that. She could see that the smirk had already deeply pissed him off.

"So, what were you doing at the park anyway?" asked his mom carefully.

Sheila picked up a chicken leg with both hands and held it in front of her face hoping to disguise her anticipation. When she looked at her uncle, he appeared almost disinterested, chewing and staring dumbly at the calendar on the opposite wall like an old bull. Their mom's left eyebrow seemed to curl into a question mark.

"On the way to school, I-I was thinking about going over to Dad's house afterwards. But at the last minute, he couldn't make it," Tim said with a shaky voice. Sheila watched him bite his lip. He knew it sounded like a lie. As Julia listened, her fork made tiny circular movements in the middle of her macaroni.

Gentrale took a loud swig of his iced tea. "Humph, wonder what he's up to these days?" he grunted, sucking on a bone.

"Try not to be so surly, Gentrale. He is your brother!" snapped Julia.

"Ain't nothing sadder than an old fool and he ain't nothing to me but an old…"

"Gentrale! Not here, not now. You hear me?" Julia cut him off sharply.

Sheila thought it a good chance to get into the action. "So, you talked to Daddy? How is he?"

"He-he's holding up okay. I think he's missing us and is very sad. Don't you miss him, Mom?" he asked, turning to face her. Julia pursed her lips. They all could see that she didn't like the question.

"S-so, you didn't go to your father's place. But, sweetheart, what does that have to do with the park? What happened?"

Sheila watched her mom's hands ball up a napkin, a sign that she was getting nervous. "Ma! Just let him tell it. Okay?"

Gentrale chuckled into his macaroni.

Tim blew air loudly through his lips. "Forget that, Sheila! This morning I-I just didn't feel like hanging with Les and them, you know? So I-I decided to cu-cut through the pa-park. That's where I ran into Mau-Maurice Rice."

Sheila placed her hands over her mouth. She tried to be calm but her voice came out in a high falsetto anyway, "Oh no you didn't! Now, come again? What were you doing over there?"

"And?" his mom demanded, standing up. Her question mark had now formed its dot.

Tim released a long sigh and hung his head. "Well, Maurice and his friends sort of ca-caught up with me at some kind of road construction si-sign," he mumbled.

"Speak up, boy!" his uncle insisted, reaching for more iced tea.

"What were you doing?" Julia asked. There was a noticeable shake in her hands.

"I-I was reading," he blurted out. Sweat poured out of his forehead.

"Reading? Ha!" Sheila snapped, rolling her eyes in disbelief.

"Yeah, I was reading this s-sign when my sneaker got st-stuck in that st-sticky black stuff they use f-for the road."

"You were stuck in tar?" asked Gentrale, food particles flying from his lips.

Tim paused but didn't look at his uncle. "That's when I felt Maurice's hand on my sh-shoulder."

Sheila started to say something but her mother beat her to it, sitting down and touching his arm. "Uh, Timmy baby. What were you, um, reading on a sign so intensely that you couldn't notice tar on the road—or Maurice Rice for that matter?"

"Let him tell us, Mom. Don't push him. There's no rush," Sheila said gently.

Tim snatched a piece of paper and pencil from the wall holder. "The s-sign said…" He wrote as he spoke. "Danger, Hot As halt." Finished, he sat back and exhaled loudly, obviously relieved to put the pen down. As everyone moved in to see what was on the paper, he spoke again. "I thought it was strange—I mean, I get *Danger* and *Hot*, but, but what about *As*? N-not trying to be fu-funny, Mom, but I thought may-maybe another 's' was mi-missing?"

Sheila yelped liked a Chihuahua, covered her mouth and jumped in her chair as if she was about to explode—wide-eyed, breathless, she sat with the demeanor of someone watching a train wreck with shameful pleasure. Her mother frowned while Gentrale had completely stopped chewing to focus his camel eyes on his nephew.

"Excuse me, Mom, but what would something like that be doing on a s-sign in the pa-park that wasn't some kind of gra-graffetti?"

"*Graffiti*, lead-head!" lashed out Sheila giddily.

"Graffiti! Then I saw *Halt* at the end and fi-figured that there must've been s-some good reason to not go any further."

For the second time, food shot from her uncle's lips. "Hell, if I saw a sign that said, 'Danger Hot-Ass,' I'd stop too!"

Gentrale jerked so hard his knees hit the underside of the table, sending glasses and silverware crashing to the floor. Tim and Sheila giggled and wriggled like cartoon characters—not so much at what Gentrale had said however, but at their mom's expression. Her mouth had stretched wide open in a mask of surprise and shock as she repeated over and over, "I don't believe you said that, Gentrale, I don't believe you said that!"

Things began to calm down as the elder's apologies took hold. "I'm sorry, Julia. I didn't mean anything, darlin'."

As everyone caught their breath and began to pick up the mess, Gentrale's expression suddenly became serious. Sheila knew it didn't sit well with her uncle that they were laughing both at his crack and at *him*. Sure that the old guy couldn't leave well enough alone, she decided to simply wait him out. She didn't have to wait long. With a sound of desperation, Gentrale pleaded with her mom, "It-it just slipped out, Julia!"

Sheila and Tim looked at each other and screamed in perfect unison, "It sounds like he farted or something!"

VOW OF VENGEANCE

Later that night in her room, Sheila lay across the bed as snatches of the scene at the dinner table played over in her mind: Tim actually writing out AS_HALT for them, Uncle Gentrale's lewd wisecrack, her mom's 'frozen scream' face. Finally she could do nothing other than roll over and laugh out loud at the memories. She tossed her *near-antique* doll, as she liked to call it, in the corner—suddenly feeling she'd outgrown such things. After all, she'd had it since fifth grade—five years ago! It was time to move on to other things, like boys and seriously losing some weight. Recently, she'd been dieting and was excited about it: drinking only sugarless sodas, opting for salad instead of fries at the local burger joint. She was feeling pretty good about her progress even if, at this point, her loss could only be measured in ounces. No one had said anything yet and of course her *asphalt* brother (ha!) wouldn't say anything unless he could turn it into some kind of wisecrack.

It was time to try on a pair of old jeans. She jumped off the bed. A loud cracking sound shot from the underside of the frame. For a moment, the thought of breaking yet another slat threatened her resolve. Shrugging it off, she caught her reflection in the mirror on the way to the closet and smiled at the beauty of her wide-set eyes, full lips, flawless brown skin and somewhat kinky hair, as she liked to say (yes, she had her sayings). After performing a couple of sexy dance moves from a music video, she shimmied over to the wardrobe and snatched up the jeans. Slinging them over her shoulder, she sashayed back to the mirror all the while, half singing, half rapping, "Oh yeah—just-a give it to me…Oh yeah—you wanna move it to me…"

Wriggling out of her pajama bottoms in perfect sync, she kicked them onto the wicker rocking chair in the corner. "Oh yeah—just-a give it to me…Oh yeah—you wanna move it to me…go girl, go girl"—a true neck-snaking, hip-rolling, corporeal if not roly-poly oneness of independence and unity—"Uh huh—uh huh."

Draping the jeans around the back of her neck, holding the ends with each hand in the front of her like a towel, she moonwalked back and forth across the room. Completely committed to the groove now, she lowered the pants into position and—exactly on the second beat— pushed a turkey thigh down one leg.

Resistance was total. The pant leg refused entry like a body rejects an organ of another blood type. In the process, Sheila sprained her little toe just before crashing into the floor lamp. Mid-flight, she tried to catch herself on the bureau, but she only managed to grab hold of the doily that was under her collection of costume jewelry. The ornaments flew in every direction like a mini Big Bang effect.

There was a knock at the door. Her mom. Sheila covered her eyes with her right hand as if to render herself invisible in case Julia entered the room. If Julia opened the door, she would've seen her daughter on the floor, on her back, with her right foot up on the bed, a necklace somehow lassoed around her big toe and her left arm leaning against the bottom half of the bureau, still holding onto the doily. But Julia didn't come in. Instead she went back to bed and Sheila stayed on the floor a long time, thinking about her brother.

If that stupid Maurice and his friends hadn't been teasing me so much, all of this wouldn't have happened. I had only said that my brother would get them for messing with me. I only wanted them to leave me alone. I didn't want Timmy to get beat-up. Darryl better not have been there! No…I can't believe that! He knows Tim! I can't believe it. I mean…he was trying to talk to me the other day at my locker until Maurice showed up. Silly boy! I bet he's embarrassed to be seen with a fat girl. Oh well…but he really is cute and smart…and with that curly hair hmm…How can he be friends with that silly boy Maurice? Well, if he can't like me for who I am, then who needs him? Oh, I wish that I wasn't like this. Tomorrow, I'm going to start

*working out, like the gym teacher said. But even my silly brother teases me!
Yeah right, 'Mr. Asphalt,' ha! That was just—just pitiful at dinner. He was
so hurt sitting there at the table. I'm not going to tease him anymore about it.
I've got to figure out how to help him with this reading thing.*

Tim lay face up on the rug in his bedroom. He'd collapsed into a sweaty
lump after only twenty pushups and thought, *Ugh—last day of school
tomorrow…finally!* Through the Venetian blinds, rays from the street
lamp outside of his window stabbed him in the eyes and made his
head pound with pain. With a groan he pulled a comic book over his
face and thought of his mother's eyes at dinner and how his sister had
pounced on him with the sympathy of an alley cat on a can of tuna fish.

*It's asphalt, SILLY BOY. Tim, when are you actually going to learn
to read? You know that the proficiencies happen the first week of school and
you've got to pass or be held back—AGAIN!*

He saw the disappointment on his mother's face and how she tried
to cover it up by shushing his sister. Uncle Gentrale had attempted to
soften the blow of his sister's words by cracking another tired joke, but
it fell flat. "Ugh…Unk. Sometimes you don't know when to shut the
fuck up," he mumbled, climbing into bed.

Tim woke up, bound in his sheets like a mummy. He lay still and
listened to the quiet. He played a game with the tick of the clock:
five to inhale, five to exhale. A sudden rustling in the trees next to
the window sent him back to the park, back to that kick to Maurice's
forehead, back to the truth…that it was a fluke, an accident, that he
really hadn't tried very hard to defend himself. The sneaker business
was a pretext, a cover for his fear. Was it because Maurice was older?
He didn't know. Then he saw it: the face of Maurice on the body of
his father, dressed in his bus driver uniform. But instead of the sad
expression that his dad usually pulled off when he had thrashed him
as a kid, this *Mau-Dad* was gloating as he tried his best to draw blood,
demanding respect with every blow. Shivering now, Tim rocked his
body side to side, but he wasn't cold…it was rage that shook him.

Motionless again, a single thought loomed into his consciousness as a dark cadence fell upon his lips.

"I'm-gonna-get-that-motherfucker, I'm-gonna-get-that-motherfucker, I'm-gonna-get that—"

FUNKIER THAN A JAMES BROWN RECORD

Like a mountain,
with a handrail.
An-a-logue
For an epic fail.

Six steps up to my door
    Just six steps to my door
Very fitting, for this
Dystopian-fairytale.

Now I'm staring in the mirror
Looking at a broken boy,
Who a Dog and his friends
    Used as a soccer toy.

Uncle Gentrale sits there sporting a big crazy grin.
    It's not compassion—he wants to get his licks in.
        So he waits.

I just want to get by him, but my legs won't let me go
So I limp on like a wounded animal across the floor.
Don't know what inspired it, I don't even give a shit
Probably the look on my face would give Lil Wayne a fit.

My mom is banging on the door—I have nothing to say
    Where would I start?
    She won't believe me anyway.
        My sister be looking at me like I'm *cray-cray*

Speaking of my sister with her big-ol-big-ol mouth
She's the major reason for things—goin' south.
She looks at me with pity in her eyes
    What were you thinking fucking with Maurice and his guys?

The twinkle in his eye
told me the moment had arrived,
Gentrale couldn't sit there
Not for a minute five
Not for a minute more.
Staying silent, he could not abide—
     So he let it fly…

Boy, you be funkier than a James Brown record!

BRINGS THE WORD WITH HIM

Early the next morning, Tim sat alone on the steps of the school.

The light had shifted and the building, scrubbed clean of graffiti, was different—as if it couldn't wait for the summer to wipe away signs of the school year. It was going to be a hot one—a breeze carrying the scent of lilacs his way held the first hint of humidity. But the beginning of summer made him think of the fall when he would have to pass the English proficiency or else. He scoffed at the thought of his teacher Jones who seemed so interested in him. Could it be the guy really thought he was dumb or something? *Nah.* The dude liked his raps and always said that he had a talent with words. But then a part of Tim didn't care what the hell Jones or anybody else thought. Leaning back onto the concrete steps, he was grateful for the time that remained before the doors opened. He had other things on his mind and needed some quiet time anyway.

The peace didn't last long. The sound of a bouncing ball made him look up. One of the twins approached in a zig-zagged line, weaving through whatever objects or debris lay in his path.

Tim stood up to check out the moves but couldn't tell which of the twins it was. He took a guess.

"What up, Squid?"

"I'm Lucy, fool. Ha! You still can't tell the difference between us? Yo, gimme some," she said holding out a fist. "Considering yesterday, it's pretty early for you. What up with that?"

Tim had to laugh at that one. "Speak for yourself, *girl*. Anyway I was just thinking about the break and whatnot. Like, what y'all planning to do this summer?"

Lucy smiled, passed the ball between her legs and came up with it spinning on an index finger. "Not too much. Mostly just hangin' out around here. You?"

"Well, after I finish up with summer school, we're talking about spending some time up at our summer house," he said with a chuckle.

Lucy sighed with what she thought an air of affluence. "Yeah, I feel you, brother, do some water skiin' on the lake. Catch some rays. *Yeah, right!*" Then she shook her head as if she'd just heard what Tim said. "Shit! You going to summer school—for real? For what?"

"English mainly," he said, avoiding her gaze.

Lucy jumped up on the stairs and crouched to take a closer look at him. "English? Shit, Tim. You the man who *brings* the word with him!"

"Maybe…I-I don't know, but you *gotta do the time* if you don't wanna *pay the fine*…so to speak, yo!" he said, standing up.

Lucy stood as well, turned around and grinned big. "Oh-oh-oh, look who else is here early on the last day of school! What up, Les? Hey, Spank-a-Lank. What y'all doin' this summer? Les, you'll be working out as usual, I guess?"

"Hey," Les said, doling out hugs to all. "*Word*—I'll be working it hard this season. I wanna be in shape for the boxing team in the fall. You still pumping, Spank?"

Spank appeared to be in a dream world of his own. "I hear *that*… huh? Who *me*? *Workin' out*? Damn, Les! You know I quit a long time ago. I got other—"

Les took the words out of Tim's mouth. "Yeah, like, other what? Other *porn* to check out?"

Spank doubled over laughing. "Awwww man! That was cold! Haaa. And ya'll can stop laughin' now, cause that shit ain't funny…yo! Tim, talk to your boy."

Les' smile disappeared. "Hey, I ain't nobody's…"

Lucy cut in, "Hey y'all, Tim's goin' to summer school. For English! Can you believe that shit?"

Les took off his baseball cap and slapped Tim on the top of the head with it. "I told you, *told* you, man—don't fuck around—that dude would fail your ass," he chided.

"I don't believe it," Spank said. "The way you can work with the word?" Spank looked at the group. They all nodded in the affirmative.

"Come on, Tim," Spank said. "I know you got a new one for us. Here's a beat—uh, uh…"

"Nah, man, I'm not feeling it, yo!" Tim said, sitting down again on the steps.

"Don't be holdin' out, boy. Give it up," Les said, hitting him again with his cap.

Tim gave him a look that said *cut it out*. "Alright-alright. This here is something I been thinking about lately. It's not finished. I'll do it but then I have to go. Little slower with that beat, Spank-a-Lank yeah… yeah, yeah, that's cool, just like that, keep it going."

Life is nothin' if not a dance
    Unpredictability at every chance.
At every turn, wiggle glide or jig,
    duck–dip–drop-or bop.
Before the first leap lunge bow or stoop,
    bend bound bob or swoop.
After any slide slither jump
    or jounce,
While thinkin' about the odd swoop skate
    or pounce.
So, you don't know what will happen next?
    Keep on dancing', kid.
After all, you never did!

Just as he gave the last line, the school doors clicked open and Tim ran into the building leaving his homies chanting in his wake, *Keep on dancin', kid. After all, you never did*. As he turned the corner someone yelled out, "Aw man…I think right about now, Tim is thinking about some *horizontal* dancin'."

The crowds in the halls made him late. Before he could enter the cafeteria, Rene pushed into the hallway through the swinging doors. Large earrings dominated her petite features and short haircut. Watching her walk away, he heard his own voice come out in a squeak. "I'm sorry, Rene. Boo. I-I was locked out."

She didn't turn around, just spoke over her shoulder, "Tim, you'll never grow up. I don't know why I even agreed to meet with you."

In spite of the warning bell, students moved slowly through the halls, taking every opportunity to pull pranks on one another, scream insults, tell jokes—anything to hold off the beginning of the day. A couple goofy gangbangers snickered loudly as Tim passed by. The word had gotten around. Everybody knew what had happened in the park with Maurice.

It wasn't going to be a good day.

THIS IS THE TIME FOR US

It's unkind
How fate strings our lives
without our say.

Brings to mind,
I may lose your love this way.

But I'm not the kind,
To let the chips fall,
As they may.
I believe,
I'll get you back someday.

You don't have to take me back just now,
Just open up your heart, somehow.

I know it's been
A very long time, since
I met you.

Have you forgot,
the feeling we shared that day?

I know you think that
I'm just a
Cray-crazy boy.

Who will never grow up,
and forget about his toys.

You don't have to take me back just now,
Just open up your heart, somehow.
This is the,
time for us.

This ain't no sappy bullshit deal.
Yo baby, you know what we had

is real.
You're one of the few
I can trust.
I'm not giving up on us.
Yeah. This is the time for both of us —
The time for us.

I've gone around, with
this love so long,
so embarrassing…so strong.
I'm watching you walk away. Is it
forever, or just for today?
Listen to your heart, yeah
I know, you done yo part. But
somewhere inside,
you've got to feel, that we'll get together
again.
For real.

You don't have to fall in love just now,
Just open up your heart, somehow.

This is the,
Time for us.
This ain't no sappy bullshit deal.
Yo baby, you know what we had,
is real.
You're one of the few
I can trust.
I'm not giving up on us.
Yeah. This is the time for both of us —
The time for us.

THE LAST STRAW

Mr. Jones stood in the corridor in front of his 2:30 study hall. He had time to notice again how the blue-white rays of the fluorescent lighting bouncing off dull beige surfaces gave the students a jaundiced hue, kind of like in an insane asylum. It was the final period of the last day of the term and, for the most part, the expressions on the faces of his colleagues could be described as a mixture of exhaustion and anticipation. On the other hand, there was an intense energy among the students as they walked, ran and skipped through the noisy corridor—yelling, laughing and even singing at the top of their lungs.

But youthful frenetic energy hadn't been the only indication of finality in the air.

That morning before his first duty of the day, he took a circuitous route through the building and saw that in the art wing, drawings and paintings had been taken down. All paints, brushes and easels had been stowed out of sight—perhaps smug and satisfied to have weathered the year well enough to be considered still useful. In the shop wing, not a speck of sawdust or shavings of any kind were visible on the well-swept floors. Foreign language texts, sorted, wiped, neatly stacked upon strong shelves, missing the caresses of their former owners, stared out longingly from behind glass doors, listening and translating for each other. While the math books, having never enjoyed such intimacy with humans, waited patiently in their storage places, calculating their next move. Passing the science labs, except for the odd shared vibration, a conspicuous silence enveloped the large collection of test tubes and vials while the Bunsen burner sat patiently in its designated station, ready for action. Only the computer stations on the far side of the room could match its level of dogged stoicism—except for laptop number five, that had been mistakenly left on, its LED flickering like a dying flame.

With all windows closed and secured, the air in the gymnasium sat like a big funky sponge. Forlorn lockers seemed to hold their breath as they stood erect, shoulder-to-shoulder in silence. Outside on the basketball courts, a residue of energy emanated from the backboards, giving testimony to the countless three-pointers and spectacular lay-ups executed over the school year.

It was the final period of the last day of the term.

Jones barely heard the familiar petulant whine of Maria, the current object of Tim's adoration. And of course he knew Tim, his daily headache on two legs, had most probably been the source of her distress. "Leave her alone!" he grunted with unconvincing authority, dragging his bulky frame into the room. Feeling the effects of the previous night's gig, he had hoped for a few quiet minutes during this last period of the day.

A tall man, Jones always felt uncomfortable at his desk. It was one of those old metal constructed relics from the eighties with plastic wood-grain laminate on top. His knees couldn't slide under it so he could never sit properly upright. He had to lean at a forty-five degree angle just to rest his elbows.

He was thinking about Tim. His heart sank at the thought that the boy had probably taken the proverbial 'wrong turn' in life in spite of the fact that he had talent and plenty of help from various teachers and counselors. His parents were a mystery. Jones could never get him to say much about either his mom or dad. He had his theories, however, and they weren't good.

His weekly sessions with the seventeen-year-old sophomore had begun after the Christmas break but the boy stopped showing up weeks ago. It was clear to Jones that Tim was very intelligent and perfectly able to improve his reading. He guessed that peer pressure was getting in the way.

Maybe a classmate had heard about Jones' tutoring sessions and

Tim was embarrassed to continue, afraid to give the impression that he cared about his education. During his own high school days, Jones remembered there existed a perverted meme that you were *acting white* if you were seen as concerned with your studies. Even though his own parents insisted that studying was his only out from the ghetto, he had worked hard to maintain a certain kind of conformity with the cool dudes at the school. Not to be seen carrying too many books around was as important as having the right haircut or latest sneakers.

Maybe Tim wanted to reserve a psychological out for himself in case he failed the reading proficiency again—the out being that he hadn't really tried. Jones' own parents were not formally educated people. They had absolutely no money to speak of, but he thought of them among the smartest people he'd known in his life. Aware of the deleterious effect of centuries of racism on the psychology of African Americans, his mom and dad consistently used language and clear age-appropriate limitations to stoke up his and his sibling's confidence. The kids of the house knew in no uncertain terms who were the children, the pre-teens and teenagers in the home. They were not confused as to who was in charge and who was responsible. They knew they were loved and—perhaps deepest of all—they knew that their parents were quite different from their buddies, that there existed an entirely different level of respect specifically for them.

His mother, while not particularly prone to violence, never abandoned it altogether as a mode of discipline. For her, the obedience and respect of her children was a matter of life and death. Once, at around thirteen years old, while standing with friends on the sidewalk in front of the apartment building where he lived, Jones had mumbled a curse word when his mother called to him from a window to come inside. Her response was as swift as her descent downstairs, which he never heard. "I am *not* your friend," she'd yelled and smacked him on the back of his head in full view of his homies. With a fistful of his collar, she pulled his face nose to nose with hers and spoke in a harsh whisper. "I *am* your mother! I will not tolerate you disrespecting me, your daddy, your sister or yourself! Before I'd let you do that, I'd take you out *myself!*" she said and slapped him again this time in the face.

Man—Jones chuckled to himself—*my boys never let me forget that one!*

He thought of their way of raising them as a kind of social armor for the particular challenges of growing up black in America. In a word, this armor could be summed up as a kind of encouragement. Sometimes the encouragement would come as pure criticism of his actions laced with insistence that he was an inherently better person than what his behavior suggested at the time. Often it would be anecdotal, a description of a situation in which a young black teen would be able to think his way out of a tough spot instead of using violence, vulgarity or profanity. Many times they would describe how to combat subtle racial slights that could cause you to behave in a way that would ultimately derail your objective, be it a job, school admission or simply passing a test.

And finally, particularly for the boys, there was *the talk.*

Why are you so late from school, Theodore? Something happened?

A cop car stopped a bunch of us just as we came out of the store.

What? What were y'all doin'?

Nothin', Mom. I'm serious. We were just goin' down the sidewalk, laughing and passin' the ball between us an stuff. The cops said that there was some kind of robbery. They checked our bags—everybody but Bob, that is.

What? Bob? Why not him?

They made him stand against the wall too, Mom, but they didn't check him. He was the only white dude in the group. The cop that searched us said they were looking for a black guy in a basketball jersey. The other cop stood on the side with his hand on his gun.

Theodore! You didn't give them any back talk did you?

No, we just answered the questions and they left us alone. Mom, did you hear anything about some black dude and a robbery? We all figured they was lyin' by the way they was laughing at us. The white dude Bob didn't see what was the big deal. He didn't seem worried or angry like the rest of us.

Sweetheart, you're getting big now. As you grow up you'll be out and about more and more and I gotta tell you this. Child, listen—shh...don't interrupt me! You're my only son. I want you to grow up to become a fine man one day. But you'll have to stay alive to do that. I'm a Christian and I've tried to raise you that way. We're not supposed to make distinctions between people based on their race or color. But many of God's children do. Now listen to me, boy. Unlike your friend Bob, you have to remember the plain hard truth that you were born black in America and while we are all children of God, some, not all mind you, of our divine white siblings would hurt or kill us for being black as easily as they could look at us. This includes the police. Maybe I should say especially them. They have the guns, the power and the state on their side. They have the power of life and death and are willing to use that power, at the slightest provocation, on black bodies especially.

When they yell stop, please stop, son. I never saw nobody outrun a bullet.

As Jones sat taking account of the boy in the oversized white T-shirt and jeans, he questioned his own motives, wondering why he cared so much. But deeply, he knew exactly the nature of his concern. He feared the boy was on his way to becoming another unarmed brother shot dead in the street. Could it be that Tim hadn't received the talk? If he had, he wondered what Tim's reaction had been. The kid didn't exactly take criticism very well. *Humph*, he thought. *Current times sure don't resemble our time back in the day. Without cell phones, the cops were able to run rampant beating and killing us—do their dirt totally undetected. But still somehow we—well, some of us—maintained a sense of hope and we expected to be helped by the adults around us, even if it was going to hurt.*

At that thought, another door from the past opened, and he was back in the office of Mrs. Pettiford.

Theodore Jones?
Yes, that's me. Mrs. Pettiford, right?
Come in, young man. Yes, I'm Mrs. Pettiford, your new guidance counselor. Hmm...let's see, um-hum. Theodore!

Huh?

Are you planning to go to college after high school?

Uh, yes…

I'm asking because I see no record of basic college prep courses in your transcript for this year. And you need a foreign language. Did you know that?

Uh, Mr. Rizzo said that I could choose the courses that I wanted and…"

Humph…Mr. Rizzo said what?

He said I could take whatever I wanted, that I'd be alright…

No, child! If you intend to go to college, we're going to make some changes in your program right now. So, again, do you plan to go to college after high school?

Yes, Mrs. Pettiford, I do.

Ok, for starters we're going to get rid of these vocational courses and put you in algebra and physics.

Aw man!—really? Do I have to, Mrs. Pettiford? I mean…

Jones smiled as he came out of his muse until he noticed that his students had been watching him. He didn't care, the term was done. D-O-N-E! All of the musical instruments had been stowed away. Only the xylophone had to be pushed into the far corner. He would be able to leave right after the bell. Tim's frisky mood was the only possible damper on the situation. But he could handle that.

"Mr. Jones," boomed the youth. Jones almost laughed out loud thinking that the boy's artificially bassed voice sounded like a basset hound talking through a cardboard paper towel cylinder. That is, if a basset hound could, well—talk. He wanted to ignore him, but now he had to pay attention since the kid had begun to raise his voice.

"Mr. Jones, I'm talking to you," he said again a little louder.

Jones pursed his lips with an air of nonchalance, released a long sigh and glanced at the clock before responding, "What is it, Tim?" he asked. His voice sounded tired.

"I have to go to the baffroom," he said, grimacing and glancing at the clock.

"There's a 'th' in that word," Jones said with a faint smile. "You'll have to wait ten minutes 'till the end of the period."

Tim pretended to whisper to a classmate, making sure to speak loud enough so that the entire class could hear. "Aw man, I have to take a piss and this guy just be sitting up there like he some king or something. Mr. Jones, I gotta go…"

Jones wanted to tell him to cross his legs. "Just wait a few minutes, ok, Tim? I've a headache, so give me a break today—whoa, where are you going? Go back to your seat!"

Instead of leaving the room, Tim swaggered straight up to the desk, swaying from side to side like a boxer, grinning, biting his lower lip. In spite of the theatrics, his classmates weren't paying much attention. It was a movie they'd seen before.

Jones raised his voice, "Tim, return to your seat and sit down. Now!"

"Yo, Mr. Jones," he said as he arrived at the desk.

"Leave me alone, Tim. Can you wait the ten minutes and be quiet? People are reading." With a knowing smile, Jones said, "Maybe you should try it yourself?"

A wrinkle of emotion rolled across Tim's brow at the mention of reading. "Yo, Mr. Jones, I know what you was like when you was in school."

Hearing that, Jones smiled weakly, thinking that he knew where this was going. They'd spoken a great deal about his school days during their tutoring sessions. They had become friendly, and he'd allowed Tim to tease him to a certain extent. Jones fancied himself as one of the 'cool' faculty, refusing to wear a tie like all the other teachers, able to banter back and forth with the kids without losing their respect. But this was a delicate moment. He didn't want to appear smug or too glib because he knew that Tim could feel disrespected and that would only serve to escalate things. Jones also knew that Tim didn't like his jokes very much and had even accused him of hypocrisy. More than once, he'd pointed out when his teacher had scoffed at school regulations while insisting that for them, playing by the rules was the only way to make it.

So, instead of cracking wise, Jones asked, "And how was I in school, Tim?"

Tim, a bit surprised at his teacher's poise, hesitated a moment, shifted his weight from one foot to the other before coming out with, "I know what you was like, Mr. Jones. You was a punk. I'm sure of it."

Jones took account of the young man standing before him. On his small chin were the beginnings of a goatee. The kid held his dark, nearly shaved head at an angle that clearly communicated 'challenge' in every way. He stood his ground and stared into the eyes of his teacher. The only signs of stress were a few beads of sweat on his brow and the shake of the ear stud in his left lobe.

Jones sat with his elbows planted heavily on the desk. His hands were facing each other as if he were praying. Much later, thinking back on all of this, Jones would note and appreciate that the kid hadn't used stronger language. Profanity would have come off as pointless, even stupid, and could have ended badly for him. Punk was a good choice and much more effective as a challenge to his teacher, five minutes before the end of the school year.

Nervous giggles rippled across the room—students were paying close attention now. Still seated, soaked in sweat and embarrassment, Jones smiled back at the youth. He felt exhausted and wanted to tell the kid to 'get out of his face' or something like that. Instead, with a weary voice, he asked, "Is that all you have to say?"

Tim hooked his thumbs in his pockets. "Yeah, that's it. You probably was a PUNK in high school!"

"Okay," he said sitting up and shifting in his seat. "Now go and sit down, please." Jones pointed towards the back of the room.

With a satisfied grin, Tim practically skipped to his seat, giving fist bumps along the way to classmates.

Jones' later reflection led him to consider that perhaps this was one of his best improvisations. That is, in spite of the surprise of the moment, he was able to keep cool, respond gracefully, maintain the tempo, and stay true to the form. Additionally, and most importantly, he executed all of this while never forgetting the main theme: his role as a high school teacher who wanted to keep his gig. However, ominously, the phrase, "Dammit, that's it! I will have to deal with this boy," did come to mind.

When the final bell sounded, Jones, as usual, stood at the door of the classroom with a tired smile. As he said his goodbyes, he was thinking of the previous night's repertoire.

"Have a good summer, Mr. Jones."

"See you in the fall, Grace."

"Take care, Mr. Jones."

"Autumn, you're leaving already?"

"Yes, you too, James, uh Tim—not-not you," Jones said, blocking the doorway.

Tim spun around on the ball of one foot and clapped his hands once and gave his teacher his best pained expression. "But Mr. Jones, I really have to leave!"

More students left the classroom. "Don't forget about me, Mr. Jones."

"Bye bye, my dear Ruby."

WTF?

"Wh-what about me?" Tim stuttered out, with panic in his eyes.

Suppressing a smile, Jones wanted to sound cool with his answer. "No, Tim, I must speak with you, that's all," he said, waving goodbye to passing students.

The air in the room was heavy from the afternoon sun. Tim flicked sweat from his eyes as he pleaded. "Let me leave, you know I gotta go to the—"

Jones let go of the door. It swung and banged shut with a freaky finality. When Tim jumped back from the noise, a strong trace of BO lingered in the air.

Catching a whiff, Jones asked himself, *What the hell am I doing*? and took a swift step towards the boy. Extending his hand, he spoke with a soft tone. "Oh, come on, Tim, I jus-just wanted to—"

Reflexively, Tim took a swipe at Jones' open hand, "N-nah man… what are you doing? Get out of here. I'm going now—*yo!*" he yelled and backward vaulted over a desk like a dancer from *West Side Story*.

When Jones accidentally knocked a trashcan into the wall, he paused and appeared to come to his senses for a moment, but by then Tim had backed himself into a corner. No more than seven seconds had passed, but both of them were breathing heavily in the heat. Jones, though, wasn't tired. For once, he had Tim's full attention—for what exactly, he didn't know. He also didn't know that the usual soft contours of his face had transformed into a mass of angular folds and lines that scared the shit out of his student. When Tim's sneaker caught under a cymbal stand, the crash brought home to Jones that he had no idea what he was doing, that he'd lost control of the situation. The thought frustrated him, angered him so he let fly an eraser at the kid's head. He missed. The boy dove like a drunken soccer goalie over the xylophone, knocked it to the floor and landed on top of it. Holding his side from the pain, Tim jumped to his feet and pleaded with Jones to calm down. Jones, without missing a beat, was already right next to him.

"I'm sorry, Mr. Jones. Really," Tim pleaded, his hands outstretched.

What now? thought Jones.

"So who's the punk now, Tim?" he said, holding back tears. He could barely stand the sight of the boy, yet he was unable to look away. Then, once again, all was still and quiet, except for their breathing. Leaning forward, hands on both knees, he finally figured out what he wanted to say. "What's the matter with you, Tim?"

"What do you mean?" he sneered. "What's the matter with me? What's the matter with *you?*"

Jones remained bent over. "Just what I asked, what's the matter with you? Why do you hate yourself?"

Hearing that, Tim's mouth flew open with disbelief. "Man. What are you talking about?" He spoke slowly as if his teacher had ceased to understand him.

"This is not the time for that, Tim. I'm serious, why do you hate yourself?"

"I don't. I to-told you!" he said wiping sweat from his brow.

Jones stood upright now. "Are you sure? I mean. It doesn't seem that you are trying to take care of yourself or your future."

Tim took notice of Jones' height advantage. His teacher had a couple inches on him. He swallowed hard. "I…um…"

"What's up at home?" Jones said, cutting him off.

"Nothin's up at home, m-man!" Tim snapped back best he could. His stutter had begun to kick in.

Once again, Jones blocked his way when he tried to move past him. "I had a voice at home. I was listened to Tim. What do you say? Are you?"

"What? Lemme out of here! Of co-course I'm li-listened to. You crazy? What do you think, man?"

Jones hesitated. "I think you believe that the world isn't interested in you. I think that you're about to give up. Well, I've got news for you, boy. Someone is listening. You exist. What you say matters and has consequences, son."

Tim pushed a small table between them and tried to slip past.

His teacher yelled, "Whoa, where do you think you're going? I'll tell you when we're done!" As Jones moved to block the boy's passage, he knocked over a giant box of pens and markers. Their impact on the floor scattered them underfoot in all directions. Perhaps he was getting through to the kid, perhaps not. But as far as Jones was concerned, Tim wasn't getting out of that corner, not yet. Adding to the boy's misery was the flag that hung just overhead between them. Tim had to continually push it away from his face to look at his teacher.

It seemed as if Tim was going to cry at any moment. "I ain't got ti-time for this bullsh…," he said, but Jones cut him off with a stiff index finger.

And for once, the boy asked the perfect question. "Mr. Jones, what's up? Wha…what are you do-doing? Fuck!" he screamed, "Come on, old man, get out of my way, I'm go-going home!"

Something about the 'F-bomb' set Jones off. "I'll show you who's the punk," he growled and lunged at the boy. When Tim moved to slip under Jones' outstretched hands, his foot rolled on top of three board markers. Like a major leaguer's dash to steal home plate, he slid forward, feet first through Jones' legs.

Without thinking, Jones reached down and grabbed Tim's left arm, clamping down upon it with his ankles as he tried to balance himself and turn around. Behind him, Tim's feet flailed wildly turning over chairs as he struggled to get free. Working hard to hold on to the squirrely teenager—he delivered his sad message:

"I'll–show–you–who–the–punk–is–Chump!
Do-you-think–that–you–
can–really–just–come–to–school–

and–do–or–say–anything?

Respect–nothing?

Not–to–day-you–won't!"

At one point, Jones could see that fear had disappeared from Tim's face entirely. The boy had ceased to be worried. Even though he continued to try to escape his teacher's grip, he hadn't kicked or punched him. With every turn of their tussle, Tim would groan with an expression that was a cross between a grimace and a sad smile. He had surrendered to what was happening even as he asked, not demanded, for his teacher to stop. After a point, as if to give his teacher a clear signal, Tim collapsed to the floor. Exhausted and grateful for the pause, Jones released his grip and leaned against a cabinet. He started to speak again but stopped midsentence to watch the boy jump to his feet, leap out of the window like Superman, perform a perfect somersault and pull up into a full sprint across the grass. In a blink, he was gone.

As he cleaned up, Jones' mind wouldn't rest.

Damn! Lucky we were on the ground floor. What have I done? A better question would be, Who's the unemployed sorry ass when the administration hears about this? Damn! Would he report me? Nah! He knew he had it coming. Maybe I wasn't the one to do it, but he surely needed somebody to put some fear into him.

He went to pick up the xylophone, but his lower back was having none of it. With a loud crash, instrument and teacher went down together. Luckily he landed on his back to the side of the thing. Lying still, he listened to the decrescendo of tones emanating from the upturned instrument like the whine of a wounded animal and wondered how cigarette burns got into the panels of the drop ceiling. The cheap carpeting was as shocked as he was at the torrent of tears flowing down his temples.

ESCAPE

Tim ran.

Images moved lazily across his mind: Jones' face—sad, furious and then sad again. They're in the classroom, the one and only session when he'd read an entire paragraph aloud without a single error. Sheila's churlish insult at the kitchen table: "You silly asphalt." His uncle's critical gaze. Out of nowhere, his mother's tired face moved in as he relived scraps of arguments between her and his dad—something about an indictment—that it was all her fault.

Back to Jones—imagining the dude climbing out of the window and sprinting across the grass in those pleated pants and black socks stopped him in his tracks. *Man, you crazy—like he really was going to come after you—ha!*

Only after shooing away a homeless man did Tim notice that he had gone in the opposite direction from home. He was standing on Clifton Ave at the corner of Bloomfield where the old pawnshop with the broken window stood, its shiny junk proudly on display. On this bright summer day, street hawkers in full force manned their stands— hot dogs, boiled corn, bean pies, toys, incense, essential oils, costume jewelry, USB drives, counterfeit CDs and DVDs were everywhere, all for sale. Car horns blared. A queue of drivers yelled at some unlucky girl in a stalled SUV until a policeman—hand on pistol, jaw set for action—arrived at the scene.

Keeping one eye on the cop, Tim bent down to help an old lady pick up some groceries she had dropped. His own reflection in a storefront window showed what looked like another homeless person in a torn oversized T-shirt and a pair of frumpy jeans. His entire left side sported a shadow of green from his roll on the wet grass. When a dull pain in his side reminded him of the xylophone, fresh embarrassment shot through him like a transfusion. Mumbling curses, he began to throw the groceries into the bags. "Mind what you're doing, child!" chided the old woman. Her homey admonition calmed him, but the expression on her face told him that she wasn't going to take any lip.

However, when a group of kids bumped into him as they ran by, he turned and yelled, "Y'all better watch where the f— I mean, watch where y'all going!"

Tim wanted to sprout wings, jump up and fly out of this place, perhaps to land at his father's apartment. Seeing those kids with musical instruments made his side hurt even more. In his mind's eye, the angry face of Jones loomed forward—his voice speaking the truth inside of him. The word *respect* reminded him of the time Jones spoke about a neighborhood shooting. A boy was shot during an argument over a basketball game. Tim was surprised to hear Jones say that it wasn't about someone being *dissed*, as he'd concluded, but that it was more about someone going for a cheap victory with a gun instead of trying to legitimately earn the respect of another person.

Suddenly he couldn't breathe or see as tears rained from his eyes and nose upon the groceries. He felt the old woman's hand on his shoulder. "It-it'll be alright, child. I-I didn't mean to yell at ya," she said with crumbly regret in her voice. Saying nothing, he finished with the bags and walked away, wiping his eyes with the end of his shirt.

Damn, man, why the fuck are you crying like some crazy fool here on the street and shit? You know the dude wasn't trying to hurt you. Yeah, you had no business getting up in his face, but he had no fucking right to—huh?

Across the street in front of Brown's Bakery, Sheila and Rene spoke with some dude wearing a single glove with no fingers. Tim thought he recognized him, but at the moment he didn't care. He had to get away quick. If his sister saw him on the street in his stained T-shirt, he would have to hear about it for the rest of the summer. Mr. Brown, who had recently caught him with a scone in his pocket, popped out onto the sidewalk. Tim nearly fell down a basement stairway as he turned to get away. By the time the storekeep turned in his direction, the only trace of the fugitive was a flying streak of blue and white.

PULLING BACK THE CURTAIN

From her seat, Sheila had a clear view of the driver and every soul that boarded the bus. She thought of her dad and wondered if—like for this driver—it had been the stress of sitting all day, saying the same things over and over and arguing with people that made him turn to the bottle every night. How boring it must be! *Yes, miss, this is the 49 Downtown Line—move towards the back, please—no, m'am, you need exact change—sorry, this transfer has expired—you have to get off the bus now or I'll have to call the police.*

Sheila looked at Rene sitting next to her and marveled at how she hadn't even broken a sweat while sweat rolled down her own temples and her handkerchief had long gone soggy. Making a run to the other side of town to Sal's Finance wasn't exactly how she'd planned to spend her afternoon. The fuck-face owned the loan her dad had taken to pay her mom's legal bills. It would be a late payment—she knew the drill: Wait in line, present the bill, act surprised at the penalty fee, claim ignorance—say she was running an errand for her mother and that she only had the money for one month. They would send her home with a receipt and a note that warned of the apocalypse if they didn't pay by a certain date. *They will just have to wait, that's all. What are they going to do? Repossess our Bentley?* Four more stops to go. They had been sitting in this sauna on wheels for too long now and they still had a five-block walk to the loan shark's office.

She peeked at Rene again out of the corner of her eye and thought, *She's really smart and looks good. I'm going to have a body like that one of these days.*

Sheila could never figure what the hell Rene saw in her brother. Yes, they were middle-school sweethearts, but they were all just kids back then.

Sheila wasn't surprised to hear that Rene and Tim were off again. She kept trying to avoid the subject, but Rene wouldn't talk about anything else. Rene was usually quite animated when she spoke, but today her hands remained in her lap, massaging each other slowly.

"I thought you knew me and Tim weren't together?"

Sheila looked over her shoulder to see if anyone was paying attention to what they were saying. "How would I know that, Rene? He hardly talks to me. So, uh, what happened between you two?"

A car with a 1000-watt stereo system paused at the light next to them. Rene leaned in close. "So, uh—what?"

"Wha-what happened?" Sheila yelled into her ear.

Lips pursed in disapproval, Rene had apparently caught the eye of the driver of the loud car.

Sheila considered that maybe her friend was trying to stare down the volume of the boom-box on wheels. Rene waited for the dude to speed off and said. "Well, it's obvious you don't wanna talk about it. I won't bore you with the details."

"No, no, girl, tell me. For real! But keep your voice down."

"Well…" whispered Rene, covering her mouth. Her expression turned serious. "It's mostly about that Maria girl."

"Oh no!" Sheila said, holding her hands to her mouth.

"What-what's up, homegirl?" Rene said touching her forearm.

"That silly boy Maurice Rice just got on. He beat up Tim in the park yesterday," she said, settling back onto her seat.

Rene shook her head side to side, "Wh-what? Why?"

Keeping an eye on Maurice, Sheila held onto the handle of the seat in front of her as if she expected turbulence. "He and his boys are always fucking with me in the halls. You know how they do. I ended up telling him that my brother was going to whip his ass."

"You what? Sheila! What the hell?" Rene whispered and pushed Sheila's arm away. Sheila let go of the handle and grabbed Rene's hand. "Shh–shh, here he comes."

The bus had suddenly emptied out a bit. Maurice, wearing huge headphones, sauntered over to them, bobbing his head to some down-low beat. "Well, well. Who do we have here? Hee–hee. S'up, Sheila? How you doin', Rene baby?"

"I'm so not your baby, Maurice. *Please!*" Rene folded her arms and looked out the window.

"I guess not—*not yet*! So, Sheila…" he said, head bobbing in time to the track in his phones…"you ain't speakin' or what?" He punched a fist into his palm like some kind of punctuation.

"Hey, Maurice," Sheila said, as stonily as possible.

"Yeah, I'm cool. Ha! Seems to me you ain't so talkative today. Not like the last time I saw you."

A couple seconds passed. The bus accelerated and jerked. People were watching now. Sheila turned towards Maurice with such force, the boy flinched. "Hey, *Scarface*, I don't have anything to say to you. Ok? Especially after what you did to my brother."

Rene cracked up. "Oh–ho-ho! Aw man—Scarface? You didn't say that…"

"Shut up, Rene," Sheila said, fixing her gaze on the thug.

Maurice held onto the overhead bar and leaned forward. Sheila frowned at his BO. "So we gonna play it like that, huh—innocent and shit? Like you ain't got nothin' to do with it?"

"Maurice—I have to go," Sheila said and pushed the boy out of the way as she rose from her seat. "This is our stop, yo! Get up, Rene."

Rene hesitated, looking a bit confused. She knew Maurice liked her and was dangerous. She didn't want to mess with him. He had taunted Tim a couple times when they were still together.

"Nah nah, get out of my way, brother," Sheila insisted, holding up her hand towards the bully as she spoke. "This is my stop," she said, moving down the first steps. "You stay on the bus and go on with your sad business. Come on, Rene, the doors are about to close!" She held out a hand to her friend.

Hand in hand, they hopped from the bus onto the sidewalk, laughed and fanned themselves with relief. The moment was short-lived. As the bus started to pull off, the asshole managed to hold the doors open enough to squeeze through. Sheila threw her hands up and pleaded with him, "Aw man, Maurice, what do you want? Don't you have somewhere to go?"

The boy adjusted his shirt. It had caught in the closing doors. Busting a major sag that day, he gave a quick tug to his waistband and came back with, "I can get off wherever I want to. Like I was just saying—I remember you giving me some kind of bullshit about your brother kickin' my ass. I only gave him a chance. Seems to me the story had a different ending."

Sheila, breathing hard, stood nose to nose with him, about two inches from his face.

"Whoa, back off girl. Rene, tell yo' girl to back off."

Rene's eyes were filled with panic as she grabbed Sheila's arm. "Come on, baby. You don't want to fool with him."

"That's right. Tell her before somebody gets popped," Maurice barked as he backed away. He held his hand sideways, pointing his middle and index fingers at them.

Sheila shook off Rene's hand. "What kind of chance was that, Maurice? You and two of your thugs holding Tim down, kicking and beating him."

Rene had taken a couple steps away from the action. "Come on, Sheila, let's go." She sounded as if she was going to cry at any minute.

"Was Darryl Campbell there?" Sheila demanded and took a step towards the thug again. Maurice backed up and held up both hands, amused. "Look look. *Hands up, don't shoot!* Ha, you crazy girl. You better get your big ass outta my face. Why you wanna know who was there? What difference…"

"WAS-HE-THERE-MAU-RICE?" Sheila growled. Her voice bounced off the buildings.

Everyone on the street stopped to watch them.

Maurice's smile drooped a little. He didn't like the way things were going. An audience was the last thing he needed if he was going to slap the shit out of this fat girl. So he answered her straight. Well, straight enough. "Maybe he was, maybe he wasn't. Anyway, he didn't do nothin'—stood around and shit. He didn't have to do nothin', you know? Your bro wasn't exactly hard work! Haaa! Word is that even Mr. Jones got a piece of him last period today!"

"What you talkin' about, man. I'll...Rene, let me go. Shit, the fool is running away now. Why'd you do that?"

Maurice yelled from across the street. "Yeah, Rene, thanks for savin' my ass from *thunder-thighs*! Hee-hee!"

BULLY

About mid-block, Tim slowed his pace. At the corner Chucky was busily torturing what looked like a middle-school kid. He could tell from the expression on the boy's face that the skateboard Chucky rode in circles was probably his. Chucky was like, "What you gonna do? Take it back if you can. Come on, pint-boy! Tick-tock! You got about sixty seconds before I leave with this piece of shit."

The scrawny motherfucker grabbed the kid's cap and put it on his own head just to aggravate the situation. Tim thought the middle-schooler was going to cry. If he hadn't shown up, Chucky would have already left with the board.

The kid's tormentor continued to circle and taunt the twelve-year-old as he spoke. "What up, Tim?" he said, making a quick swerve to avoid the kid who tried to take advantage of the distraction.

"Hey, man, why don't you give the boy his board?" Tim smiled as he spoke to lighten his words, but his eyes weren't cooperating.

Chucky had to stop and flip the board backwards to avoid the kid's latest attempt. "Whoa-ho-ho, my little brother. Nice try. Now you got about thirty seconds. Tim, what you talking about? What's it to you? You know this dude or something?" he said and jumped right back on the board.

Tim put a hand on the chest of the middle-schooler to chill him out. "Yeah, I know him and his family. He's cool, man. Now stop with this bullshit and..." This time when Chucky came around, Tim snatched the cap off of his head and stomped on the edge of the skateboard. The punk jumped off just in time to land on his feet. He wasn't happy.

"Shit, Tim," he screamed. "You almost made me..."

"*Fall?*" Tim said in a dramatic high falsetto, holding a hand over his chest. He sent the boy off with his cap, skateboard and a fist bump, both laughing their asses off.

"Man, that's some shit you pulled. I gotta fly now, but payback is a bitch," Chucky said, turning away. "I guess I'll catch you at Spank's throw-down."

Tim watched the kid cross the street. "Oh yeah, I'll be there, Chucky. See you then."

Chucky yelled over his shoulder, "You can bet on it." His words echoed off the brick and concrete.

Tim shoved his hands into his pockets and whistled while he walked—he wanted to appear unflustered, cool. But he was mad as hell and ashamed. Soon his walk became a trudge, his tune a noise of disgust. Leaning upon a large city trash receptacle he took a quick sniff at his armpit. *Dag, you stink! And what's going on here? In the last thirty minutes you had to escape an ass-whipping, slip by your little sis on the street—and who was that dude with the glove anyway? Running from an old man in an apron don't even sound good and what the fuck was I doing with Chucky and that kid? Ew, what's that?*

Curiously, he had walked three blocks without seeing much of the neighborhood, like the balloon merchant, only ten feet away, nearly overwhelmed by a rowdy brood of siblings or the kids in the playground he'd just passed. He hadn't even seen the old lady sitting in the window of the brownstone in front of him. Somehow the stalled car with the overheated radiator and barking terrier in the back seat had missed his attention. And he may have never noticed the busload of onlookers behind him had he not followed his nose to the half rotting pigeon staring at him from inside the trashcan.

All of a sudden, something in his belly wanted out, and wanted out fast. Shocked at his guts suddenly erupting, he held on tight to the wire-mesh rim as his throat stretched open to maximize passage of the chunky, bitter spew. Within seconds the corpse was no longer visible. Only a slimy wing protruded from the stinky slop.

When he finally looked up, the bus passengers had lost interest. His audience had been reduced to an old mangy cat and a wild-haired bus driver. When the vehicle pulled away, the hiss of the air brakes dismissed him with a sound of disgust. Nevertheless, feeling better and grateful for the napkin in his pocket, he smiled. Turning on his heel, he kicked a can into the gutter and decided to walk the two and a half miles home. He needed time to think.

REGRET

It was an hour later by the time Jones got to his car, half expecting to see Tim waiting in the school parking lot with a couple of his boys, perhaps to eye him menacingly, lob an F-bomb or worse. No such luck, the grounds were clear.

It was hot and his AC was on the blink. Jones sat heavily in the driver's seat, grabbed a towel from a gym bag and vigorously wiped his entire head and neck dry. As soon as he was done, sweat began to collect on his forehead and upper lip. In the rearview mirror, dark spots on his shirt reminded him of the futility of his tussle with Tim. He reclined his seat as far as possible, waited for the ache in his lower back to subside and thought of a time when his dad had chastised him, the only time that he'd actually struck him. It was an accident really—his mom and dad had been arguing when he came into the room and asked for permission to go outside.

His dad said, "Not now, son. Get outta here! Can't you see yo' mama and me be talking?" Jones vaguely remembered thinking, *If not now, when?* But what he actually clearly recalled was hitting the floor hard, sitting up and screaming at the pain on the side of his face. He also remembered the confusion and shame on his dad's face when he ordered him to get up and go to his room.

Over the years Jones came to understand that, in spite of his father's violent reaction, he was a child who was listened to. In that slap, Jones understood that what he said mattered, that his parents were listening and that his dad stood for something. Or at least didn't stand for disrespect from his kids. He wondered about Tim—did his parents stand for anything? Probably not. So how could the boy believe that he, his study hall teacher, cared? How could he, if he couldn't be sure about his own parents?

"But then, what kind of fucking help was that Ted Jones?" he asked himself aloud. The sensation of failure hit him so hard he checked again to be sure that he was alone, as if his shame could leak out of the car and be seen by others. Reclining the seat a bit more, he inhaled deeply and held his breath. His exhalation came out in short bursts from his gut until they'd turned into uncontrollable contractions. Only the patient pigeons, hanging about for the odd tidbit, heard the peals of laughter bouncing off the brick surfaces of the school building. He started the car and headed for home. However, this time Jones wasn't surprised by the moisture in his eyes because he knew that whatever the motivations behind his actions, young guys like Tim needed to know that it was at least *possible* that someone could give a shit.

The door to his apartment, swollen in its frame from humidity, felt more like a crisis than an annoyance. His back was starting to ache again and he really didn't need this now. After a good swift kick, the thing swung open with a bang.

Rays of the late evening sun bathed the sitting room in light and exposed swirling dust in the still air. As he clicked on the AC, he paused for a moment and imagined layers of faraway constellations in the array of particles. Ever since he was a kid, stars made him think of science, science—education, education—school—*ugh, I really lost it in there with that boy!*

Thirsty, he scooted to the fridge where a lone six-pack lay in wait on the bottom shelf. The pop of the tab and frosty kiss of the tin sent his taste buds into an orgasmic frenzy. For the third time within about an hour, wet tears flowed from his closed eyes.

Before he had finished off the first can, the last day of school, the sweat, the rumble, bang and clang came back to his mind in stark lines, like the unfinished story that it all was. It felt almost unbelievable. He watched the scene in his mind as if it had happened to someone else.

A few beers later, nature finally called. Sitting on the can in a hoppy happy haze he mused about the last remaining beer, and whether leaving it for another time was the right thing to do. Chuckling to himself, he thought, *this is one injustice that will not stand!* Before easing into a nod, Jones thought of when he'd met Tim Thornton for the first time.

Uh, excuse me, but you Mr. Jones, right?

What? Speak up, young man.

Oh, uh sorry. Are you Mr. Jones?

Come, step into the room. It's too noisy out here in the hall. Yes, that's me. And you are?

Um, I'm-uh… Tim Thornton. Can I use your pencil sharpener?

Nice to meet you, Tim Thornton. But I don't know. Can you use it? Do you know how?

Aw man, that's so old! May I use your pencil sharpener?

Sure, see the walk-in cabinet with the double doors over there? Freshman, right?

Uh, yeah, I'm a freshman. Where'd you say it was?

It's inside the cabinet. Yes, that's right. Open the door, that's it. See it?

Uh—Mr. Jones, I can see it, but it's on the inside of the other door. It's full of stuff in there. Wh-what I gotta do?

What's that, Tim?

What do I have to do to use the sharpner, yo?

Uh—you have to climb in!

Jones laughed himself into consciousness and nearly fell off the toilet. *I couldn't believe it when he actually disappeared inside that thing. I guess he never saw the release chain. Probably the boy never got over that one completely. I suppose he's been trying to get me back ever since.*

PROPOSITION

Dang! *The boy is handsome*, Sheila thought when Darryl came out of the darkened building. Having waited an hour outside the service exit of the library, she had begun to feel a little stupid. Especially since she saw him just the day before with Rene. Only now she remembered the odd look on his face when they all spotted Tim on the street across the intersection. Determined to get down to business, she took heart in the fact that no gangbangers were in sight and most importantly—*no Maurice*! He didn't have a basketball with him, so there was no game to rush off to—he couldn't just blow her off. *Take a big breath*, she thought, *Game on*!

"Hi, Darryl!" she sang out across the parking lot, hot with embarrassment. *What, he's not going to stop?* "Hey...Darryl Campbell, wait up! I know you can hear me!"

Darryl turned around slowly, left hand in his pocket, right hand brushing his upper lip as if he had bristles to play with, jeans halfway down his butt. "Yo, what'sup, cuz?" he said, words sounding like they were stretched out in a hammock.

"Don't *cuz* me, Darryl," Sheila said with one hand on her hip. "We both know that you don't really talk like that. And why don't you pull up those stupid pants. Your boys aren't around. No need for *street-cool* here."

Darryl pinched his nose and looked down the street in each direction to see if anyone had heard. Holding his head off to the side, he reached out to touch her shoulder.

"Yo, girl, why you bustin' on me like that? What did I do to you?" he said with that smile of his, with those perfect teeth.

Ohh, she thought. But it was more of a deep down feeling than a thought and for a moment, it caused her to hesitate, even reconsider what she'd come to do. The boy had smiled at her after all. "Darryl, I know you were there day before yesterday when Maurice beat up my brother in the park. And I know you knew he was my brother too."

The flash of panic in his eyes told her that it was true. "Whoa-whoa...hold up, hold up, girl. What are you talking about?"

"No, I'm not going to *hold up.* I don't care if you want to continue with this clown act. Knock yourself out. But you're going to listen to this!" she insisted, pointing at him as she spoke.

Darryl half laughed through a loud snort, shifted his weight onto the other foot and looked around. They were alone on the street. Only a curious dog stared at them from a window. It was beginning to get dark. He took a step towards her. "Listen to this, b—"

Sheila took a step in as well. Standing nose-to-nose, it was clear that they were about the same height and she had the weight advantage by about twenty pounds. "I wouldn't go there if I were you," she growled.

"Okay, okay, sister," he said, taking a step backwards, chuckling softly as if there was some joke between them. "What do I have to listen to that's so important? Besides, I didn't touch him. Look, I'm sorry about what happened, but I was totally on the side, not a part of it. Yeah, I don't even think the dude saw me. I mean like, did he say something?"

"No, he hasn't said a thing. And don't call me *sister*, okay? Stop that!" she said, batting his hand away. He had tried to pinch her cheek as she spoke. "Anyway, I know for a fact that you were there, and I'm pretty sure he didn't see you. So, he doesn't know you were there—but I do! And since you did nothing to help him then, you have to do something for him now!" She liked her tone now.

Darryl scoffed. "Huh? Like what?"

"I know that you try to keep your good grades a secret so you can hang out with those silly friends of yours," she said, poking him in the chest with two fingers.

"And-and so?" he said looking at her poking hand.

"And so, you have to help Tim with his reading." Darryl slapped her hand away when she tried to poke him again. At the same time, he grabbed his belt buckle. His jeans were about to fall to the ground. His voice exploded in a high falsetto. "With whaaaat? *Shit*."

"His reading, fool. Are you deaf? Soon he will be at the library every day. He has to pass the reading proficiency in September," she said, wiping her mouth, worried about calling him a fool.

Darryl guffawed at the news. "And why's that a problem?" He leaned back on one leg and scratched his chin. "Oh yeahh...he's *STU-PID!*"

Sheila took a minute as if she could stare down Darryl's boldness. But his curly hair threatened her resolve. Suddenly she wanted to forget all of this mess, take his hand and stroll down the sidewalk like lovers making future plans. But then an inner voice screamed at her...not now! She leaned in again, close this time and suppressed a smile. The boy smelled good.

"If you don't want Maurice to find out about your tendency to study and your geeky job here at the library, you better agree to give Tim some real help every day that he comes. You have to make sure that he is able to pass that proficiency. You got it? You know what would happen if those silly boys heard about you."

"Aw man," he said, turning to face the other way. "I'm no fucking teacher."

Sheila came around to face him again. "No, but you are somebody with a secret that wants it to stay like that. Right?"

"Hmm..." said the fake thug, rubbing phantom chin whiskers.

LIKING IT

While he stared at himself in the mirror, Tim brushed his teeth and stood on one leg in 'tree pose'—something he'd seen in a yoga book. He laughed out loud thinking of his trip to the library with his uncle six weeks ago at the beginning of the summer. Gentrale would be shocked to hear that Tim had become kind of a regular at the joint, reading the news online almost every day.

Gentrale had said that he needed someone to accompany him to the library—claiming he needed help, that he had to research something important. Yes, that's the word he used. *Research.* Tim had to think about that for a minute. He was a little suspicious when he agreed to go. And, he was embarrassed to be seen, so he suggested they sit in a remote corner near the wall.

It didn't matter. Gentrale was in a great mood as he planted himself in one of those big leather chairs and read the local paper aloud as Tim followed along. After reading an article about the recent robberies in town, they made a trip to the card index and then down the aisles. A few minutes later, they were reading the details of famous robberies in the U.S. from a couple huge hardcovers. At one point, a library employee, a dude named Darryl, reminded them of the library policy of silence. Later, the guy returned with a bunch of cool illustrated books.

Darryl suggested they go online and search *The Most Stupid Burglars Ever.* A couple hours later, Tim and Gentrale were eating ice cream and laughing about the guy who wore a transparent face mask during a bank robbery and about other failed heists. Tim liked that word *heist.*

Yes, it was his uncle who tricked him into going to the library in the first place. But it was Darryl who got him through those doors every day. If it weren't for him, things would have been different. Tim kept quiet about all of this, telling himself that it was none of his family's business: *It's on me, yo! Like if I can't pass that proficiency, it will totally be my problem.*

There was another problem though. He couldn't shake the feeling that he knew the library dude from somewhere.

He stood grinning at the toothpaste flowing down his chin, but nearly choked when the bathroom door suddenly swung wide open.

"What are you doing?"

"Sheila, get the fuck out of here!" he barked. Toothpaste rain speckled her glasses.

"I'm going to tell Mom about your filthy mouth. And—take that toothbrush out of your mouth." Looking towards the floor she said, "What the—" She pointed at his legs.

"Oh, uh—forget that!" he said, putting his foot down. "Leave now, please. I have to eat something and get down to the gym before it gets too crowded."

"Oh!" she snorted. "So now that you're done trying to grow some brains you want to grow some muscles?" she said, flexing a bicep.

"Girl, that's none of your business. Now get—" he said, trying to push her through the door.

Sheila pushed back. "Ha! That's good and all, Timmy, but you look like Al Jolson with that toothpaste—"

"CLOSE THE DOOR!" he screamed at the top of his lungs. This time, his sister allowed him to push her out.

Who the heck is Al Jolson?

A moment later, it was Gentrale at the door. "Tim! You done fell in the toilet boy or what?"

"Ahgottahandleonit," Tim mumbled on his way back to his bedroom. The phrase made him think of his dad all boozy and swollen.

It was something he always said. Remembering that, Tim felt a little sick. He threw on his clothes, grabbed his gym bag and ran out of the house as if he could leave the puffy-faced memories behind.

Out on the sidewalk, the sun felt as if it would pierce his skin. Sweat poured out of him as he trudged forward, moving his book-laden gym bag from one hand to the other. There were still about three weeks to go before the proficiency and he had to pass it. The thought of failing almost made him turn around and run back home. Sheer determination kept him going. He couldn't listen to any more of his sister's shit. He really didn't want to hear: *So Mr. Asphalt, what are you going to do now?*

"Fuck her," he grunted. "What I do is none of anybody's business."

BEST LAID PLANS

Even though Spank lived on the eleventh floor of the Southside projects, you could hear the beat of his stereo from the street. Tim didn't come down here much. It was way too easy to get into some shit with the police. If the cops didn't get you, the dudes on the corners could easily interpret your presence as either a problem or a threat.

The elevator was a toilet. No seriously, there were bottles of piss in the corners of the four-by-four box. Tim ran up the eleven flights, six of them without lighting in about a minute flat.

"*Wasssssup*, Spank?" Tim sang breathlessly, letting his greeting substitute for a long-needed exhalation.

"S'up, Tim? My man. You made it!" Spank shouted back, reaching to hug him.

Tim, sweaty from his run up the stairs, pushed away quick. "Yeah. It's Saturday night, bro, I have to get in a good one before it's all over. Only a couple more weeks before everything starts up again."

Spank looked him up and down. "Whoa, brother, don't be bringin' no school shit up in here. Hey, s'up with the muscles? You be working it, huh?"

"Yeah, brother. Gotta do what I gotta do, you know! Ooh-wee, you got some smoking honeys up here tonight. But seriously, you have to change that track. I mean…"

Spank yelled across the room, "Yo, Betty! Bring this boy something to put in his mouth so he can shut the fuck up! Haaaa."

Tim couldn't make out Betty in the crowd until he was bumped in the chest by two huge breasts in a tube top. "Hey, Tim, how you doin', baby?" she said with a scary smile. "Ain't seen you for like forever. What you want, beer or some of that other shit going around? Hey, where you going?"

Before she'd finished saying whatever she had to say, Tim had moved on. He'd thought to catch a glimpse of Maria in the crowd. "I'll get with you later, Betty," he yelled back at her. When he didn't see his favorite Guatemalan, he joined in the group bump and grind. No room for any kind of stepping, only hands overhead, hip and booty moves allowed. Tim felt the effects of the heavy marijuana cloud hanging in the air and soon was giggling at a couple blitzed-out girls talking about an upholstered chair.

Yo, Kathy—chill, baby. Put your foot down. You know the deal. Spank's mom will spaz-out if she sees shoe marks on the furniture an' shit. Humph, I don't know what he be worried about. This ain't exactly House and Gardens...haaa...shhh-shhh, here comes Spank now.

Tim nearly lost it when Spank spoke up. "I heard that shit. Ya'll can get y'all's asses outta here if you don't like the conditions."

"Hey Spank-a-Lank, what the hell is that?" Tim pointed towards the corner.

Spank waved a hand at the thing. "Aw man, that's uh-uh, an old weaving machine. My folks don't know how to throw nothing away."

"What do you do with it?"

"You weave stuff, fool!" he said and pushed through the crowd towards the DJ. "Wait a minute...I'll get back to you homie. Hey, Maaarcie...pump it up, girl. I wanna be feelin' it."

The bony girl at the booth spoke into the microphone. "You talkin' to me, Spanky Butt?"

"Your name still Marcie, right? I can't hear the music. Turn it up— turn it up..." he chanted, bringing the whole room with him. *Turn it up—turn it up.*

"I thought you were going to talk to Spank all night, Timmy," Maria said, tapping him on the shoulder from behind.

"Maria! Oh, so now like you talking to me, huh? Giving me the eyes and shit. What changed since the last day of school? Wait, first gimme some of that spliff."

"Okay, but take it slow, baby." She handed it over.

Tim took a deep pull on the blunt. It sent him into a coughing fit.

"Haa…shit, I told you to go slow, bro. That stuff is strong," she said, patting him on the back.

Tim doubled over from the smoke. "Oh man! This—ain't just weed. I got to talk with Spank. He must be experimenting again," he said, taking another drag.

Maria's hand froze in mid air. "Experimenting? What the fuck are you talking about, dude?"

He held the ace out to her. "Last time it was Windex. He swore that it extended the shelf life of the shit," he said, trying to talk and hold his breath at the same time.

Maria slapped at his hand as if he held an actual roach. "Ew! Windex? You're serious? I don't believe—I can't believe that shit."

Tim smiled and grabbed her around the waist. The skinny DJ had just hit them with a slow jam. "You don't have to believe it. It's better that way," he said turning her around to kiss her on the neck.

Maria wriggled free, turned and looked him in the eyes. "Anyway— why you want to bring up ancient history? Forget about it! Come on, dance with me," she said, pulling him close again. "The last day of school was so long ago. Besides you were being an asshole and you know it!"

"I was being a *what*?"

She held on to him, ignoring his attempt to pull away. "Insisting on going to the bathroom ten minutes before the whole term was over and shit."

Tim held her tighter now, their moves became more exaggerated as the music became louder. "True that—I guess. But Jones was trying to dis me. You saw it."

"Maybe, baby, but you didn't have to get in his face like that. Did you even see how he looked at you when you went up to his desk?" She had to stop talking to move Tim's hand that had traveled way too far south. "It's no wonder he kept you after class. I would've paid to be a fly on the wall. So, out with it, brother! What happened after we left you in the room?"

Tim released his grip suddenly—having to grab her again to break her fall. Now he was pissed. Somebody's cell was ringing. "Why you so worried about it?" he yelled.

Maria was already on her phone. "*Hey*, Daveed! Yeah…nice!"

Tim turned around.

She grabbed his wrist. "Wait—wait a minute, Tim. I have to take this call. My little sister's at home alone."

"Yeah, whatever," he mumbled, happy for her touch.

She put her phone away, he couldn't figure out where. "I thought you were about to leave me again, Timmy."

"Nah, girl. Everything cool at home? Come here," he said, taking her hand." Another slow one floated through the air. "And don't call me Timmy!" he said with a silly smile on his face.

"Okay, Teeeiiiim!" she said, pinching his cheek. "Yes, everything is fine at home. How is it with you? I thought maybe you had seen Rene over there!" she said pointing across the room.

Tim jerked around to see. "What? She's *here*? *Now*? Where?"

Maria slapped him across the back of his sweaty neck. "Got you! Nah man, she's not here. Try and chill, okay?"

They laughed, embraced and—after a while—simply moved to the music without speaking.

In fact, the entire room swayed in silence to the seductive groove. At the mention of Rene, Tim's thoughts went into a tailspin. But the problem with tailspins is that they are usually preceded by a series of breakdowns and followed by a crash. It occurred to him that breaking up with his girlfriend was just another one of his failures.

Maria spoke very softly. "So, what happened with Jones?"

"Why you wanna know?"

"Just curious, that's all. Something didn't seem right when he kept you from leaving that day and…"

"He didn't keep me from leaving nowhere. I hung back 'cause he wanted to talk to me," he said, not breaking their rhythm.

Maria spoke carefully now. "Sooo, that's it? You guys just talked?"

Tim had had enough of this shit. "What the fuck is this, anyway? You training for the police or something?" he said, pushing her away.

"Oooh, baby, go get yourself something to drink. Uh oh, here comes Maurice—I mean uh—Fidel."

Tim leaned in close to her ear now. "What? You been talking to Maurice?"

Fidel's spooky voice cut through the noise. "Yo, Tim! Come on in the back. Spank wants to speak with you about something."

"Ye-yeah okay. Hey, Maria. I'll be back in a minute."

She waved him on in a cutesy manner. "Yeah, yeah...*sure*, Timmy. Oh, *hey*, Saraj! Hey, *sweetie!*"

"Whoa, bro! Take it easy. That table has legs, but it's not going to get out of your way, no matter how *bad* you think you are!" Fidel smiled as he spoke. He looked funny.

"There's so much shit everywhere. You'd think the dude would at least clean up some..." Tim said. As they entered the next room, Fidel's jacket opened enough to expose a nine-millimeter in the pocket. "Oh shit, Fidel! What you going to do with that?"

He pulled it half way out. "What? This?" he said. The funny smile was back.

"Nah, nah, man, don't put it away. Let me see." Tim reached out as if to touch it.

Fidel closed his jacket. "Fuck you! Mind your own business. Spank wants to see you in the back room. That's all this is about." He turned and pushed through another door.

Tim followed. "Yo, just don't be pulling that thing on me!"

Tim could barely see for all the thick smoke in the room. Cigarettes mostly. They had run out of weed a long time ago. The group sat around a card table. Spank gestured towards a chair.

Tim sat down and chuckled. "What's going on? Some kind of meeting?"

"Not without you, brother Tim. Uh...close that door, Fidel! Okay, fellas, we gotta problem."

"Tim, you know Fidel and his cousin Chucky."

Tim returned the cold look Chucky gave him. "Yeah, I kind of already know Chucky," he said with a faint smile. "So—what's up, Spank-a-Lank?"

"You got any money?"

Tim leaned back in his chair. "Yeah, like, *of course.* Uh—*no!*" he said laughing.

Spank's hands lay flat on the table. Side to side, they looked like a black bat splayed out in front of him. "Exactly," he said without smiling.

"Exactly what?"

"We don't have no money either. But it's only 10:30 and we're already outta beer an' shit!" He turned his hands over as he said this.

"Uh…sorry. I ain't got no beer on me either!" Tim said, noticing that he was the only one laughing.

Fidel broke in. "You know Rasheed, right?"

"Fr-from the liquor st-store?"

"Yes!" they all said in unison.

"And so?"

Spank slapped the table. "And we figure since he's a friend of yours, you could get him to front us some beer tonight," he said, taking a drag on a butt.

"You mean, like, on credit or some shit like that?"

Chucky laughed, his face scar formed a tight S. "Yeah, hee-hee, I like that. On credit. That's funny."

The light finally clicked on for Tim. He looked dead at the scrawny dude as he spoke. "I don't think so. Besides liquor stores close at ten, *dawg,*" he said and tried to stand up. Fidel pushed him down in his seat and wagged a finger at him as if to say *be a good boy.*

Spank spoke real business like. "Yes, we know that. But maybe you could convince him? He lives upstairs over the place."

"Ha! *Man,* that fool is blind on gin and dead asleep by now. Nothing's going to wake him up."

"You say nothin'?"

"Yep, nothing." Tim relaxed, feeling the matter was closed.

Spank picked up a deck of cards as he spoke. It practically disappeared in his giant hands. "Cool then. What do you say, Fidel?"

"Yeah. It's cool with me."

Tim leaned back in his chair. "Wait-wait-wait…what the fuck y'all talking about?"

"Tim, my man! We knew about Rasheed," Spank said, with a smirk. "We just needed some confirmation from you. We gonna stop by the joint and *borrow* some of his stock."

Tim waved his hands. "No-no, I don't think that's a good idea." Everyone in the room exchanged looks.

"I'll tell him, Spank," Fidel said with a dead serious tone.

"No, I'll tell him."

"Yo!" Fidel yelled, fixing Spank with his eyes. "I said, *I GOT THIS*! Tim, we didn't bring you in to ask for your opinion. So, what you *think* doesn't carry much sway here. Understand?"

Tim looked at the bulge in Fidel's jacket. "Yeah, man. Chill okay? No problem. W-when y'all going?"

"What do you mean *y'all*, dawg. You goin' too!" Chucky said, letting his southern accent slip in.

"Is there a problem, Tim?" Spank's down-to-business tone was back.

Tim looked at Fidel sitting next to him. The creepy dude didn't return his gaze. Instead he just stared straight ahead at the wall and listened to the conversation. "N-no…Spank-a-Lank. I was just…who's that coming in?"

A girl from the party pushed into the room. "Uh…*Spanky*, when you comin' back out to the party? I mean…"

"CLOSE THE DOOR, BITCH. WHAT DID I TELL YOU LAST TIME!" Spank yelled. "Alright, let's go! Hurry up! Fidel, you drivin'—right?"

Fidel shrugged. "Yeah, I guess."

"Okay, get a hussle on, Tim," he said pointing to the door. "Let's go! Me and Chucky in the back, Fidel, you and Tim in the front seat."

RINGTONE

They rode in silence, listening to the quiet of the dark streets. Fidel drove under the speed limit and hadn't turned on the stereo. They'd already seen one police car and didn't want to attract attention. Suddenly Fidel hit the steering wheel with the butt of his hand. "Aw man…somebody farted. Say something, Spank!"

"That's your breath, Fidel. How's that? Just concentrate on not speeding…just like you're doing. We don't need no problems tonight."

"Hey y'all," Chucky said. "I gots me some fine honeys waitin' back at the spot. So, we need to make this quick." He paused for a moment, laughed and then said, "I think Maria is waitin' on Timmy boy. What say you, big cuz? You feel me?"

"Ah yes! Maria. Ooo la la, Tim," Fidel said taking his hands off the wheel to do a little dance in his seat.

Tim tried to change the subject. "Fidel, Chucky—y'all cousins? For real? Hey, Spank, is that somebody's cell ringing?"

♪ *Chuck-keeee, Chuck-keee, pick-up swee-teee…* ♪

"Oh-oh-oh! Or should I say—ho-ho-*ho*! Is that Maria? Ha!" Fidel half spoke, half sang. The entire car shook as they bounced in their seats and sang, *Chuck-keeee, Chuck-keee, pick-up swee-teee…*

Spank snatched off Chucky's cap and slapped him with it. "Put that motherfucker on silent, yo. Tim! What did you say?" he sounded angry.

The ringtone had freaked Tim out. "Yo, Spank, I-I don't see what's so fffff-fuckin' funny."

Fidel glanced at Tim out of the corner of his eye. "Ahhh-ha! Shit, Chucky, I can't believe you got her to record that!" he practically screamed.

"Chucky? What you sayin, dude? Speak up!" Spank said, nudging him in the ribs.

"I-I don't ssss-see wha-what sss-so ffff-fun-ny."

Spank couldn't keep the laugh out of his voice. "Aw, man! That's cold—makin' fun of somebody's defect and shit. That's not cool."

Fidel chimed in. "Well, Spank-a-Lank, at least with our boy Tim in the car, we'll always find us a handicap parking space! Ahhh-haaa."

"Oh shit, Tim my man! Everybody's bustin' on your ass now! Shhhh! We're here. Slow down, Fido!"

"Fido my ass! I'll break your face, *Spunk!*"

Spank shook his head and waved a hand at the back of Fidel's head, "*Aw, man!* Could y'all tell *Mr. Sensitive* I'm just fuckin' with him?"

Chucky stuck his head out of the window. His voice echoed off the buildings, half of which were abandoned. Only a couple cars were parked. Except for a couple addicts and prostitutes, no one was on the street. "Damn, check it out, the place is all dark, shit. Tim, what's it like in the back?"

Tim had to crawl out of a deep sulk to answer. "Uh—it's dark back there too. But you can get in through the bathroom window. It's really small so it stays unlocked. Uh—you probably could get through it though," he said, turning around to look at Chucky.

"Why you smilin' at me, bitch? *I gotta go?* Spank!" he said, snatching back his cap. Why me? I ain't…"

"You heard the man—cause you can get through the fuckin' window. Maybe you should've eaten your Wheaties when you were a kid," he said, opening the door. "Come on, let's go! Tim, you stay with the car. I'm calling your cell now—answer it. Ok? Now, don't hang up. Just listen and let us know what's goin' on out here on the street or upstairs. Lemme know if you see anybody moving around."

Tim was still dealing with his sulk. "Ye-yeah…okay." He got

another look at Fidel's piece as the thug got out of the car. "Yo—yo," he said. "Be cool with that, that—you know! Chucky, talk to your cousin."

Chucky's eyes got wide. "Oh shiiiiit! Fidel, I see you be ready!"

"Shut the fuck up, Chucky! And you, I told you before, *Timmy boy*, to mind your business and keep your eyes open."

"Yo, don't wo-worry about it, da-dawg," Tim said as coolly as he could.

"It's not me who will have to worry if things go south," Fidel threatened. "I'm not going tell you again. Let's go, y'all."

Tim watched the trio disappear into the shadows. His thoughts wouldn't let him rest. *How the hell did I get myself into this shit? Sitting here like an ass—asphalt—listening to some fools trying to break into a liquor store...what the fuck can they be talking about?*

The windows above the store were still dark. Rasheed was surely dead to the world. The phone had only a couple bars of juice left. Listening to their bullshit, he wondered if they would make it back before his battery went dead.

Shh...be quiet y'all.

Oh—oh shit, man, I think I cut myself.

Shut up, Chucky, keep moving.

Here's the back door.

We don't want the door, we looking for a small window to the bathroom.

It's here somewhere, I can smell it. Fidel, where are you?

Ahmmmm-riiiiight-heeeerrrrre beeeeehiiiinnd y'aalllll!

Shit! Quit fuckin' around, Fidel.

Yo- yo-yo, here it is! Cool! Ok, Chucky, get over here!

Man, I don't wanna—

What? Shhh! Psst...Tim. Everything's cool out there?

Having entered the first stage of a nod, it took Tim a minute to reorient himself. Spank's voice surprised him. "Yeah-yeah man. Everything's cool. Y'all sounding like y'all fucking around. Hurry up!"

Just chill and keep your eyes open. Fidel, put that shit away and hold open the window. This ain't no cops and robbers and shit. Okay cool, now help me with Chucky. Awwwwright. PUSH!

Ahhhhhhhhh! Oh—shit, oh shit!

Sup, Chucky? You alright? I can't see you.

Ooh, oh yeah, I'm alright. My foot went in the fuckin' toilet. Splashed shit all over. Shhh...y'all it ain't funny, yo!

Well, I ain't sittin' next to him on the way back.

Shh...Chucky, open the fucking door. Push on it, dawg, it's not locked.

Tim couldn't help but wonder if the line had finally gone dead. No one had said anything for a couple minutes. *Damn! Sure is quiet in there. Wonder what they doing? Probably drinking. What's that? A light? Oh shit! THE COPS! Ugh...where the fuck is my phone? Got it! Shit! I gotta get out of here. Oh, who's that? Ha, just a bum. Ok think, dawg—easy does it, turn-off-the-ceiling light, wait for the dude to walk past, now-open-the-door—slowly—close it. Walk, don't run, you're almost to the corner—MADE IT!*

Tim jumped at the hissing static noise the phone made just as he rounded the corner. It was Spank talking to him.

He peeked back around the corner once just to confirm to himself what he'd just seen. Fidel's old black Dodge was sitting next to a hydrant. *Damn! Why hadn't he noticed before? Too late for that shit,* he thought.

"Psst...psst...hey y'all—the cops are coming. I see lights. I'm getting outta the car." The phone crackled again.

Don't go anywhere, man. We're coming now.

Tim had already made it halfway down the block before he responded. "Must have been an alarm or something. Anyway Fidel got the keys. I'm out."

VISIT WITH DADDY

As they ate, the drip drip from the sink's faucet annoyed Sheila, but she said nothing about it. The place stank of mold and old farts and the canned beans over rice didn't help anything. But it was cool. The early August heat had little effect on her dad's subterranean hovel.

Even though Tim had been very descriptive of their dad's place, she'd mostly heard the hurt in his voice. Now she understood that it had been more pity than hurt. Here now—pity and its principal sidekick sadness were loafing around her dad's dungeon like chronically obese demons. And they were hungry. She could feel herself under attack from her first step onto the concrete floor. The low ceiling and dankness squeezed out of her any sense that she would leave with hope for something better.

Maybe she simply wanted to see her dad, talk with him and laugh at his silly jokes. He had a talent for mimicry. She particularly loved the way he could impersonate their uncle Gentrale. At the mention of his brother, Victor would go straight into a routine that they'd come to know well—his take on Gentrale's penchant for laughing at his own jokes. Her dad was on that same roll right now and she, chewing her beans, struggled to keep her mouth closed.

Sheila was enjoying herself until he picked up the vodka bottle from the floor. From that point forward, each punch line was punctuated with a shot and a snort. His movements became increasingly uninhibited and fluid as if he were alone in the kitchen recounting old memories to himself. Partly out of fascination, she didn't interrupt him for quite a while. Yes, he was an alcoholic, but curiously she'd never actually seen him drink. Suspecting that she herself was delusional, she told herself that Victor, by hiding it from her, wanted to shield her from the sorry truth.

The jokes became cruder, the cackling louder, the bouts of coughing longer. It seemed to her that he'd stopped seeing her, that her presence had been reduced to another reflective surface like the walls, the fridge or sink. She'd stopped eating as her head came to feel like a tank being filled with, with—bullshit, the only word she could come up with.

"Dad?" she finally said, surprised at the whiney sound of her voice.

In the midst of a long swig, Victor jumped in his seat as if he'd forgotten that he wasn't alone. "Huh?"

Sheila put down her spoon and tried to catch his gaze. "What happened between you and Uncle Gentrale?"

Her dad's lips made a pop sound as he took the bottle away. "Aw, girl. You ain't interested in no ancient history. Bes leave it alone."

"Unk says you disappointed him," she said, leaning forward and resting an elbow on the table.

"He said wha..?" Victor mouthed a curse word. "I'll stomp that fool—humph, talkin' behind a man's back like that!"

"Aw, Dad, he wasn't exactly doing that," she said, rolling her eyes.

"What exactly then did he say? Get yo' story straight now, girl."

Sheila spoke as she put her dish in the sink. "He said something about being really sad when you abandoned them back on the farm. That they were in a real bad way for a long time and…"

"Abandoned them? Sh…it wasn't my fault! I…" Victor let out a giant burp.

She stood behind him and placed a hand on his shoulder. "I'm not blaming anyone, Daddy. I'm just curious about you and him not talking for all these years."

Victor shrugged and looked at the bottle as if he expected it to say something. "Since yo' uncle got him a little time at the school when we was young, he thinks he can go around castin' dis-dispersions and…"

"Aspersions," Sheila said dryly.

"Huh?" he said, turning around to look at her, being careful not to disturb the hand that still rested upon his shoulder. The touch comforted him. "Damn, you like him in that regard, goin' around correctin' people's speech. Anyway, he always thought that he was a slightly higher cut than the rest of us. I just couldn't stay any longer. Had to get up and out of there. A man's gotta do what he's gotta do. I know you heard that one!"

"Just like a woman does, Daddy!" Sheila said, smiling big.

"What? Whew...you be somethin', girl. Look at you! Growin' up so fast. Yes, I suppose for a woman as well, today! That's why I'm so proud of you and your progress in school."

Sheila sat down again and didn't interrupt him as he slurred on about his hopes for her, how proud he was of her and her accomplishments: honor roll, vice president of the debate team. Her father's words took hold of her, caressed her. They sent her back to when she was a child on the swings. Victor, with every push, would render endearments in her ear. With each exertion, the change in his voice embraced her: you are my—heart, my—sweetie pie, you are the—smartest, the—strongest, the—prettiest girl in the universe. She hadn't known what he meant by universe at the time. Years later, she came to understand that he probably didn't either. But to her ears at the time it all sounded really good.

The crash of the vodka bottle on the floor snapped her out of her daydream. There wasn't much in it to talk about in the first place, but the old drunk, as he knelt down to collect the largest shards, carried on as if he'd lost a child. A finger of the stuff lingered in a large corner piece.

Sheila held her breath as she watched him contemplate the unthinkable before chucking it in the trash. She wanted to help him but was paralyzed in her chair as she listened to him tell her that after he'd left the farm, something bad happened, that it was something that he didn't want to talk about.

"If you wanna talk to somebody about it, you can go and talk to your uncle or maybe even yo' brother. I think they talk. But don't ask me anything 'bout it no more. Okay?"

Her promise to not ask him about it swept away the courage to ask him why he left Tim and her and their mother.

THE GLOVE

Tim liked the evening hours of the library during mid-August. With a week since Spank's party and that mess at Rasheed's, he could finally revel in his own thoughts, whose only competition was the tick-tick of the giant wall clock. There were so few people in the joint, it was as if mice were scurrying around in slippers while bookworms lounged in their pajamas. He didn't think it exactly, but sitting at one of the heavy wooden tables, he sensed the patience of the computers—silently waiting to transport, inform, educate. He laughed when he thought of the carefully stacked newspapers, remembering something Darryl had said the day before about the paperboy.

Yeah man, every morning that poor kid delivers freshly printed papers, full of old news.

Picking up a daily, Tim chuckled again and thought, *Dag! If a newspaper was a person, he'd probably be in a funk most of the time. Maybe even in therapy!* Having recently read an article about psychology, he imagined an animated copy of *The Star Ledger* on the therapist's couch.

So, what's on your mind today, Mr. Ledger?
It's always the same dream, doc. I'm delivered to my customers and…
Yeah, go on…
I-I tell them what I know! But it's always stuff they've already heard!
Yeah, Mr. Ledger, it's the same-old shit dream. You have to get over this business or else.

Surprised at the echo of his laugh, Tim shushed himself, having forgotten that except for a few others in distant corners, he was pretty much alone. His eyes fell upon the massive card index that stood proudly in the corner of the room. Unlike the newspapers, he imagined that it wouldn't have problems of insecurity since chaos would be certain if for example it were spontaneously abducted by extraterrestrials.

"S'up Tim. I thought you weren't going to show today," Darryl said, half whispering.

So deep was he in his muse, Tim hadn't heard the dude walk up and jumped in his seat. He turned quickly to face him. The glove on Darryl's hand made him forget all about aliens and shit. "Yeah-yeah, I know, I'm late. Got hung up at the house," Tim said, eyeing the glove.

Darryl leaned on the table, scratching his chin. He rolled his eyes. "That's what you said day before yesterday, dude."

The glove was right next to him now. He couldn't resist asking. "So, Darryl—like, wh-what-up with the glove?"

Darryl's sardonic smile faded as he took his hand from the table. "Uh, yeah, nothing really, just an image thing I'm trying out."

Tim pushed his lips out from his teeth with his tongue. "Hmm… yeah, I got that! Something new, huh?"

"*Kinda-sorta*, yeah."

Tim stood up. "Li-like how long you been sporting that thing? I-I don't re-remember seeing it before."

Darryl turned away and nodded hello at some students just entering the hall. When he faced Tim again, he looked a little annoyed and his smile was a little crooked. "A man has to keep evolving —you know?" he said, exhaling heavily as he spoke. Then his voice seemed to catch on something like a thread on a nail, "Like—why are you suddenly so interested in this glove, yo?"

Tim sat down again and leaned back on his chair, balancing on its rear legs. "Aw man, forget about it. *Chill pill*. Okay?" he said. "So, what you got for me today?"

"Aw man, I'm cool. So, how goes the yoga? Is that why you're late? Did you get yourself twisted up in a knot this afternoon?"

"Veeeery funny. It was just one little article the other day and now I got to hear about it forever. Huh?"

Darryl went to help three girls who'd just arrived. He scooted back to Tim's table. "Oh, I know the article you were checking out! Yeah, the one full of fine honeys doing the down dog!"

"It's downward facing dog, *dawg!*" Tim deadpanned.

"You know, Rene was here today," Darryl said casually.

Tim jumped out of his chair and stood next to him. "What? Did she ask for me?"

Darryl sat down and gestured for his friend to do the same. "I *feel* you, bro. She's a nice girl—real nice. In a way she did ask for you. Mentioned that she'd heard you were coming here every day. I told her yeah, you'd probably swing by sometime today. She let it drop at that." His expression was purely mischievous as he spoke. Chuckling at Tim's open mouth, Darryl hopped up from his chair. " I have to get back to work, man. I'll be back in a few with something good. Okay?"

"Aw, man!" Tim said, lacing his fingers behind his head. "That's cold to leave me hanging like that. Alright, I'm here. Catch you in a few," he said pulling some worksheets from his back pocket.

A sharp click-clack of high heels on tile announced the arrival of the librarian, famous for never looking at you as she spoke. "Hello, Darryl. Hi, Tim. I'm happy to see that you've settled into a rhythm of sorts," she said, inspecting the bracelet on her arm.

"Oh, hi, Mrs. Shepard. A *rhythm?*" he asked, trying to catch her eye.

Now the librarian seemed to be studying the face of the big clock as she listened to him. "Yes, eh-hem. I meant to say that you are showing a new determination and consistency with your studies. This is good news!" She clapped her hands together softly exactly on the word good. It made Tim nervous. "Darryl, when you're done with Tim, I need you in the reference section. Okay?"

"I'll be right there, Mrs. Shepard," Darryl said. They watched the sway of her hips as she clacked her way back to the other side of the building.

"Yo Darryl," Tim whispered. "Yo, like, there's a wrestling section up in here?"

Darryl's eyebrows shot up. "Hee! Man, you're crazy! It's *reference* section. But never mind that, we'll get over there later. For now, let me ask you a question. What's the difference between these two phrases…"

Tim couldn't be sure, but it seemed that Darryl's movements had become stilted, less fluid, and the dude had somehow lost the glove. When Darryl hi-fived him for having figured out simple and past perfect tense, Tim couldn't help but see the reddened mesh imprint at the base of each finger—the point where the glove stopped. He accepted the compliment and said nothing. There was hardly time to say anything, for soon it would be closing time and he still had twenty pages of exercises to complete. Eventually he laughed it off, thinking to catch up with Darryl later in the *wrestling* section.

THIS CHANGES EVERYTHING

At first Tim hadn't recognized Chucky—never could've-would've imagined the punk sitting inside a library let alone reading anything. The runt and some dude he didn't know sat a couple tables away. He did his best to ignore them. But then the whispering began.

"Psst, hey, Tim. S'up?" Chucky whispered.

Tim stared at his book, scratched his temple. "Nothing, just hanging, you know."

"What you doin' up in here? I heard you can't read. Got you some nice *picture books*?" He pronounced it *pitcha books* with a goofy southern accent.

"Nah man," the other boy chimed in, matching Chucky's drawl. "He's entertainin' himself with one of those *National Geogliphics*. Ahhhaaa!"

As they giggled behind their magazine props, Tim corrected him. "It's *National GEOGRAPHIC*—st-stupid."

"Oooh! I do believe he called you stupid, brother," Chucky said, grinning broadly, a missing front tooth on full display, as well as the S scar on his cheek. "I-I-know what's up with him. Hey-hey, Tim. Ho-hoping to run into Maria?"

And so it went. Darryl had surprised Tim with some new readings. Today's topic: Marsupials. With a snort Tim thought, *Yeah, Chucky looks like a cross between an opossum and a wombat. Damn! Something told me not to come late today. Now I have to deal with these fools. I sure hope Rene doesn't come in here now. Well, he ain't said nothing about Rasheed's yet—that's good. Maybe he's not here to fuck with me.*

People had begun to leave. The silence in the joint had become so thick that he could hear an echo after each tick of the giant clock.

Vague blunt noises came from distant corners of the library. No doubt it was Darryl throwing books around, but the sound alarmed Tim. Closing his eyes, he leaned heavily on the table and held his head with both hands. A good whiff of Chucky's BO had given him a headache.

"Yo, *Tim*," whispered the thug, shushing his boy who wanted to get into the action. "Yo, Tim. Tick-tock-tick. I heard that Mr. Jones showed you what time it really was back in June. Showed you who was the real *punk*." Tim froze in his seat as the pounding in his head intensified and his heart sank to his stomach. He wanted to leave, but then where would he go? Couldn't let these crazies follow him home. So he stayed put, stared at his book and hoped that they would get tired and leave.

A text came in. It was Les.

S'up?

Tim wrote back:

I'm at the library taking shit from that chump
Chucky. Don't know if I can take much more from
the scrawny motherfucker.

"Did you hear me, fool?" taunted Chucky with an airy falsetto. Tim didn't have to turn his head to know where they were. His nose told him that the duo had moved to the very next table. At the same time, two girls who were seated on the other side of his table got up and left. He couldn't be sure if it was for Chucky's stink or a sense of trouble in the air.

"Psst…yo, Timmy boy, I heard that he beat you down in the corner while you rolled around on the floor going, *Ooh, aaah, what are you doing, Mr. Jones?*"

Tim couldn't move. Shame seeped into him like old greasy water.

Chucky dropped the falsetto. "So you don't hear me, huh? Well, hear this. What about Rasheed's? Tell me about that shit, motherfucker!"

Sweat rolled down Tim's back from the nape of his neck as his body shook with rage. Okay, it was true, everyone knew about the last day of school. Maybe now was the time to get this shit straight, face up to what happened with Jones once and for all. Putting down his book, he looked Chucky in the eye and hoped to God that he wouldn't stutter.

"So what about it?" was all he could get out. Mrs. Shepard, who pretended to read as she listened to their conversation, completely missed the surprise that swept over Chucky's face like a fast-moving shadow.

Leaning in, he whispered, "Oh, so it's like that, *bitch*? Accordin' to you, leaving us and shit was okay? You should *know* Fidel wants to see your ass. The police towed his ride since you left it parked next to a hydrant. We had to walk back to the party. Seemed that you knew all along there was an alarm in the joint. Said so yourself on the phone. So in your eyes, that was *cool*?"

Finally understanding what the punk was talking about, Tim's heart jumped in his chest. "Na-nah, man. I didn't—"

In a flash, the dude was up and in his face. Cold spit hit Tim on the cheek. "Fuck it! You can try to watch yo' back outside, motherfucker, but it won't do you no good," Chucky snarled.

They ran out the exit cackling like chimps on helium. Chucky's southern drawl echoed from the walls. "Tick-tock, *Timmy boy*."

Tick-tock-tick, mocked the clock on the wall, reminding Tim of his last two fights, if you want to call them that—Maurice and Mr. Jones. *They were more like crucifixions*. He smiled at his new vocabulary word and hopped to his feet when Mrs. Shepard rang her little bell, the closing signal for the day.

Everyone left by the rear service exit—a narrow hall with cinder block walls and fluorescent lights. Tim hoped that only an empty parking lot awaited him.

The air was hot and humid and the lot was vacant. He imagined the sound of a pipe whistle from an old Clint Eastwood flick. "The town is empty, no bad guys in sight," he sighed with relief and turned towards home.

But no. Thirty feet away Chucky and a couple of other dudes were so busy talking they hadn't noticed him.

A text came in. It was Les again:

Get out of there.

Now the boys were coming his way. They resembled a pack of hyenas in their approach: one from each side, Chucky down the middle. Tim had intended to stand his ground but then one of them clutched something in his hand.

He bolted straight into traffic.

The pack, stopped by a wall of passing cars, watched as their prey stood on an island in the middle of the street. Chucky sent his boys to the traffic lights at the opposite corners. Tim stepped out in front of a City Transit Bus, the company his dad drove for—with his hands above his head. It stopped with a hiss and a stream of curses from the driver.

Running blindly into a Dunkin' Donuts parking lot, he slammed shoulder-first into an SUV. Pushing off with both hands, ignoring the pain in his arm, he stumbled past the drive-up window, turned the corner and made a hard right onto King Street. The dude that sat next to Chucky in the library was about fifty feet behind. Running full tilt now, Tim pushed by pedestrians and children at play. He couldn't shake the dude even though his legs burned like hell. Then he saw it—about fifty feet ahead: his next move. It turned out to be a snap to hop over the low front-yard fence. The hoods sitting on the porch didn't have time to react. Careening down the alley into the backyard like a madman, he never saw the Doberman lying silently on the ground. What he did see were teeth lunging from the shadows, but the rock and roll of a chain told him there was no danger.

Up and over the back fence, he found himself standing in the cover of trees listening to a cacophony of barking dog and shouting homies searching for the running boy.

He didn't move.

Then he heard the goofy voice of…Chucky. "Hey, hey hey, he's in the park, I'm goin' around the other side."

He sprinted into the blackness, happy to find that the terrain was flat. Running, pushing leaves and branches out of the way with every step, his mind raced ahead of him before it took a turn back to the beginning of the summer.

He saw himself still trying to read that damned sign, except it was Maurice's face in the place of the missing letter—he's in the hole his dad calls home, listening to his father's drunken regret-gorged drivel—now he's walking up to Jones' desk, but this time, when Jones asks him if that was all he has to say, he hauls off and slaps him hard across his big pursed lips.

The mental image of slapping his teacher focused his mind just in time to see a half-buried stone stop his left foot dead, leaving the rest of him to hurl forward like a dummy in a crash test. Mid-flight, Chucky appeared out of nowhere, held out his arms as if to break the fall of the flying boy but instead jumped out of the way. Tim saw only Chucky's S-shaped scar as he went down.

Face down in the mulch, he caught his breath and braced himself for the beating to come.

A musty green aroma filled his nostrils. Only the sound of a couple of crows crying overhead broke the rhythm of the crickets.

Tim felt the toe of a sneaker in his side. "So, bitch. Thought you was gonna get away, huh? Shiiieeet. Nah-nah, motherfucker, tonight's your night. This here will be an ass-whipping you'll remem—"

♪ Chuck-keeee, Chuck-keee, pick-up swee-teee... ♪

In the end, it wasn't the ringtone that stopped Chucky mid-sentence, it was the feral cry of the boy on the ground that transfixed his ass—as he watched Tim pick up the half-buried rock and put all his natural born weight into landing it at his temple. Just before the punk blacked out, Chucky licked his lips and fingertips—intrigued at the coppery taste of his own blood.

The last thing the fool must have felt was the spray of hot spit on his face, the last thing he must have seen were Tim's lips screaming what must have been the last thing he was going to hear in his short miserable life.

"Fucking ASSHOLE!"

A text beeped in—it was his dad:

Home now. Gonna cook some cabbage. Come on over.

DEALING WITH IT

It was ten o'clock at night and still hot as hell.

Tim sat on the concrete steps of his dad's apartment building, stared at his phone and wondered how long it would be before some of the local gangbangers would take an interest. A couple hooded dudes had already passed by. *It won't be long*, he guessed. *Maybe I better get my ass inside.* But then, he would have to talk—he wasn't ready to talk—not yet, not to his dad. Yet he couldn't think of anyone else he could speak with—that is, if he could explain it. At that moment, explaining it to himself was proving to be a serious problem. The harder he tried to piece together what just happened with everything else that went down over the summer, the more it all seemed a blur, as if he was being drawn down the center of a whirlpool of disappointing images.

Like the dejected sound of his uncle's voice at the end of his freshman year, when it was confirmed that he was again in academic trouble. His mother was so crestfallen. It felt as if the kitchen was going to implode upon them. And that damned smirk on Sheila's face didn't help one bit when he tried to defend himself. Oddly, his only relief was his dad who was still in bed sleeping off a binge. He had hoped that this fact would provide some kind of morbid interference against the full force of his mother's outrage and disillusionment.

When the hooded dudes appeared on the other side of the street for the second time, Tim stood up and paced back and forth on the concrete stoop. He thought of the time in sophomore English class when he'd stumbled on the word *annihilate* pronouncing it *annihila-tee*. He groaned at the memory of his classmates giggling behind their books. Since then he'd searched the term online and found it a perfect description for what he'd managed to do to the countless chances that Mr. Jones, his self-appointed tutor, had given him. The more Jones tried, the angrier he had become. Jones' attention felt like a criticism of him, his life and particularly of his father who could barely read the label on his vodka bottle.

Yes, he had given Jones a hard time, being the class clown most days and a general fuck-up on the others. Like the time when he'd shot ten or twelve spitballs through a plastic straw at Lucy who, like a mechanical target, moved back and forth just outside of the classroom window. Everybody loved it because it took at least ten minutes before Jones figured out what was going on. It was the only time that he'd sent Tim to the principal's office.

Things got worse after he'd stopped showing up to Jones' tutoring sessions. Like the time in study hall when someone hit him upside the head with a chalky eraser. Instead of retaliating, he rubbed the white stuff all over the dark skin of his face.

"Oh shit…what'see doin?" cried a boy in the class.

"Look, look! Oh God!" screamed one of the cheerleaders, giggling hysterically as Tim pushed the eraser down his crotch and stalked around the room like a horny zombie singing *I Will Survive,* copping feels from the girls, who for the most part, squealed in fake protest.

After a while, it seemed that no matter what, Jones always found a way to not throw him out of the room. *How could that dude be for real? He couldn't have been all that worried 'bout me. I don't believe it. Probably was looking out for some kind of extra credit or promotion or something. Yeah, something like that,* he thought.

Then the memory of losing his job at the drug store came at him so fast that his body lurched to one side as if to jump out of the way of the recollection. When friends of his were caught shoplifting on his shift, he could never shake the suspicion of his boss. As for his mom, he'd made up some story, even though he was sure that his sister had heard about it but curiously hadn't said a word.

One argument with his uncle Gentrale had stuck with him. It was one of those groggy mornings just before the beginning of the summer break when he couldn't get out of bed in time for school. Wanting to avoid the old man's bitching, he attempted to slip out the back door undetected. But his wise elder, on to him, laid in wait in the kitchen.

"Whew! You skipped your shower, didn't you!" chided the old man pointing to a chair with his cane.

Totally surprised, Tim simply sat down. "I-I—wanted to get out of the house quick. Seemed like you was going to be a while in the bathroom. I di-didn't want to r-rush you."

"I wasn't going to be that long. And what?" Gentrale took a step back. "You put on fresh clothes without bathing? You're stinking of cigarettes, boy. Look, eat your food and then jump in the shower. I don't want to see you 'till later on this afternoon. Okay?"

Tim was ready with a quick answer. "Since when you can tell us what to do? You not my father! You his brother and…"

Gentrale cut him off with a stern look. "That's right. I'm his brother, even if it's hard to believe we came from the same place. That means you and I come from the same place. He's not here now. He's in trouble, like he's been for most of his life. But I *am* here, and I told your mama that I'll help her the best I can, and that's what I'm doing. Now, after you eat, you are going to get out of my face, bathe properly and take your sorry butt to school."

Thoroughly pissed off, Tim jumped from his chair to look his uncle in the eye. "Oh, s-so now I'm s-sorry, huh?" he said, his voice cracking on the last syllable.

The old farmer didn't even blink. He used to wrestle hogs bigger and a lot scarier than his nephew. "Yes, you are indeed a sorry soul if you don't start taking yourself more seriously, taking life more seriously. You're no baby no more, Tim. The time is coming when you'll have to take care of yourself."

From the way his uncle had just stood there, staring at him, he remembered seeing in those ancient eyes—

A combination of pity and pain,
leaning heavily on a cane.
Mouth a little damp,
drooping to one side—
Bald head reflecting the light from the wall lamp.

For the moment, he could stop pacing. The dudes on the street had lost interest in him. Nevertheless, Tim crouched in the unlit corner of the stoop as he relived being shaken to the core by the doubt on his uncle's face and hoped against hope that his dad would know what to do. Now he had to deal with his own set of insecurities: he was almost eighteen and just about two years behind in school, that is if he didn't pass the proficiency two weeks from now.

At any rate, he had just killed somebody and probably wouldn't have the chance.

He would be in jail soon.

AND THE REST OF THE WORLD ASPIRES TO THIS?

Baby boomers sending us to war,
Politics moved by bored TV stars.
The Christian right sees disorder
south of the border,
Maybe with a big enough fence
You could mask **mass indifference**.

After a big dip
The economy is startin' to grow
Hardly noticed by some…**The Haves and have Moz**.
But unlike
jobs, jobs, jobs,
Their greed never seems to slow.

And the rest of the world aspires to this?

The poorer the community
The more churches and liquor stores.
Tools of inequity
Desensitize the ability
to criticize, and
blunt the hope for more.

So the ghetto be still
pumpin' bumpin' 'n grindin'—out
Historical-
  sterical misfits.
  It's hard to believe
  Even to conceive, that
  The rest of the world aspires to this.

The global economy
Seems to make fun of me,
My work,
My time
My energy.
Waistlines grow as does
the nation's po'
Student debt gone crazy
Along with endless war
        Somebody scream!
   It's hard to believe
   Even to conceive, that
   The rest of the world aspires to this.
It's another week...
Blue on black murder.
   hardly time to speak,
   or surrender—
Hands up, don't shoot...

Broken windows
No child left behind
Stop and Frisk, uh oh...
   Was that a gang sign?
Livin' in the shadows
of those who think they ain't your kind,
   Think they are white,
   Think they are better.
   Entitled
   Privileged,
   Who think a black life don't matter

Bleeding out on the street is a drama so blasé—
Bleeding out on the street is a drama so blasé—
Bleeding out on the street is a drama so blasé—
Bleeding out on the street is a drama so blasé—

It's hard to believe
Even to conceive, that
    The rest of the world aspires—
It's hard to believe
Even to conceive, that
    The rest of the world aspires—
It's hard to believe
Even to conceive, that
    The rest of the world aspires—
It's hard to believe
Even to conceive, that
    The rest of the world aspires to this?
Do you?

AHGOTTAHANDLEONIT!

Tim hated the dilapidated apartment building where his dad lived, with its giant metal door, graffiti, and stink. He especially hated how the cyclone fence surrounding the joint stood perfectly erect, as if the trash and garbage in plain view needed to be protected. Staring at his dad's name next to the buzzer made him think maybe his old man was finally happy. After having lived for so long in precarious situations at the whim and mercy of others, Victor Thornton had become very particular about his name being displayed on his place of residence.

The dudes across the street had suddenly come back and were looking at him. He pushed the button.

"Yeah?" rasped an old voice over rowdy laughter in the background.

"Uh, is my dad there? Tell him it's Tim," he announced, the crack in his voice matching that of the intercom.

"Yo, Vic! It's yo' boy Tim at the door!" yelled the voice into the apartment. Even through the cheap system, Tim could hear the grin in it.

"Well, fool, buzz him in," his father hollered back.

With a dull metallic click, the heavy magnetic lock disengaged. Leaning on the door, Tim pushed into the dark hallway—an airborne cocktail of cleaning agents, urine and boiled cabbage hit him in the face. The swathe of light coming in from the street lamp quickly became a wedge and finally a sliver. The door shut behind him with the sound of a vault. *This place is like a crypt*, he thought. As he watched the outline of his shadow disappear, a loud scream shot through from the rear of the building. He tripped over something metallic in the darkness, but managed to catch hold of the banister to the spiral staircase leading to the basement.

He waited and listened. Nothing. No one opened a door and more importantly, there were no more screams. Still holding onto the railing, he made his way down to his dad's apartment, pausing on each stair, feeling along the dank wall with his other hand. When he tripped the light sensor, a hundred-watt bulb, shooting its load into every crack and crevice of the tiny space, blinded him momentarily. Comically, the solitary door at the bottom of the stairs swung open really fast. In the doorway stood Baggy, childhood friend of his dad. Grey dreadlocks gone fuzzy a long time ago, matching well-groomed beard, hi-top sneakers, red shorts and T-shirt—he could have been a refugee from a Rastafarian geezer basketball league. His broad smile revealed at least six missing teeth.

"Hey hey hey! Who we got here?" he sang. "That you, Tim? Man! I must be gettin' old! How you doin', boy? Uh—what's that in your ear?" He seemed genuinely curious.

"Uh, hi Baggy. I'm fine. It's uh—an ear stud, you know. How are you? I didn't know you was here. *Hey, Dad!*"

Victor stood on the other side of the room wiping his hands with a kitchen towel. "Hello, son. What took you so long? It's pretty late and you're a mess! Somethin' happened? Baggy, what were you gonna do, chat him up in the hallway? Let him in!"

The humid, shotgun apartment was only partially underground. When his dad had just moved in, Tim thought the two windows high up on the wall, just beneath the ceiling, looked like a couple of closed gray eyelids. *Yeah…no wonder they ain't open. Some places you should see before you die, but this here feels like a place you go to die.*

It had been three weeks since Tim's last visit. He never imagined that things could get worse. But they had.

His dad was drinking again.

"Come on in, boy! What you waiting for?" slurred Victor.

"Maybe a formal invitation?" chimed in Baggy, stepping aside from the doorway.

Victor moved a folding chair away from the card table. "Don't mind him, Tim. He's a little, you know…*WEIRD*! Now sit down and relax."

"Aw man, Dad. Don't bust on Baggy, he's cool," Tim offered, trying to get in on the joke. He turned the chair to sit on it backwards.

"Get him straight, boy," Baggy chuckled through old mucus.

In the corner, his dad's old TV still sat on top of a couple of milk crates. An unknown beefy guy, who seemed to have hopelessly lost something up his nose, sat at the card table in the middle of the room. Next to his other hand, a shot glass of something brown lay in wait. Instead of speaking, he eyed Tim suspiciously. Tim eyed him back. The nose finger took a break to pull on his ear as he glanced at Baggy, who nodded with a little smile on his lips.

A huge bottle of whiskey sat next to a rocking chair that faced the television. The air smelled of cooked cabbage. Someone was snoring, but Tim couldn't figure out who it could be. The mountain of furniture in the adjoining room hadn't changed—piled up willy-nilly since the move-in three months prior. Only a rat-sized space along the wall allowed a person to move from the sitting room to the rest of the apartment.

Almost immediately, his dad disappeared through the opening to check on the cabbage that was cooking, leaving him alone with Baggy and the mute thug. The snoring was getting louder.

"So, you be 'bout seventeen now, huh?" asked the old man with the dark puffy circles under his eyes.

"Yeah, that's right," Tim said, trying to take in the whole room and figure out where someone could be sleeping.

"Nice *earring*," said the beefy guy, taking a swig of his drink. He and Baggy looked at Tim's dirty clothes and then at each other.

"Oh uh, th-thanks. It's an ear stud, *yo!*" Tim responded, surprised to hear the guy speak up, not sure if he was teasing him or not.

"Must be about finished with school. That true?" asked Baggy.

"Nah. Not yet," Tim said, shifting in his seat. "Got the proficiencies and another year before…whoa! What the *fuck*?"

In a flash, Tim was squatting with both feet on his chair shaking and pointing at a blanket in the corner. Baggy and the beefy guy didn't seem to notice anything. Tim's voice broke as he screamed, "Hey, something moved over there, under that blanket!"

The blanket spoke in a growling crescendo.

"You guys gotta keep it the *fuck DOWN*! I'm trying to SLEEP OVER *HERE*!"

Tim fell backwards off his chair. As his legs lurched up towards the ceiling, his saggy-baggy jeans lagged behind, exposing way more boxer short than was ever planned. The blanket sprouted a wooly head and arms as it rose and stood to face the wall before turning around to see Tim scrambling up from the floor.

"Damn, you guys! That was cold blooded! Aw, man!" Tim couldn't even hear his own voice for the hoots, hollers and high fives exchanged in rapid fire from one drunk to the next. When his dad called from the kitchen, he had the perfect reason to run out of the room.

"What's goin' on in there?" barked Victor over his shoulder. He was at the stove.

Tim stood in the doorway and hunched his shoulders. "Aw, nothin', just Baggy and them having some fun with me."

Victor pushed by Tim, leaned into the hall and spoke to himself, "I think it's time for those motherfuckers to go now."

Somebody's phone rang. Victor turned suddenly and looked at his son. "Hey, I think that's you. You gotta a new ringtone? Sounds like singing or something?"

Tim jumped and fumbled through his pockets. "Nah, its not sss-so new."

Victor studied the distorted expression on his son's face for a moment before leaning out again from the kitchen doorway. "Yo, fellas, get y'all's shit and split. I'm serious, I hangin' with my boy—you hear me? Get outta here. I'll have to see ya'll later. Okay?"

Turning towards the stove, he didn't look at Tim. It was clear he didn't want to speak yet, so they waited in silence for the rowdy bunch to leave. His dad had been binging again. The smell of stale alcohol and puff around the eyes and midsection told the whole story—or most of it. Adorned only in the top half of his City Transit bus uniform and boxer shorts, Victor grunted as he moved to and fro in the small space. Tim worried that his father's arthritis had flared up again.

They listened to the front door shut with a bang and jangle. As the aimless trio made their way up the stairs, drunken gargoyle giggles emanated from the stairwell through the apartment.

Tim spoke up. "So, this is it, huh?"

"What you talkin' about?" answered Victor over his shoulder.

The folksy curl of a smile in his dad's voice almost made Tim laugh. "I mean. This is your new life, the one you left us for? Is it the freedom you wanted? This is *it?*" The sound of a loud single chop came from the cutting board like a curse word.

Letting go a long sigh, Victor spoke. "I know that you startin' to feel your oats, maybe impressed with your own BO and all, but it sounds like you 'bout to open up a can of worms Tim that you bes leave be. So, how did the school year end up for ya?"

Even having expected the question, Tim felt on the verge of blubbering and blabbering to Daddy just how big a fuck-up his boy had been. And more specifically, he wanted tell him what kind of disaster his son had left in the park. He wanted to know if Victor could help him out of this mess. But he still wasn't ready to talk about it. Something stopped him cold. Perhaps that something was the fact that he already knew the answer to his question. So he lied. "It went okay. I have to study up for the reading proficiency in September and…"

Victor cut in with, "Your mama? How's she doin'?"

Tim looked at his dad swaying side to side as he chopped. "Wha—?"

Victor paused and turned his head a little to the side to say, "She gotta new *friend* yet?"

"Dad! Were you listening to me, or what? I wasn't talking about Mom, I was in the middle of telling you…" He folded his arms and sat heavily in a chair.

"Yeah yeah, I hear you, man. You gonna take the proficiency in the fall. Yeah, I heard you." At the sound of Tim's loud exhalation, Victor glanced over his shoulder. "Wh-what? Now come on, Tim, don't go into one of your sulks on me."

"Yeah, yeah—I guess you heard me!" Tim said, mocking his father's tone. The chopping stopped. Tim could see his father's eyes in his mind before he even turned around.

"What's yo' problem, boy?" His voice sounded more like a threat than a question. Then, putting down the knife, he pulled up a chair and softened his tone. "What's up, Timmy? What happened to your clothes? Looks like you been rolling around in the dirt. Did you cut yourself? Is that blood?" Tim could hear the quiet surprise in his dad's voice. He folded his arms to cover his shirt, sat as still as he could and focused on his sneakers. "Do-don't call me that," he whispered, holding himself close.

"Alright," Victor said, burping and fidgeting with a dishcloth, like he didn't know what to do. "Okay, tell me, Tim. Obviously you're okay, but is—is somebody else sick or somethin'?"

He reached for a water glass half-filled with a clear liquid.

Tim watched his dad turn the glass up to his mouth and felt the hope drain out of his body. He was angry now and glad for it, relieved to be pissed. Then he didn't have to worry about crying. "I'm sick, Dad. Sick and tired of you living over here like this, in *this-this*—"

"Hole," volunteered Victor, looking at his hand, working on a torn cuticle.

"Yeah, man. You li-living in a ho-hole!" He felt his body start to tremble. He slapped his thighs, half stood, sat back down and blew air through his lips. "And you even know you live in a hole! Why'd you leave us? Like I asked you before. Is this what you wanted? *For real?*"

"Aw, man," Victor mumbled as he jumped up to tend to a pot that was boiling over. "Tim, I didn't leave you or your sister. Your mama and me couldn't make it no more. All that stuff I said 'bout being free was just trash talk in the middle of arguing. You know 'bout that. Don't mean nothin'. Ain't got nothin' to do with ya'll kids. What I need you to do is to concentrate on your studies 'cause that's the only thing that will get you up and out of here, out of this life. You hear me, boy? Don't you worry 'bout me. I'll be all right. Just need to get my head straight and..." His voice dropped off. He stared at his hands.

Tim slapped the table. "How you going to do that, Dad—with whiskey or whatever that stuff is? Please don't go down that road again!" he said with deadly seriousness, shocked at how sorry he felt for his father.

Recently, Tim had learned that the name Victor meant victorious. But the guy sitting at the table with him, pondering his question, looked anything but a winner: pantless, bloodshot eyes so gorged with hurt and shame that Tim had to look away. Leaning over, he held his head in his hands. He thought, *Oh shit, I am so fucked. Like Uncle Gentrale said, the dude's in trouble. I think he's in another world and wouldn't have a clue how to help my ass.*

More than a minute passed before Tim looked up at his dad. When he did, he found a familiar scene. The corners of Victor's mouth had turned downward, his right eyebrow arched as he glanced at the back of his left hand. Tim's heart sank because his dad always made the same moves whenever he was about to lie to him. He waited and let him do it anyway.

"*Ahgottahandleonit*, son..."

PASSING DOWN THE PAIN

Victor stared blankly into space as he chewed, sopping up cabbage juice with wads of Wonder Bread. His mind hadn't yet registered it, but he was totally focused on some faded Looney Tunes stickers on the wall— hapless Elmer Fudd aimed his oversized shotgun for yet another futile shot at Bugs Bunny, who unsurprisingly showed little concern.

The imaginary standoff was no match for the very real showdown with his son. After Tim said what he had to say, he ran out of the apartment. Victor's *ahgottahandleonit* lingered on a cloud of perspiration. He smiled and mumbled, "Humph, the boy is growin' up fast."

He leaned back on his chair and looked around the kitchen. The tiny room triggered memories of life back on the farm. Most people, living with nine others in two rooms, learn lessons of adaptation and tolerance. But Victor wasn't like most people. He certainly wasn't like his big brother Gentrale who would lie down for almost anything. Yes, Victor was different—he had a plan. Thoughts of his brother, together with the effects of the booze sent him into a dark place, a place he usually avoided. He leaned heavily on the table, drool oozing from his mouth as his head began a slow descent toward his forearms. He closed his eyes to the memories, paralyzed like someone unable to move before an oncoming train…

Little Vic is breathing the soup they called air during the summer in Orleans Parish. He's on the farm with his seven siblings. They are picking a short crop of cotton, baling hay, slopping the hogs and milking the cows. Brother William has fallen out of a tree and they're laughing at him.

Now he's in the field. The compacted grass is short stacked and spaced evenly into neat rows. Between the cotton plants, the brothers are playing gotcha' with their sisters.

Now they are pulling traps from the Mississippi, taking in the largest haul of crayfish he's ever seen. The brown water is cool—they take a dip even though Papa could show up anytime and there would be hell to pay. The current is strong—they have to be extra careful not to be pulled downriver.

Thoroughly pissed-off, Tim karate kicked open the giant metal door of the apartment block. He wanted to shake the image of his half-conscious father sitting at the kitchen table in his underwear. Victor was as sad as his friends were funny. As long as he lived in that hole, Tim figured, he couldn't expect anything good to come out of the situation. He couldn't expect any help either. At the sidewalk in front of the building, he leaned upon the cyclone fence to catch his breath. "FUCK!"—he screamed and listened to his voice bounce wildly off the buildings. *Lucky those hooded dudes ain't around*, he thought. Interlacing his fingers on top of his head, he muttered to himself, "Chucky, why did you have to push the shit to the extreme? Stupid motherfucker…oh shit, shit," he said, looking upwards, turning around a couple times. "What the fuck am I gonna do? And Dad? Ugh, *Ahgottahandleonit*—bullshit!"

Victor jerked out of his daydream when his plate crashed to the floor. For a full minute, he stared at the greasy mess. An idea pushed through the haze of his thoughts: *Check the vodka bottle.* As he got down on his hands and knees, his joints played a symphony of pops—and cracks, accompanied by the rock and roll of a saltshaker that found a new place under the stove.

Exhausted from the clean up, he sat on the floor, took an endearing glance at the fifth, reached for the contoured container and caressed the bottle with the delicacy of a lover. From the way his legs were feeling, his drinking glass, just as well, could have been in another galaxy. Frowning as if in pain, he turned the bottle up to his mouth, undaunted by the vodka dribbling down his stubbly chin. *Well, for me anyways, it won't be the first time to take a swig from the bottle,* he thought and passed out...

Younger brothers, William and Booker are splashing him. Little Vic dives under the surface to escape their assault and swims towards big brother Gentrale. He wants to dunk him from behind.

Tim pushed off the fence and walked slowly. Something inside told him to get moving. This wasn't the time or place to have a fucking breakdown. It was midnight and he had to be careful. The sidewalks on this side of town were wider, the trees older and larger, but the forlornness of the gutted out buildings and vacant lots was undeniable. At the very next corner, hooded figures—some urban sentries, others independent entrepreneurs—manned their territory and hawked their pulverized dreams. Never without a beat going in his head, Tim dialed down his rhythmic gait a couple notches at the sight of these dudes. However, not completely—stopping all together would have attracted attention. He made sure to avoid all eye contact and hoped to God that they would be uninterested in the brother in the muddy clothes passing through.

Just outside the door of the kitchen, piled to the ceiling, sat all of his shit, as Victor liked to put it. The mishmash, consisting of a bed, lamps, chairs, ladder, tool box, dining room set, two trunks, rolled up rugs, tables, suitcases etc. was like an abstract modernist painting come to life.

Suddenly, the drunk came to and scurried out of the kitchen on hands and knees like a rodent through the darkness...

Little Vic is on the cool bare earth of the barn now, creeping along on all fours. Unexpectedly his dad enters the barn with landowner McClerkin. Little Vic puts his hand to his chest to quiet down the sound of his beating heart. He waits. They won't be long and then he can get to his hiding place and back before dinnertime. It's his turn to bring in the fresh water.

He's watching his father closely now. The swagger is absent. His voice is laden with a heavy conciliatory tone. There's a problem with the six-month audit, a ten percent deficit of cottonseed has to be made up. Standing there in his dirty overalls, his father seems awash in shame and fear. Never returning the white man's stare, he agrees with the decrease in the family's allocation of the weekly yield. McClerkin is calm.

Tim came upon a little commercial strip, its sidewalks lined on both sides with hole-in-the-wall bars. A promenade of stylish night crawlers and bar flies moved slowly up and down the sidewalk as music pumped out of every doorway. In the middle of the street, what would normally be considered traffic resembled a parking lot full of pimped-out clunkers.

Tim, bouncing to a hip-hop beat in his head, paused to take in the scene. A stray cat found his pant leg and rubbed its body against it. Absentmindedly picking up the pitiful creature that purred lustfully at his touch, he smiled but then realized that he'd reached the limit of any kindness he could extend.

"Fuck *all* this shit!" he screamed and slung it into the traffic.

Victor collapsed onto his knees and elbows about halfway through the passageway until the shock of a large cockroach crawling across his hands got him going again.

If Baggy had been still hanging around, he would have seen his friend barrel into the living room only to collapse unconscious onto his belly.

McClerkin is holding a curb bit. Its leather strap hangs limply to the floor. The man is pointing to the ledger in his other hand, but Little Vic's dad is watching the one with the horse tether. The white man is smiling now.

Judging from his City Transit shirt, caked with sweat and dust, Victor figured that he'd been out for a while. Leaning heavily on the card table, he pulled himself onto the rocking chair that creaked in protest from his weight. In the middle of this onslaught of fragmented recollections, a vision comes to him: an angry sea at dawn; the words *abandonment* and *betrayal* ascend over the horizon in the form of two glowing black suns. The sway of the rocker forces him deeper into his muse.

Little Vic watches,

 the hand of McClerkin make a slow ascent.

He watches,

 his father stand perfectly still and let the white man wind the leather strap around his neck. Twice.

He watches,

 McClerkin tie a knot and jerk his father to the ground. The white man is leaning in close now, whispering into his ear to be sure that not even the cows can hear.

He watches,

 the breast of his father heave as if he's having trouble breathing. But the man isn't finished talking yet.

He watches,

 HIMSELF, throw a milking pail at the head of McClerkin.

He misses and runs out into the dusk…

The memory pushed in on Victor like a stampede and he kicked the floor hard—too hard. The cheap rocker sent him heels over head. Blind with panic, the drunk jumped to his feet screaming, "I didn't mean to leave you, Pops!" and ran out of the apartment into the stairwell. The door slammed shut behind him.

Blackness.

A thick spider's web caught him on the ear. It wasn't but a couple seconds of reeling around in the dark before his head found the low hanging beam under the stairwell. All went quiet, except for his snoring that echoed against the stone walls…

It's dark. Little Vic trips and falls down an irrigation ditch. Listening for angry footsteps, he sits quiet 'till the coast is clear. Two minutes later, he's bringing water to the dinner table.

Embarrassed to look at his dad, he can barely eat for what he's just witnessed in the barn. He shakes with shame in his seat for running away, abandoning his father. It's too late now to make things right, too late to put the seed back.

Victor shivered and woke himself up. Every bone in his body ached from the dank cold of the stone floor. Remembering the matches in his pocket, he checked himself for bugs—especially spiders—and found the opening at the bottom of the door where he kept a spare key.

He picked up the vodka bottle again hoping to shake the shame in Tim's question. *Why had he left them?* He wondered if the answer was that he was simply one of those people who doesn't stick around, who gives up and walks away, had always been that way...

Little Vic is behind the cottonseed barn, placing bags of seed in his hiding place. The air is full of dust and the noise is deafening. Crying, he reaches into the back of the barn, scooping cottonseed through a hole in the boards. Final count, twelve, thirteen sacks of misery.

He's running—he's carrying a pillowcase. Inside—his other shirt, a sandwich and the money from the sale of the seed. He's remembering his trembling hands, counting the dirty cash.

As if on a rhythmic loop, Tim's father's last words—*Ahgottahandleonit*—repeated in his mind. The harder he tried to push them away, the clearer their form and rhythm became. Like a gas, a pulse escaped from his lips, as if it had become too strong for his body to contain. Explosive syncopated high and low consonants combined into a series of juxtaposed patterns, held together with a lot of wheezy rhythmic breathing made for an infectious groove. He never heard the squeal of tires, the thump of the cat's body on the hood of the passing car nor the curses that followed.

"Ahgottahandleonit," Victor grunted and took perhaps the longest swig of the day. With each burning swallow, he refused his body's need for oxygen and became more determined to finish the bottle. Why not? He was just another fucking loser who had left his family stranded. The gray eyelid windows looked on sleepily as he completed his mission, wobbled to his feet and made haste to the toilet...

Little Vic is on the phone listening to his big brother Gentrale tell him that something terrible has happened.

As if he could dilute the message, he's holding the receiver slightly away from his ear. Little Vic lets Gentrale's words hang in the air for a while before he slowly pushes the hook down.

Tim never saw the cat shoot up the windshield and over the roof of the moving vehicle. It sprang off the roof of the car behind that, fortunately, had already stopped. He didn't look back as he moved down the sidewalk away from the melee, blending into the gathering crowd. Hands clapping, stepping in time, he had transformed into a lanky wind-up dancing doll—a toy store fugitive on the loose.

> Ahgotta**handle**onit son...
> Ahgotta**handle**onit.
> Ain't 'bout bein' free,
> It's 'tween yo mama an' me.
> Ahgottahandleonit son...
> Ahgottahandleonit.
> You worried 'bout the whis–ky?
> **Don't think about it.**

Back on the farm, back in the day,
Nothin' was ours not even the tools.
We worked the land, but had no say—
no power to refuse.
We lived on credit,
That's what they called it— 'cept for,

we couldn't get out of it.
The nine of us lived in that tiny hole,
I was the only one sayin' we deserved more.
At night we slept two to a cot

spent our days in the fields—
fo' real.
With no escape or place to fail,
We worked like dogs in our open-air jail.

I hid in the barn
creeping along the floor.
In came McClerkin,
Man, I was shaken.
But then I saw yo' gramps
Standin' bent like he got the cramps.
The leather 'round his neck
Wouldn't let him stand straight.
A strap for a beast
Now a tool of hate.
I'm lookin' at my daddy,
There's no smile, no swagger.
He speaks real low,
Like a truly humble nigga.
The cottonseed is down,
There's no explanation.
McClerkin jerks the belt,
He wants a solution.
Daddy, awash in shame and fear—
Takes a hit to the weekly yield.

This hole in my soul done got so wide
I shiver at the thought of looking inside.
I don't wanna see how I lost my head,
Stealing the seed, running out on my peeps
    —ditching the homestead.
One desperate move,
sent my brother in motion
to meet those fools,

now our family's broken.
But this ain't so new.
When I look at you
I see the same ol' story
in a modern venue.

You come in my place.
With a heart full of anger.
The story's on yo' face,
Another boy heading for danger.
You in need of my help,
I don't know if I care
I'm too drunk really—
So I sit in this chair,
With a bottle—lookin' silly.

We poke around the edges
But then I get distracted
Our talk becomes protracted
Maybe you over-reac-ted?
I know,
it's hard to see.
I'm just passin' on
the pain of my legacy.
Baby, can you feel me?

Ahgotta*handleonit* son…
Ahgotta*handleonit*.
Ain't 'bout bein' free,
It's 'tween yo mama an' me.
Ahgottahandleonit son…
Ahgottahandleonit.
You worried 'bout the whis–ky?
Don't think about it.
Ahgotta*handleonit*.
Ahgotta*handleonit, onit, onit!*

"Aw man, Dad…did you really have to leave us?"

THEY CAN'T TAKE THAT AWAY FROM YA

It was early afternoon. Tim sat at a crowded library table reading the news online. The joint was unusually busy—a welcomed distraction from his thoughts. Nothing—no mention in either of the local papers of anybody found anywhere. It had been three whole days since he'd left Chucky in the park, left the stink and lies of his drunken father in that stupid apartment.

But just that morning, he'd had breakfast with his dad who had hit him up on his phone first thing. He showed up to his old man's door without even answering his text.

When his tutor suddenly arrived to say that there was a call for him at the desk, everyone turned to see who was in trouble. At least that was the way Tim felt about it. This had to be something. You don't get called on the library phone for chitchat. "Wh-what's up, Darryl?"

Too busy to fool around, Darryl shrugged and said, "Just take the call, man. It's your sister," and rolled a cartful of books away.

Tim suspected that he could have been dreaming again or it was the police. Surely something had changed. The proof of it was Mrs. Shepard—she looked directly into his eyes as she handed over the receiver. Weirdly, she appeared about ready to burst into laughter. Tim thought that maybe it was for the whispering girls at the corner table. He could hear them riffing through lewd scenarios for the mysterious phone call at the library desk.

"He-hello, Sheila? What's up?" he said, afraid to let the receiver touch his ear.

"Why is your phone off? You have to come home now!" she screamed.

The sound of her voice sent Tim into a panic sprint towards

the restroom, pulling the entire phone base off the desk along with practically everything else. "So-sorry about that," he said to the librarian as he picked up the mess. "Yeah I know, I know…it's a landline."

Oh shit! he thought. *Could this be it?* "Why? Wha—happened? Why didn't you call my cell?"

His sister exhaled into the phone. "I just said that it's turned off, boy! It's Daddy, Tim. He's gone."

"Sh—gone where? I-I just saw him this morning—he ma-made me breakfast!"

"Well, he's dead, Tim! Get your butt over here. Now!" she said, and hung up.

He would have broke down in tears right then and there if Mrs. Shepard hadn't with a simple touch on the arm sent a jolt of static electricity through him. He wondered about that touch for a long time, playing the scene in his mind again and again, each time seeing himself flinch like a fish. He could never decide if the shock was more from her hand on his skin or the fact that before that moment, he hadn't noticed her eyes and how beautiful they were.

Just that morning, his father had cooked up a giant stack of pancakes, scrambled eggs and ham. They watched adventure movies, exchanged funny stories and even talked about girls. It was like old times except that this time, his old man was talking different. "Timmy, whatever you do in life, do your best. Make sure to get yourself an education 'cause they can't take that away from ya!"

He walked the long way home and bathed in the memory of their last meal together. His dad had been so funny, talkative, full of life. For the first time in a while he didn't leave his hole feeling sorry for him.

A familial patchwork of narratives around his dad ran through his mind. Somehow they always led to Victor as a kid watching a white man beat down his own father, Tim's grandfather. Piecing together stories he'd imagined many times, Tim's internal eye moved circuitously from the face of his dad, to the face of his grandfather, to the white man's face and so on. But this time they were all in Jones' classroom.

His teacher inhabited the body of the white man and he—Tim—stood in his grandfather's overalls. Tim was so deep in his muse that when landowner/Jones came to thrash him, he lurched blindly to the side and slammed into a kid on the street. Before the dude could say anything, he'd sprinted away.

He slowed to a walk when he arrived at the corner near his house and imagined himself gliding along a couple inches above the surface. Nothing could touch him. A breeze kicked up the sweet aroma of lilies from the neighbor's front yard, and he heard his dad's voice in the soft rustle of the leaves on the trees, saying to him the things that he'd always wanted to hear from him, but never did:

You can do it, Tim—I have faith in you.

I'm proud of you.

I love you, son.

He wanted to deny, delay the pain that was coming. He also needed to settle with Jones.

WHERE'S TIM?

Things were way too festive for Julia. Victor was dead. D. E. A. D. No matter how many people showed up or how much food they consumed, there was nothing anyone could do about it. Looking at the six or seven cakes sitting next to a banquet of home-cooked meats and vegetables on the kitchen table, Julia thought, *Damn! 'Scuse me, Lord. The body ain't even cold yet. Seems like they had this stuff already cooked and ready for when Victor would finally kick the bucket.*

Julia smiled at the sight of her daughter in the doorway. Sheila walked into the room and hugged her for a long time. Everyone watched them in silence. "Oh baby, baby, baby…it's going to be alright. You know that, don't you?"

"Yeah, Mom. I know, I know. You need to sit…" she whispered, stroking her mother's hair.

"Where's Tim?" Julia asked, her eyes glassy with tears.

Sheila pulled her mom's wet face into her neck and hugged tight. "I called him at the library. He's on his way. Don't worry."

"Oh Lord…how is he going handle this? You know he's a delicate boy."

"I talked to him, Mom. He sounded okay to me. He'll be here in a minute. Oh! Mom, you're shaking! Give me your hands—let me help— are you alright?"

Julia stood straight, wiped her tears and thought, *He's just like his Daddy. Oh no! Forgive me, Lord.* "So you have talked to him? Never mind, darling. I'm going to my room for a bit. You tend to things, okay? No-no, I'm good, Leola, Tissie…Joe…I'm fine. I'll be right back."

She nearly fainted when she closed the door behind her. She lurched towards the bed, tossed aside some of the clothes that covered it and collapsed face down on top of what remained. A loud familiar squeak came from the far wall. She'd forgotten to close the closet door again—in her mind's eye she could see the cheap closet leaning hard to one side, threatening to collapse. It would have to wait.

It had been a crazy morning. Getting the call at work, asking permission to leave, waiting for the bus in the heat. It didn't matter, she'd become used to the hot days and the wait gave her time to make calls and arrangements. She hadn't planned for so many people to show up. But it was no use thinking it could have been any other way, once Aunt Tissie got wind of it. By the time she got home, the first faces had already arrived, sitting with Gentrale who'd begun a silent vigil. The air in the room sat very still—heavily perfumed from the fresh cut lilies in new vases. Thank God someone had dragged out the fan from the basement.

Julia squeezed hard what she thought were her daughter's hands and opened her eyes to the sweet smile and crooked teeth of Aunt Tissie.

"You-you alright, Julia?"

"Wha—? Who? Aunt Tissie? I must've been dreaming. Whew!"

With a firm hand on Julia's forearm, Tissie cooed, "Whoa, don't get up. It's been a long day. Lie down a little while longer. I'm not going anywhere." A young eighty something, the only facial lines visible were crow's feet in the corners of her eyes. She reeked of Chanel No. 5. Her flowered dress fit snuggly around her waist while a slender gold necklace competed with matching bracelets for attention. At the sound of a crash and laughter coming from the living room, Julia said, "I'm glad to hear that everybody's enjoying themselves."

"Oh, child. Don't let it get to you. They just trying to distract themselves. We all are. Especially me. I don't claim to know what's in the Lord's mind, but it don't seem right for an old auntie to outlive her nephew."

The curtains swayed solemnly as if in agreement. Julia watched their shadow move across Tissie's face. "So, how are you, Auntie?"

"Don't worry 'bout this old bird. How are you is the question? I know what it's like to raise kids alone." She moved her head side to side slowly as she spoke.

"I'm not exactly alone, there's Gentrale—" At the thought of Victor's brother, her son came to mind. Julia covered her face with her hands.

"Oh, don't cry, darling," Tissie said, pushing Julia's hair away from her face. "Don't you worry yourself, girl. Tim'll be here before you know it."

"Yeah—you're right. Anyway, like I was saying, having Gentrale here has been a blessing."

"Well, that's something, I suppose," the old biddy mumbled. "But he's getting up there himself. Oh, I can remember them as kids—seem like yesterday," she said, working a pair of knitting needles in her hands. "Uh, Julia baby, how you intend to make it from this day forward? I mean all that legal stuff is, uh, behind you now. Right?"

Julia looked at her husband's aunt long and hard. Grateful that they didn't have an audience, she smiled and relaxed in the luxury of not having to save face. For once, she could think before responding. "Yes, Auntie, that's all over with now. I got a job at a factory and everythi…"

Fearing she'd stepped over the line, Tissie cut her off. "I-I didn't mean to offend," she said nervously.

Julia pushed up onto her elbows. "No, Auntie! I've got plans to get out of here with the kids and…"

"Nothin' to do with that man in jail, does it?" She didn't look at her niece this time.

In a flash Julia was on her feet—hands on hips, nostrils flaring, set for battle. "What are you talking about? And where'd you hear anything about some man? Where you get off asking me something like that?"

Tissie's knitting needles went into a frenzied sprint. "Oh! I-I'm sorry, honey. You right. It ain't none of my business. I mean…"

"You damn straight, it ain't," Julia yelled and turned to leave. When the bedroom door failed to open on her first try, Julia placed her foot on the wall for leverage. The thing swung open with a crick and a bang.

"Sheilaaaaaaa! Where the hell is Tim? Well, go and find his ass!"

STRESS

"Well, how long he's been here? Why didn't you tell me? Let me through, ya'll!"

His mother's voice sounded thick and wild as it cut through the crowd. He had figured it would be like that so he'd deliberately slipped in the back door to avoid making a scene. But all his efforts were in vain.

"Tiiiimmmy!" she hollered. She grabbed him around the neck with both arms and bawled full force, squeezing him as tight as she could. To his surprise, it made him feel better. "Ooh, Timmy…I'm so sorry, baby, so sorry…ahhhh. You going to be alright. You know it, don't you?" she blubbered into his neck.

Tim didn't dare to look at anyone. He kept his head down and spoke into her neck. "Yeah, Mom. I-I'm alright, I guess. Where's Sheila?" He wriggled his face free of her shoulder.

All eyes were on them. He wanted to cry, but not like this, as if it were a performance.

So he held her tight and planned to run out of the house as soon as she released him. A whiff of jasmine oil tickled his nose. His heart skipped a beat. *Is that Rene?* he thought, but when he turned his head to look, his sister was practically on top of him from behind, strong arms trapping him around his waist, leaning her head on his back. Sobbing her ass off. "Timmy!"

Speechless, sandwiched between the two of them, he stood there soaked front and back.

His own grief pushed inside his chest like a volcano. *Don't do it, dawg. Don't do it!*

In desperation, he turned and looked for his uncle Gentrale who sat alone in a corner not speaking to anyone. A seamless piece of an idea came to him and it made him feel better—

Blue suit saggin'.
Seams strainin'
to reign in
the grief of a
brother in his
     waning—years.
Bow-tied, recently deodorized—
matching handkerchief peeping
from a breast pocket
     of his ancient outfit.
Silver grey hair
sprouting wildly everywhere
'cept from the crown of his deep chocolate head
     that shone like a coffee bean.
Tapping ratty wingtips to a secret song,
swaying side-to-side,
hands and chin long,
resting on an African cane,
     as he stared into the distance.

Gentrale returned his nephew's gaze, nodding with appreciation for the care he saw in his eyes. They had become close in spite of their numerous rows. He genuinely worried about the boy. After six weeks of summer school, instead of showing signs of getting it together, it appeared that ambition had been wrung out of him like water from a sponge. No wonder, he reckoned, Julia could fly off the handle so easily. The girl was on her own, tired and discouraged—pretty much helpless to raise her children right.

His mind turned to his dead brother who in many ways couldn't help turning out like he did. While what happened down on the farm, back in the day, had affected them all badly, it was Victor who'd actually witnessed his father's shame. Since he could never be sure how he himself would have reacted, he couldn't really blame his brother for running away like he did—not completely.

But then, there was the matter of Booker.

Gentrale closed his eyes at the memory of the torn-up body of their younger brother who—out of despair over Victor's departure—had gone into town to get drunk and returned a corpse.

Some good ol' boys who didn't like the looks of the uppity nigger tied him to the back of a pickup and drug him for a quarter mile down a country road. Some tried to put the blame for Booker's death on Victor for leaving his family as he did.

Gentrale figured it was pure guilt that fueled Victor's anger, cussin' and drinking—he must have infected his own son with hopelessness. The way his nephew had been talking back and sneaking in and out of the house without a word seemed to confirm his suspicions and made his head hurt.

Over the years Victor and Gentrale hadn't been very close. But here, on full display, was the fact that there had been a deep connection between them. Now only the pain remained. Gentrale hadn't spoken a word all day, so Tim, like everyone else, was surprised to hear the old man call out to him. It gave him the perfect escape route from the grip of his mom and sister.

"Timmy!" Gentrale croaked. The sorrow in his voice cut through the crowd.

Tim wrestled himself free and pulled up close to his uncle. "You alright, Uncle Gentrale?" he said, wiping his brow.

Gentrale pointed and curled his index finger. As Tim moved in closer, he leaned towards his ear. "Yes, but get me outta here! Okay?"

Ten minutes later they had slipped out of the rear door into the backyard. Gentrale paused and stared at the rows in the soil where a vegetable garden had once existed. He locked elbows with his nephew, made a start and paused again just as Tim lurched backwards to brush off a hairy caterpillar from his lapel. Gentrale shook his head with a sad chuckle.

"You know, yo' father and me used to live on a farm down south."

"Hey Unk, didju see that thing?" The distracted look in Gentrale's eye told Tim that his uncle's mind was somewhere else. He wasn't thinking about caterpillars. "Ye-yeah, I know—musta been a whole different life, huh?"

They started to walk again. Gentrale sighed loudly. "Completely different. Sho can't say it was better. Even though it was considered modern times—shoot it was the 50's and 60's. Even with the war goin' on, the country was thrivin', yet we were living something poorly. We were damn near slaves," he said, taking Tim's arm again as they turned towards the alley.

"Tsk, come on, Uncle Gentrale! I never heard…" His uncle turned quickly and fixed him with his eyes. His whole body jerked rigid. "Boy, don'tchu be suckin' yo teeth at me if you plan on keeping 'em a while longer!"

"I-I'm sorry, I wasn't tryin' to say that you were lyin', but…slavery?"

"Timmy, you can't know the whole story, but you should've heard plenty by now. Share croppin'—which for a black family back then meant slavery. Or close enough. We hadta give over ninety po-cent of our crop just to be able to stay on the land, have work and a place to live." His words brought them to a dead stop. Tim, not seeming to notice, stood silently staring at his sneakers. His jaw was working like someone in deep thought. Gentrale said nothing. He watched the boy and let him chew on what he'd said for a moment before jerking his arm.

"Come on!" he whispered.

They ducked into the alley that led to the street. The narrow passageway was partially blocked by old toilet fixtures and broken baby furniture. They had to move slowly. When Tim heard his mom calling out to them from the backyard, he held his arm out to his uncle. "Shh…take my hand."

"Don't you worry 'bout me, son. Better you look out fo' yourself. Psst! Wait, boy! Somebody's coming out onto the front porch. Quiet."

"Ok, ok…now keep your head down, Unk. Let's go!"

Crouching behind the tall hedges, they scooted over to the neighbor's front yard. The sudden fresh spring in Gentrale's step told Tim that his uncle was going to be fine. He almost laughed each time he'd glanced back at the old codger, whose arched eyebrows, wild elbows and frozen grin were the only indication that he was running. Gentrale was having fun, even if it was true that the more energy he committed to his hustle, the slower he went. At the sight of the next door neighbor, Tim stopped short and stood upright. Gentrale ran right into him and flopped to the ground like a rag doll.

"Hi, Mrs. Green," called out Tim as casually as he could, extending a hand to his uncle.

The neighbor eyed them curiously, over her glasses. "Timmy. Mr. Thornton, you okay?" she asked, watching closely as Gentrale brushed off his pants.

"Uh, of course. I'm fine, Daisy. How you doin'? We just passin' through," Gentrale said as sweetly as he could.

"Make sure to watch out for my violets over there. You're gonna trample 'em if ya not careful."

"Will do, Mrs. Green. Have a good day," said Tim, waving at her as he pulled on his uncle's sleeve.

It was four in the afternoon and the leaves on the trees were so still that Tim wondered if bugs could suffer from heat stroke. He also wondered if there would be any police hanging around the Chicken Shack.

"What are you thinking, son?" asked Gentrale, hooking back onto Tim's elbow.

Tim wiped his eyes with the end of his shirt. "You know, I just saw him this morning."

"Oh yes. So I heard. How was he?"

"He was good. Better than I'd seen him in a while."

"Hmm…not be drinking, I suppose?"

"Yeah! I mean no! And there wasn't no liquor around either. I thought that was strange for an alcoholic."

Gentrale jerked and stopped. "He wasn't no alkee," he said hoarsely. Water had collected in his eyes.

Tim pulled his uncle to a dead stop on the sidewalk and turned to look at him. "No? Come on, Uncle Gentrale! If he wasn't an alcoholic, then why—ugh!"

"Why what, exactly?" Gentrale said, tugging his nephew's arm. He could feel a tremble in it. They resumed their walk.

"S-so, when he was living with us, w-why did he and mom battle it out everyday about his drinking?"

"They were fighting about a lot of other things besides that, Timmy. Believe me! But please, please don't get yourself worked up 'bout that old business, boy. Yo' mama didn't know how to talk about the deeper stuff. The drinking, humph—was easy to see, easy to point to." Releasing his grip on his nephew, Gentrale wiped his brow with a handkerchief.

Tim flicked sweat from his face with his hands. "W-why then were all his friends drunks? Why did he keep such big bottles of vodka around all the time?"

The insouciant wise-ass laughed hard at this one. "Because—yo' daddy preferred to drink in company. Ha! Aw my-my goodness, Timmy boy. Those friends of his were terrible, weren't they? That Baggy though was one funny son-of-a-gun! I'll give him that!"

Other than the feeble cackles of Gentrale, the street was quiet. His uncle was right, of course, but Tim resisted laughing. Instead, he worked hard to distract himself by squinting hard to see the hot air rise from a sidewalk grate. This time, when he spoke, it sounded more like whining. "W-well, if he wasn't no alkee like you say, why then was he usually drunk whenever I went to see him?"

On that one, Gentrale gave a loud snort and fixed his eyes across the street at a couple skateboarders whizzing by. Sighing, he almost seemed to lose interest. "Oh, I don't know, Timmy. Can't say really. But I can say this: he was no alkee, he just liked to drink. That's all. Had a tolerance for the stuff. Wasn't no alcoholic."

Tim smiled at how sure his uncle sounded.

A cop car screamed past them down the street. Tim jerked but masked his alarm by nudging his uncle in the ribs. "Hmm, that's good to know. But this mornin', he-he was—different. Like he had to tell me a lot of important stuff in a hurry. It was like he knew that he was out of time. Was he like that when y'all was young? I mean, for example, did he seem to know things?"

For a while, they simply walked arm in arm, saying nothing. Gentrale had gone off deep in thought. Tim nudged him in the ribs.

"Well, Unk?"

"Eh-hem. Yes, I was thinking 'bout whatchu asked me. I can r'member back on the farm. Yo' daddy was always going on 'bout how he couldn't see no difference in our lives compared to how our folks was describing the olden days, when life for us black folk was really hard. As soon as he got his legs, so to speak, he up and hauled ass out of there. He was one year older than you—eighteen. I remember it 'cause it was July of 1968, three months after they killed Martin Luther King.

"One night, after that mess in the barn concerning the white landowner and Papa—yo' granddaddy—I know you heard about it— Victor was talkin' somethin' fierce 'bout conditions 'till all nine of us in that two-room shack begged him to shut up. We didn't beg him exactly. We jumped him, all of us. I even had his arm behind his back. He finally closed his trap. Next mornin', his cot and him was gone. Humph, ten years my junior and he knew somethin' I didn't at the time. That's fo' sure! Dunno why I hung around for so long."

"Ha! So, it wasn't real slavery!" exclaimed Tim, clapping his hands.

Gentrale stopped short again and looked at his nephew from head to toe with pity in his eyes. He was angry. "Is that all you got out of what I just said? Knucklehead!"

"Ahhh-ha, aw man! Gotchu, Uncle Gentrale. You're really pissed off!"

"Watcho mouth, boy! Now…let's sit down here for a bit. Ahh, oooh, whew…these ol' bones need a rest. Run over to the store, Timmy, and bring me back a Coke. Here, take this, buy whatever you want."

They'd paused at a bus stop. Half of the Plexiglass panels were broken or torn out. The remains of a public telephone hung dumbly on a street lamp pole. A wire mesh trash receptacle overflowed with debris. A city map decorated with permanent markers outlining sexual images remained visible. Tim worried about leaving the old man alone. The police cruiser parked in front of the Shack worried him too, but Gentrale detested fast food joints, claimed they made his clothes stink. Anyway, it was just a couple of colas and he would only be a minute. He returned in what seemed like seconds smiling victoriously. His uncle's face lit up as he reached greedily with both hands for the can.

"Damn, that was quick! Did you beam over there and back, Timmy?" he quipped, taking a long swig.

"It's a fast food joint, man! Get it? Dag! Now, what was we talkin' 'bout?" he asked as he helped Gentrale up from the metal bench and aimed him back towards the house.

An old black Dodge with its stereo blasting careened up to the curb. Fidel sat at the wheel, chewing on a toothpick. He didn't look at Tim. Spank called out from the back seat. "Yo, Tim! S'up?"

It surprised Tim. He looked at his uncle who leaned on his cane and deadpanned him like a pro. Tim wanted to sound friendly. "Aw, man! Spank, what's up, cuz? Ain't seen you sin-since the—party." After that night at Rasheed's, something inside him had hoped that he wouldn't see these dudes again.

"Ye-yeah, cuz, that's right. Since the fucking—party," Fidel sneered, never turning his head.

Gentrale spoke up. "Timmy, we need to get back. You know? In case your mama needs us. Come on, let's go, son."

"This yo' pops, Tim? For real?" Spank exclaimed from the car window. Then he said to his boys in the car, "Oh man, that dude is dusty!" It seemed the junker would fall apart from their screams.

That was enough friendly tone for Tim. "That was funny Spank-a-Lank, but y'all about to step in some shit here. That's my uncle, my father's brother. His name is Mr. Thornton. So, tread lightly, motherfuckers."

"Timmy! We don't need no trouble here. Let's go!" Gentrale said, pulling him by the arm. As he turned to go with his uncle, Fidel killed the engine. Suddenly, you could hear the kickball game going on in the street right next to them.

Spank's high-pitched laugh mocked Tim in a girlie voice. "Ooh, tread lightly...breaking bad on us, Tim, or should we call you Mr. White?"

Even Fidel cracked a serpent-like smile for about a half second. "Yo, Tim. I would appreciate it if you see my cousin Chucky, tell him to make a presence. People are looking for him. Maria asked about him yesterday." Fidel sounded really pissed, but he managed to smile again when he said Maria.

Tim was worried but as long as the thug had both hands on the wheel, he could handle the tension. Obviously no one had found Chucky yet—he would know if Fidel suspected something. But that Maria crack really fucked with him. He turned and faced them again. "Let me ask y'all so-something. Fidel, Spank—you listening?"

Spank looked at Fidel as if for some kind of cue. Before they could respond, Tim continued, "Do I look like the Lost & Found to you? Just leave me the fuck alone. Alright?" Tim took Gentrale's arm and turned towards home. He heard the car start and the boom of the fifteen-inch woofers.

Fidel yelled over the music, "Yeah, I ain't forgot that shit you pulled at Rasheed's. Word on that!" When the car tore off down the street, Tim peeked over his shoulder, relieved to see that they were gone.

They walked in silence and let the tension of the encounter subside, each wondering what the other would say next. A half block later, Gentrale solved the mystery. "Yep, your old man was no alcoholic—an asshole, maybe, but no alkee! 'Scuz ma French!" he quipped.

Tim laughed hard—happy to ignore the elephant in the room. "Hmm...yeah, uh, like what happened, Uncle Gentrale? I mean, between you two? Seems like y'all hadn't spoken for ages. And Dad never wanted to talk to me about it."

"Humph. I don't blame him," Gentrale said.

"Come on, Unk. Did y'all fight? Can't imagine what could happen so bad 'tween Sheila and me—I mean…Sheila and I!" he said wondering why his uncle looked at him so curiously. "What?"

"Sheila and me works just fine, Timmy. And I'll let it slide for now that you pretend to know less than you do. I'll say this. Let's hope that nothing so heavy comes up 'tween you two. No matter what, try to remember that she's your sister, and she deserves your respect. Even if it seems like she doesn't deserve it, her place in your life should be respected. Without respect, you can break y'all's relationship, just like you can with anybody else—hmm."

"Sounds like you saying that Dad seriously dissed you at one time," Tim spoke softly. He didn't want to sound like he was blaming his uncle.

"You could say that. But worse…he dissed my place, my meaning in his life." Gentrale practically coughed out the word *meaning*. Feeling his uncle's arm shake as he spoke, Tim didn't know what to say. He let the slow pat and scrape of their shoes on the pavement accompany their thoughts.

A bus with a single passenger came out of nowhere and sped by like an ambulance. They walked past an empty playground. The air was still.

"What you mean by that?" Tim asked.

"What?"

"Your place in his life—your meaning?"

Gentrale let go another long sigh. He took a deep breath before speaking. "We are all capable of evil, son. Don't be fooled. All of us! But almost always the opportunity to own up to our mistakes comes around. With your kin especially, you should take advantage when it does, to do and say the right thing, take your part without any double talk. Your family'll forgive you. Because when you forgive a family member, more than with people unrelated, you be forgiving yourself for your own misdeeds. Now, that's all I have to say on the matter. The man isn't even in the ground yet. God bless him." He shook his head slowly.

"Hmm. My teacher Mr. Jones was going on and on 'bout respect and stuff on the last day of school. Was saying that we can't be going 'round saying and doing stuff as if what we say or do don't matter. We have to think about the conse, conse…"

"Consequences," Gentrale said, without looking up.

"Yeah, the consequences. Like, what could happen if I did such and such? Or how somebody would feel about it? Saying you got to think about other people. He was pretty serious. Sounded like he was talking about plain old selfishness to me. Was what happened something like that?"

"Yeah, it was something like that and it broke our family. 'Cause, unfortunately, your daddy couldn't or wouldn't come clean with what he did after it was all out in the open. Absolutely didn't show no remorse. Deep down, I believe that he was sorry for abandoning us like he did, but was too weak to face it. It was terrible and well…I personally was dying for him to fess up so that I could get on with respecting him again. He didn't know it, Timmy—he was already forgiven, he only had to ask for it. He didn't. Now I can't say no more. Except that it sounds to me that you got yourself a good man for a teacher! Stay close to him. I'd say."

"Hmm…yeah, I guess so—too bad about y'all and all. Hey look, I can't handle going back in the house now. Tell Mom I went to see Les. She'll understand," Tim said, having already skipped away a couple yards. He didn't see the police cruiser that silently passed behind him.

Gentrale saw it though. Through a forced smile he called back to his nephew, "I'm sure she will. Here comes the bus. Hey! Where you going? You walking?"

Hopping over a hydrant, Tim yelled back, "Yeah man…see you."

He never heard his uncle's response. "See you later, Timmy. Love you, boy."

SOME MEMORIES SUCK

At barely five o'clock, the air was sweltering and Ol' Sol hadn't shown any signs of retiring. Tim smiled at the kids on their afternoon play shift and thought that for a shadow, the summer meant a lot of overtime. As he remembered chasing down his own shadow on broken sidewalks, his smile became a giggle, his walk a jog. The dark boy shape on the pavement matched him stride for stride—until the wombat face of Chucky loomed into mind.

Maybe the dude wasn't dead, had played possum 'till he'd left, like he did when Maurice and them kicked his ass. The delusion made him sick, unable to think or see for the water welling up in his eyes. But deeply he knew that those tears were really for his pitiful father who had fucked up and died on him just that morning. The stark cold reality was that there wasn't room inside him for two dead bodies at the moment.

As the darkness soothed him, the memory of the one and only summer his mom let him go on painting jobs with his dad seeped into his mind. He was twelve years old and about to start middle school.

Tim! Take out four gallons of flat white from the trunk and bring 'em over to the scaffold.

Is this them, Dad?

Yeah, that's them. What you thinkin' about, boy?

Was thinking how cool it would be to have my own painting business like you. I mean, even you say I gotta steady hand.

Come over here. Hold out yo' hands—go on, let me see them. That's right.

What are you doing, Dad?

Eh...turn them over.

Daaaaaad!

Turn them over like I said—come on.

Let go my hands. Stop!

Now ain't that a co-accident!

A wha…?

You 'bout got the same markings on yo' hands as me!

Oh, you mean coincidence!

Those ain't working hands, Tim! You don't want to do this, boy…and get off that scaffold! Yo' mama'll kill me twice if I let you go up on that thing. Make sure to stay in school, son.

It was an exceptional summer—before he'd been kept back the first time, before his dad started working for the bus company and the arguments, before his dad moved out and started drinking heavily (or was it the other way around?), long before his mom got into trouble with the law, before his dad and uncle really stopped talking. That summer was special, because the sad simple fact was that, afterwards, there were no other such summers.

The very next spring was a harbinger of what was to come.

Mama, where we going?

Tim, you, me and your sister are going to stay with Aunt Betsy for a bit.

What? Where's Daddy? Why he ain't driving us? Why we in a taxi, Mom?

Your father is busy tonight. He couldn't take us.

Busy?

See, I told you, Sheila. He's busy tonight.

Hmm…Ma, I heard y'all hollering at each other. Daddy said he didn't care where we went. Did he throw us out?

No, sweetie, like I said, we're going to visit a little while with Aunt Betsy. Everything will be fine. Promise.

See. I told you! Maaa, Sheila's hitting me!

Girl, keep your hands to yourself. You hear me!

As was the following year.

Yo, man, wait up!

Oh God! Just a few more steps—aw, man, please let me get to the door.

Hold up, Tim. I know you heard me.

Damn! How come he knows my name?

Don't run, dawg! It's only a few more feet…shit! Here they come.

Yo, Tim. You Dim? Ha, get it? Didn't you hear me yelling back there?

Nah, I didn't hear nothing. What's up?

Eh-heh…hmm…uh, my main man Shawn wants to see your player.

What? He can't see it from there?

He actually wants to uh—hold it. You know.

N-nah man, I c-can't do that. What's with him? Why he grumbling and shit like that? He can't talk-or something?

He don't like to talk much…and he really don't like people saying no!

Well, I can't le-let him hold my player. He can listen with the phones for a minute if he wants…whoa, back up man…yo check it out, up there on the second floor! See my Pops in the window? Hey, Dad! Come down quick! They trying to take ma play—

No one was in the window.

BUTT-CALL

"Hey Tim, s'up?" called out Lucy from the playground across the street. She'd just hit a three-pointer, all net. *Damn, how long I been sitting here?* Tim wondered and hopped to his feet.

"What up, Lucy? Didn't see you when I walked up."

"I must've got here after you did. Didn't see you either—been warming up for a little game with Chucky," she said, sinking one from the foul line. "He should be easy work. Ha! But the dude is late and he's not answering my texts. Tim? You listening, bro? Where'd you go? What are you looking at?"

Tim stared at the cloudless sky as he spoke. "So, he was supposed to be here right now?"

Lucy kept dribbling in circles. "Yeah, that's what I said. S'up with you?"

Tim sat on the blacktop, hugged his knees as some kind of buttress against the memory. Blood, mud and an S-shaped scar invaded his mind. *'So, bitch. Thought you was gonna get away, huh? Shiiieeet.'*

Tim closed his eyes and spoke in a monotone. "His cousin Fidel's been looking for him too. Man! That's an evil motherfucker."

At the mention of Fidel, Lucy stood still with the ball on her hip. "Yeah, man. A serious cold draft follows that dude around. Ha! It's seriously crazy how he wears that stupid jacket all the time," she said, sinking another basket.

The three-pointer pushed back the darkness a little for Tim. "Whoa, girl. Next you'll be feeling frisky enough to actually challenge somebody!"

Lucy spun around, dribbled the ball between her legs to say, "What are you talking about? If you're feeling it now, get your ass up!"

Tim rose slowly. A text had just come in. Les was waiting. "Nah, I gotta go. Ain't got time…"

"Timmy is a-fraid, Timmy is a-fraaaid!" sang the dancing dreadlocked girl, twirling the ball on a finger.

"Okay, I'm feelin' it now," he said.

Lucy grinned, showing a set of perfect teeth. "So, name your poison, Timmy—uh, Tim! Twenty-one, one-on-one or just a friendly game of Horse since you all dressed up and what not." As she spoke, she moved side to side, shifting her weight from one foot to the other. With that long hair, Tim thought she looked like a big cat.

"Ladies choice. No, I mean it. Whatever. I need to make this fast," he said crouching down, pulling up his pantlegs.

"Ok. It's one-on-one. Ten points, no taking it back, just straight out. Cool?"

"Yeah, like I said, whatever. You can have the first out."

"Hmm…nice! Touch?" she asked, smiling sweetly, bouncing the ball to him.

"Yeah, yeah—touch," Tim said impatiently, leaning a little to the left as he bounced it back to Lucy who immediately dashed hard to his right. The next thing he saw was the last bead of her dreads when she shot by him for a perfect layup. Her grin lit up the backboard like a floodlight.

"Whew! Aw man, Tim. I think you're going to remember this day!" she teased, speaking through her teeth. "Touch?"

Tim cocked his ear to her tone this time. He hadn't heard the sarcasm before. "Yeah, yeah, sure. TOUCH," he barked, heaving the ball at her face.

Embarrassed, he took a quick glance over his shoulder—no one was watching. She caught it. "Me seems my boy has got his back up. Must be tough being checked by a sister!" she taunted, bouncing the ball into play.

Tim stole the ball before she could get too close and sank an easy jumper to even the score. Lucy tied her dreads back—a signal that things had become serious. Tim, surprised that he had to really play to stay in the game, was about to take off his shirt when his cell buzzed. His heart jumped, he could hardly believe the caller ID. It was Rene.

"Ho-hold up, Lucy—I gotta ta-take this," he said, turning towards the curb.

Lucy hurled the ball hard against the backboard. It bounced into the street. "Aw man, Tim, look what you made me do. I was about to take you to the hoop for real." Her voice echoed off the buildings. Hearing this, some kids on the next court cracked up.

Tim held a finger up to shush her as he jogged through the gate. "Don't worry abou… Hello? Boo?"

"Oh–uh…Tim?" the voice sounded confused.

"Rene! What's up, Boo? I was…"

"Tim, I didn't mean to call you. Ugh…I mean the phone must've dialed you by mistake…"

Tim smiled as he went straight into his *smooth* mode, as he liked to call it. "Oh! So, like it was a butt call, eh?" he half sang, kicking a soda can in the gutter.

"Don't get any ideas, brother, I uh…"

"Yo! I wanna see you—" he said, walking in a tight circle.

"I don't think so! I mean, I *really* don't think so."

Tim almost dropped the phone. "I need to talk to somebody."

"Maybe you should talk to whoever is trying get in touch with you right now. What's that buzzing? Is that another phone? Only drug dealers have more than one phone! Timmy! Do you hear me?"

As Tim watched Lucy practice her layups, he reached into his pocket. The buzzing stopped before he could do anything. *She was getting good*, he thought. "No, uh, th-that's Les' cell. He le-left it at the gym. I was on my way th-there wh-when you called."

"Oh, so now you want to talk to me? Well, it's clear that you've—"

Turning towards her house, Tim waved bye to Lucy and lied to Rene. "I'm nearby. Can-can I come over? You home?"

"Yes, I am. But I'm babysitting my little sister and… *Timmy, hello? Are you there?*"

SUNFLOWER YELLOW

Rene's family apartment was situated over Wong's Market. He wondered how a tacky storefront could sell everything from Oreos to pantyhose to meds for a runny nose at such seriously high prices— everything except fresh produce, of course. They even had a liquor license. Therefore, from beef jerky to Wild Turkey, Captain Crunch to salami for lunch, the average customer was covered. When he was in Rene's living room, he could hear each time the entrance door opened and closed as it hit the little bell suspended over it. Open for business twenty-four hours.

"Hey, you got here pretty quick. Were you around the corner or something?" She placed her hands on her hips and her left eyebrow shot up suspiciously as she spoke.

"Oh, yeah…I mean no, I wasn't 'round the corner, I was—" *Hmm… no bra!*

Following his eyes, Rene folded her arms in front of her. "Don't think. Sit. I'll be right back. I have to check on my baby sister."

He sat amid baby toys that dominated the little room. It was hot. The blades of the electric fan moved as if there were weights on them. Doilies were under everything, protecting the cheap furniture from the cheap vases, ashtrays and lamps that sat on them. Being particularly careful of his shoes, he leaned back on the ruddy couch and extended a leg to take in the family photos displayed all over the room. He always got a kick out of them: Rene as a newborn, toddler, young child—not a cute kid. Her mom was another story. His favorite shot of her, the one in which she posed seductively with Rene's dad at the beach, sat on the end table.

As usual, his mood would sober up when his eyes fell upon Martin Luther King staring solemnly off into the distance.

"Ok, here I am!" Rene announced, bouncing into the room.

Whoa! What's this?—bra? Shit! He sat up quickly taking account of his ex-girlfriend, dressed in her cheerleading skirt and top. He couldn't be sure about anything, except that there she stood smiling at him, holding two bowls. Her tapered brown eyes and petite muscular physique threatened to overwhelm him with the pain of their so-called breakup. But what really drove him crazy was the combination of her deep brown skin, high cheekbones, full lips and a short *au naturel* haircut.

He wanted to jump up and kiss her right then and there, but that would have most certainly gotten him thrown out onto the sidewalk in front of Wong's.

"Are you still a freak for fruit salad?" she asked with a smile.

"Yeeeessss! That's me, Freaky Tim!" He took the bowl and howled like a hungry hound.

For a minute or two the only sounds in the room were clinking spoons and the whir of the fan. They were both perspiring from the heat.

"Tim, don't get me wrong, but why are you here? Are you ok? You look good. I heard that you've been working out."

Tim smiled and moved his head side to side like a boxer. "Yeah, kind of…so, you been keepin' up with me, huh?"

Now it was Rene who smiled. She reached out and brushed the top of his head with her hand letting it follow downwards along the contour of his face. "I also heard that you've been putting in some serious time at the library. Is that true?"

"Dag. My sister's got a *big* mouth!"

"Hmm—maybe, but I was glad to hear it. What's this stuff about Mr. Jones and then Maurice in the park?"

Tim, done with his fruit, sat hunched over, leaning on his knees. He hadn't expected this.

Rene fanned herself with her hand. "*Uh-oh*, never mind, I can tell from the look on your face that you don't want to talk about that stuff—sorry. So, seriously—why *did* you want to see me?"

"My-my dad—di-died today," Tim said, still looking at the floor.

Renee threw her spoon at him. "Oh no you didn't, Timothy Thornton! Now what are you going to do? Try and pull some *fresh* bullshit on me?"

She was ready for battle, but the panic in his eyes stopped her. The fruit bowl shook so hard in his hand, he'd almost dropped it when he yelled back at her. "I'm serious, Boo! Dad passed this morning. I just left my family at the house. Me and my uncle couldn't take it no more. So we escaped."

She held up a hand to her mouth "Whoa, whoa, what? Wait—I'm sorry to hear that, Timmy. What happened?"

Tim spoke into the bowl. "It was a heart attack—his third. He was in bad shape."

"And your uncle? He's older. Isn't he?"

"Ten years. They wasn't exactly on speakin' terms."

"Speaking terms." Rene corrected.

"*Huh*?"

"Never mind," Rene said quickly. "Sounds like my own family. I can imagine…"

Tim yelled. "Oh, I get it. *Speaking* terms. Ha! Fuck you, Boo! I don't wanna talk about it anymore. I was already sad as shit about us and now this—ugh!" He leaned his head onto his knees and let his arms fall to the floor. Suddenly comfortable, he relaxed and stayed like that.

A couple minutes ago, he thought Rene had eaten her fruit standing up because she didn't know what to do, where to sit. But now she did. "Come here, Timmy." Cooing like a mother, she sat on the couch and hugged him tight. Of course, the news would have hit her hard too.

After all, they'd been together close to a year. She was around when his dad moved out and had cried all night with Sheila in her room. Yes, she was close with the family until she broke up with him. *You confused, boy*, she'd told him that night. Rene was so quiet now, he wondered if she still thought of him as confused. *Nah—if she was thinking like that, she'd still be on the other side of the room.* When Rene sighed long and hard, sending her hot breath down his collar, he thought, *Alright, dawg—don't get no ideas! But damn, the girl sure smells good.*

"Take deep breaths, Timmy," she whispered into his ear, shutting her eyes.

His had been closed for a while. Boo was always *the one*, and yet he couldn't remember how he'd blown it with her. Yes Maria was nice, sexy and all, but this girl here—Rene, had his heart. *But now, none of this shit matters because eventually somebody is going to find Chucky and my ass will be changing address real soon—and not to Chicago.* How he would ever get her back he couldn't imagine under the circumstances. She, like his mom, will be crushed when everything blows up. On that thought, he inhaled deeply and listened to the ding of Wong's little bell downstairs. Until…

"Yo, Boo."

"Hmm…?"

"Boo?"

"Tell me, Tim."

"I miss you. You know it, right?"

"That's just the grief talking now, man. Stay still, be quiet." She pulled him closer and then jerked rigid. "Don't get any ideas. Ok?"

"Yeah, yeah," he said, taking a huge breath, imagining that he could inhale her inside of him. She was wearing the Egyptian Musk oil he'd given her—*two-dollar* bottle. He was so deep into her neck now that the next time he spoke his voice was muffled. Her left hand had gently landed on his right bicep and stayed there.

"I saw him this morning. He wasn't drinking at all. He was clear, but kind of strange."

"Strange? How?"

"I'm sure he knew his time was 'bout up. He was saying stuff."

Rene's hand on his bicep went into a steady stroke.

"Stuff?"

"Yeah, like study hard and shit. But he always said stuff like that. This time was different though. It was like he was trying to make up for lost chances, you know? All of sudden, he comes outta his face with some shit like, *Tell yo' mama that I love her and always loved her.* Just like that, *yo!* Then like always, he would wonder out loud if she had a new man. Like *I* knew somethin'." When his voice broke, Tim pulled away, sat up straight and wiped his eyes.

"What is it, Timmy?"

"I-I told him this mo-morning not to ca-call me Timmy."

Her hand touched his shoulder. "But *I've* always called you Timmy. *Timmmmie.*" She cooed again, but not like a mother this time. He leaned back in again closer, lower, real low. He wallowed in her embrace as she continued to caress and squeeze his bicep. Her other hand stroked his hair. He felt better with every pass. When he leaned back, his hand had rested upon her abdomen. They were breathing in sync. Rene's top had risen about an inch above the top of her skirt and his pinky had actually made contact with belly flesh. At that, Tim released his longest and deepest exhalation—matched molecule for molecule by his ex-girlfriend. Listening to her heart that was beating faster now, he moved his little finger back and forth with the gentleness of a butterfly's antenna, barely brushing the moist peach fuzz just below her navel.

That's when he saw the packet of Trojans wedged in the waistband of her sunflower yellow panties.

PARANOIA

Im>U: What are you doing? Are you still in your room? It's been two whole days since Daddy—you know.

Sprinter2000: Yeah, believe me, I know. What do u want?

Im>U: What do I want? I don't want anything. Just wondering how you're doing?

Sprinter2000: Don't worry about me. What's up?

Im>U: Look, it's hard for me too. But locking yourself up in there all day isn't good. I don't think Daddy would want that. You're not drinking in there, Timmy, are you?

Sprinter2000: What? Why you asking me that? And how you know what Dad would want? Anyway, it hasn't been all day, I went to the library this morning.

Im>U: That's good. Did you work with Darryl?

Sprinter2000: Nah, I tried to do something, but couldn't concentrate, couldn't take it, so I came home.

Im>U: I have to talk with you about something.

Sprinter2000: Some other time. I got shit to do.

Im>U: Oh, so like, now we're cursing each other out online?

Sprinter2000: Sorry.

Im>U: You're not sorry. Anyway, what do you have to do that's so important? You just said you couldn't work when you were at the library.

Sprinter2000: Like I said, don't worry 'bout me. It ain't your business anyway. I gotta go. C U

Im>U: Hold up. Wait...I'll come home and we'll talk. Okay? Is Uncle Gentrale there?

Sprinter2000: Forget that! I got a lot on my mind, believe it or not.

Im>U: Yeah, yeah, Timmy, I know, believe me, I know. Just chill, okay? I'll be there in a few. I just remembered that Uncle Gentrale went to visit his card-playing friends. He'll be gone awhile.

Sprinter2000: What do u mean, like, you know? You know what? You don't know nothing.

Im>U: Okay, okay. I don't know nothing. But please don't try to tell me you have to go work out. I mean like...if you're going to the gym all the time, how come you still so scrawny?

Sprinter2000: Scrawny, huh? I will punish you for that! Word! What's so important? Something happened? You heard something?

Im>U: Nothing happened!!! What? Was I supposed to hear something? About what?

Sprinter 2000: Just saying.

Im>U: Never mind. I need to talk to you. When I get there, I'll make you some food. You cool with that?

Sprinter2000: Okay, if u really are going to hook up some eats. Otherwise, I'll just go to the Chicken Shack with Les.

Im>U: Yeah, I'll hook you up, no worries. Don't have me come back there for nothing. Okay? C U at 2.

Sprinter2000: I'm here.

It had been five days since the killing.

Tim sat on the floor in his room. His mind couldn't rest. Not even the five beers he'd thrown back real fast could help him. Seeing the word *scrawny* on the screen simply blew him away. Maybe his sister had heard something? *She was good at keeping secrets, the sneaky bitch*, he thought and then regretted it. But she had never called him *scrawny* before. He had always thought of the skinny dude Chucky like that but hardly ever talked about it—'cept for maybe to Les. He wondered if he had ever mentioned his pet name for Chucky to Sheila?

That morning at the library, Tim had used a lot of energy trying to ignore the furtive glances of the librarian. He had a lot to catch up on before his study drill with Darryl, but couldn't help wondering if it was his imagination that Mrs. Shepard had been staring at him. What could she know? Yes, she was around that night when Chucky threatened him, but she hadn't come out into the parking lot—she hadn't seen a thing. However, when he'd moved to an upholstered chair to wait for Darryl, he couldn't deny that she took regular checks on his whereabouts.

Then he thought of the surprise visitors who appeared. Maybe Mrs. Shepard knew they were coming. They tried to appear casual, but it was obvious that they had been waiting for him. It impressed him that they were detectives and not just regular beat cops. They asked a lot of questions. Recounting the exchange made him feel suddenly weak. He stretched out on the throw rug and covered his face with a comic book.

Yeah, I'm Timothy Thorton. I'm seventeen.

78 S. Eighth Street, First Floor.

Me, my mom, my sister and my uncle. Nope, my dad died yesterday.

Heart attack. Thanks.

Barringer High School.

Sophomore this fall, if I don't pass the proficiency in September. Yeah, I'm behind a couple years.

Yes, that's why I'm here. I'm studying for it. Yeah, almost every day.

Darryl Campbell.

He's my tutor.

No, I don't pay him.

A friend?

Yeah, I guess.

Yeah, I was here that night.

Yeah, I know Chucky.

Uh-huh…he was here. I talked to him, yeah.

About? Uhm…nothing. They were just into teasing people. You know!

No, I didn't know he hadn't been home for three nights.

What? Nah, nah…we didn't get mad or nothing.

Oh? That's what Mrs. Shepard said? Well, it wasn't like that.

It was like we kicked it back and forth some 'till Chucky and his boy left.

The other dude?

No, I didn't know him. Never saw him before.

Parking lot? Man, do I look like I drive?

N-no, I didn't meet nobody in the parking lot afterwards. I stayed 'till
9:30, closing time, left, got a burger and went to my dad's place on Central.

About one o'clock in the morning.

Everybody was asleep in their rooms when I got home. I went to bed.

Nah, I didn't see nobody 'till the next morning.

Yeah, you too, officer, have a nice day.

It puzzled Tim that the cops hadn't asked about the third guy. Then he answered his own question—they probably didn't know he existed. No doubt, Chucky's goofy friend hadn't mentioned the other boy. From the sound of their questions, the guy hadn't done much talking at all.

The vibration of the cell in his pocket surprised Tim. He felt as if every molecule of his breath threatened to leave his lungs at once. Lurching to his feet, he stuck his head out of the window where he found the alley spinning, his head its axis. Pushing back into the room, he turned and sprinted to the bathroom. As he held onto the bowl with both hands, he filled the air with gasps and moans until the inevitable relief came.

On the way back to his room, the walls of the narrow hallway appeared to collapse upon him as if he were in a funhouse.

His head hurt *bad*. He needed to sleep.

He's yelling at what looks like a big tattooed scarecrow lying on the ground. He's kicking it now, first on the soles of the sneakers, the calves, the knees, in the side, then a final nudge on the shoulder. He sees now what he didn't want to see, smells what he didn't want to smell: blood oozing out of the side of the head, the rock—an island in a red sea, sitting next to it. A crow cries at the full moon from which the boy's cheap jewelry is throwing off wild asterisms in every direction. He sees himself pulling the body by the leg under a large bush. He watches himself pick up the cell phone that falls from the body, put it on silent mode and stick it in his own pocket. He looks around, pulls it out again and takes a picture of the corpse. Now, except for his shoes, you can't see Chucky. Now he's kicking loose dirt over the scrawny motherfucker—he removes the sneakers and places them on his chest.

Chucky's so fucking dead.

Tim skulks out of the park, expecting at any moment to see the other two boys, but no one is around. He walks quickly, he doesn't care where he is. He only wants to get far away from that thing in the bushes...there's an underpass—more like a tunnel with a deep echo. He enters it. He's alone. It's humid and completely dark. He stops, braces himself against the curved wall and screams long and hard. Finally a drop of bile, when it comes up and then down the wrong way, sends him into a coughing fit. In the middle of it, Chucky's smirking face comes to mind.

Curiously it calms him. Finally, as the last sonic reflection of his hacking dissolves into silence, he waits to catch his breath.

He's not so sad.

SHEILA AND TIM TALK FAMILY

"Timmy! Are you in there? Come on and eat," Sheila said, standing just outside of his bedroom door.

Aroused from a deep sleep, Tim could barely make out what his sister was saying. His own voice cracked as sweat poured out of him into the stuffy room. He supposed his body was still adjusting to carrying the big lie around. "So—what's up? Is Mom alright?"

Sheila gave a single loud knock on the door. "Come on, boy! I went to a lot of trouble. See you in the kitchen."

He found his sister dressed in a big loose yellow blouse over shorts and sandals. As they talked, he watched her bite her lip like their father. She had her *tells* for sure, but there was no lie to come, which could have meant that something buried was about to come to the surface.

Sheila's hair was pinned up away from her neck to show off a fake tattoo of a heart. He couldn't be sure but it looked like the name *Darryl* was written in the middle of the thing. Tim wondered what that was about.

"I went to see Daddy a week or so before he died."

"Oh yeah? How was he?"

"He was drinking again," she said, fussing with her hair.

Tim played with his sandwich, taking out the pickles. "Yeah, I know—been drinking for a while too. B-but day before yesterday, in the morning, he was sober. You know? Uh…*so*, t-that's what you wanted to talk to me about?" he asked.

When it came to something important, Sheila usually had trouble getting started. Tim knew he couldn't push her because she was perfectly capable of dropping the whole thing if he pissed her off.

Instead he decided to stay cool and listen. Which was easier said than done. He could barely sit still in his chair. At any minute it felt as if his legs would—on their own—break into a sprint and carry him through the door at full speed.

His sister eyed him. *It's too early for her to know something. The cops didn't even know anything. They only asked about Chucky because he hadn't been home for three days. It has to be something else.*

Sheila took a deep breath and paused as if something had caught in her throat. "Do you know why Daddy and Uncle Gentrale didn't speak? I mean, what was behind it all?"

Tim, relieved by her question, scratched the side of his head and leaned back in his chair. "Some idea, yeah. S-so, that's what you and Dad talked about?"

"When I was leaving, he said that I should talk to you about what happened if I really wanted to know. Well, Timmy, I see the surprise in your face. So, don't mess around. *Give it up, boy!*"

Pulling together the pieces of the sad family story for his sister made the events all the more real for Tim. It was like looking at an old dusty puzzle that no one had been willing to put together before.

He told her that Victor, as weak as he may have appeared to them, was actually a principal source of strength in the family back on the farm. He explained to her as Gentrale had explained to him that they were sharecroppers and that their dad could never make peace with the near-slavery conditions they had to endure. Always quick to point out the injustices and indignities of their everyday lives, their father's griping provided a respite from the crippling monotony and physical strife of their work. His constant complaints and sense of humor focused and allowed all nine of them to dream and have hope for something better. He described what he'd understood about an unexplained shortage in cottonseed and, as a result, how the landowner had dogged their grandfather in the barn with some kind of leather strap. He watched Sheila's eyes widen when he told her that their dad had witnessed the whole fucking thing. Other than Victor and

Gentrale, only an Auntie Naomi, now pushing a hundred years on earth, survived the brutal toil of their lives on the farm—or so they'd heard. The others—Auntie Sister, Aunt Sedona, Uncle James, Uncle John and Jessie—had suffered early deaths from various causes.

But the one that stood out was the murder of their uncle Booker. Over time, the family had come to the understanding that their youngest knew what he was doing when he went into that bar in town where mostly white dudes drank. All it took was for him to look at somebody the wrong way. The elders called it *suicide by mob*, born out of pure despair after Victor had abandoned them.

Tim and Sheila sat quiet for a while listening to the squeal of tires from the front side of the house followed by the siren of a police cruiser careening by.

"There was something else," Tim said hesitantly.

Sheila had been sitting there twisting her fingers as she listened. Tim's sudden hushed tone scared her. Her first impulse was to cover her ears. She had heard enough. Instead, through what sounded like a whimper, she said, "Okay, okay—hurry up, get it over with."

"Now…don't get mad at me but—I'm pretty sure Dad stole that seed. The shortage was discovered just before he ran away. He would've needed money."

Sheila jerked rigid. "But, uh–no, Tim, no! I was gonna tell you to shut up before, now it's time for you to stop, I mean…how would you know that? It couldn't have—"

"I don't know. I'm just guessing. Unk only talks about Daddy abandoning the family and the loss of respect between them. Shit…aw, man, I'm sorry I brought it up."

When Tim finished talking, Sheila, looking as if the blood had drained out of her face, got up and moved to the fridge for ice. "I'm sure there's even more to it. But Mom clams up pretty good when I ask her about it. I don't think she has a clue."

Tim, slowly nodding his head, played with his food and muttered, "Probably not."

There was a pause and then *it* finally surfaced. "I saw that girl Maria. She told me about Mr. Jones, big brother," Sheila blurted out.

Hearing Jones' name, Tim turned over his soda in his lap. As he jumped up, Chucky's phone beeped and vibrated in his back pocket. The surprise sent him ass down, feet up onto the floor in the middle of the mess. "Fuck!" he yelled.

Sheila handed over paper towels to her brother, but she couldn't stop laughing "Timmy, you klutz! Watch your mouth. What's the matter with you?"

Tim lifted himself up from the floor. His jeans were soaked and his mind was spinning. He didn't know what to do except go in the bathroom and clean up.

After five minutes, Sheila approached the door and spoke through it. "Tim? You alright?"

"Yeah-yeah-yeah," he said, staring at the screen of Chucky's phone. He wondered how he hadn't noticed the texts that had come in:

Where are u? **Fidel**
What up Chucky? U hiding out? LOL. **Spank**
Chucky Sweetie, text me okay? **Maria**
Charles, don't worry your sister and me okay? Let us hear from you today. **Mom**

"What are you doing?" Sheila said, knocking again.

Tim had been standing in the middle of the bathroom reading the messages over and over, especially the one from the boy's mother. "Uh-yeah...coming out in a minute. What else did Maria say?"

"She told me how you got into Mr. Jones' face, that he kept you after school on the last day! Is that true?" she said suppressing a giggle.

Tim opened the door and walked past her. "Yeah, it's true," he said, totally resigned now. "But that's all I'm going to say about it. Okay? Don't ask me nothin' else about Jones. I'll see that dude soon enough." The next thing he said sounded like a plea. "Yo, Sheila?"

She'd followed him back to the kitchen. "Yeah?" she uttered softly, feeling a little sorry for laughing at him.

"You re-really think Mom never worried herself much about Dad's and Unk's history?" Tim said, voice catching again.

"Well, I wouldn't say she *never* thought about them. But, eh-hem, Mom's got enough secrets of her own."

Sheila's tone of voice made Tim turn around and sit again at the table. "What you talking about?" he said through a sneer.

Now it was time for Tim to listen as she told him how their mom got into trouble for embezzlement, something Uncle Gentrale described once as *some kind of stealing*. Having deliberately ignored the details as they leaked out over time, Tim struggled to imagine his mom gullible enough to be taken in by some guy at work. But, by the time she was arrested, there were a lot of unresolved questions regarding her partner, a man who'd since been charged and sentenced. What Tim did know was that by the end of the case, she couldn't find a decent job. Only low-paid-below-the-tax-radar-kind-of-gigs were available to her. Their dad, with his drinking, couldn't support them on his salary alone and their lives went to pieces.

Somewhere along the way their mom got religion and joined a storefront church. Sheila cracked him up with her impersonation of the holy testimonials she'd witnessed in the run-down joint. For a minute, they were both prancing around the kitchen, pumping their hands to the heavens and chanting hallelujah to a double time gospel beat.

Then Sheila got serious again. "Tim, you know Daddy was jealous. Don't you?"

The question caught him off guard. He could only hang his head in agreement. Sheila reminded him of the big fight in which their dad referred to their mom's professed lord and savior as her *new* boyfriend. However, it became clear that religion wasn't all that was bothering him. In that argument, Victor shut down the whole conversation by bringing up the mystery behind the co-worker who'd gotten her in trouble. *Humph, so now you think this one's gonna save ya, huh?* Tim couldn't be sure if his dad saw the embarrassment that had settled on their mother's face, but he and his sister did.

For a long time after that argument, a shroud of sadness had descended on his mom's every word and gesture. She never fell into complete despondency though. He and his sister were always able to reach her, make her laugh, no matter how impossible the details of the case or how long it dragged on. It wasn't said outwardly, but he knew they still mattered in her life. Unconsciously, he later understood, they were fighting for their mom while being resigned to losing their father to alcohol. Two years later, the charges were expunged, enabling her to apply for proper jobs. However, with his dad drinking more of his paycheck each month, things didn't change much.

All of this reminded Tim of the separation and how his mother looked when their father walked out on them. For seven days the only sounds that came from her were when she was asleep or in the bathroom. Otherwise, she spoke to them with her eyes or simple hand gestures. He and his sister, without even talking about it, didn't question it. In his heart, he was afraid she'd never speak again.

Sheila sported a little pout as she spoke now. "You know, nobody ever heard anything about that guy who went to jail because of that case."

"Well, he was a criminal, a con man! Mom was just working there," Tim said. His anger soothed him.

His sister leaned on the sink and moved her head side to side as if to refute whatever he was thinking. "Sorry, Timmy, mom knew that guy. She even knows that he'll be getting out of jail this year. I think that they were lov..."

"Shut the *fuck* up, Sheila," Tim screamed in her face. "That guy was a no-nothing to Mom. She wouldn't do no shit li-like that. She wasn't cheating on Dad!"

"Okay, okay Timmy...I hear you. But..."

"No b-buts. You ma-may be hearing me," he yelled, jumping up from the table, "but I'm not hearing you and I ain't le-letting you sit there and say somethin' like that. You got it?"

Sheila moved to the other side of the kitchen. "Yeah, I got it, Timmy. Now will you sit down. You're scaring me. What's wrong? What? Where are you going?"

The screen door met the frame with a crack like gunfire.

THE KNIFE

Without a word, Les stepped aside to let Tim into the apartment. A thick funk of BO hung like a wet tarp in the air. "Yo man, I heard. Sorry," he said holding out a hand. Tim took it. They touched shoulders. "I texted your sister when you didn't answer your cell. She told me about your pops. That's *craaazy*, man! Don't know what I'd do if it was mine. Hey, why you not at home? I'm sure your mom wants you to hang close these days."

"Like you said, homie, it's *my* pops that's dead. I don't need another one right now. *Okay?*"

Les held his hands up. "Whoa—partner. No problem. Come on in the back and chill."

"That was days ago, bro—two, three—I don't know. She'll be alright," Tim said, following Les down the narrow hallway.

"Who?"

"My moms, yo! What? You didn't hear me?" Tim paused at the door.

Les looked up to the ceiling and sighed hard. "Alright-alright…go on, I'm listening."

"You know my pops was really out there, man, a little crazy—never without a bottle nearby. It was ss-some s-sad shit to see. I told him once he was li-iving in a ho-hole, man." Tim paused to snort up a flood of mucus. "Aw man!" he said, holding his nose. Look— I need your bathroom, bro."

Staring into the small mirror that hung over the toilet, Tim frowned at the reek of stale alcohol from his urine. The dark brown color of his skin had taken on a grayish quality, his tiny goatee appeared off center and there were balls of mucus in the corners of his eyes.

"Damn boy, you sure is ugly!" he mumbled, moving to the sink. The warm water felt good. On his way out, he stepped onto the scale and was surprised to see his weight down a couple pounds.

Les yelled from inside his room. "Everything okay, homie? Do I need to come and check on yo' ass?"

Tim came out of the bathroom and stubbed his toe. A shiver ran down his spine to see a good-sized rock holding open the door to Les' room. Just like that, he was back at the park and the stink of blood and grass engulfed him. His own voice startled him. It sounded artificial, toy-like, as if he were speaking through plastic vocal chords. "I'm okay, I guess. Yeah, my mom might be looking for me, but I ain't looking for nobody. Don't wanna feel nothing. You feeling me, dawg?" he said and stepped further into the messy bedroom.

The bed was completely covered with clothes. Les probably hadn't hung up anything the entire summer. Tim wondered where his friend actually slept. In the corner, the weight bench suffered the same fate except that at each end twenty-pound plates were stacked on top of it.

About nine pairs of sport shoes stuffed with dirty socks competed for space in every corner. Perhaps out of desperation for relief, he let the small window fan remind him of Rene. Thinking of Boo made him smile. He sat on the corner of the bed—under control now.

"What you smiling at?"

"Yo, I heard something 'bout some new gear," Tim said through a cheesy grin. But the grin didn't last long. How the hell could he have missed the fingerless glove draped over the weight bar? Envy elbowed out agitation when Les plucked two pairs of hand stitched Grant sparring mitts from under the bed. Licking his lips, Tim said, "S'pose you don't have to go to the gym to workout now, huh? Got anything cold to go with that?" He wanted a beer bad, but couldn't figure out where Les stashed them. Then, from out of nowhere, the dude handed over a cold one.

"Can't be giving up going to the gym. I can do only so much at home," Les said, never taking his eyes off the mitts. "Yo, what was up with you this morning so important that you couldn't pick up the phone? Finally got next to Maria?"

Half-listening, Tim looked around for what else he might have missed. A medium-sized folding knife on the bureau drew his gaze in for a moment. "Aw man. I was in the library—forgot to charge my phone. O-oh, speaking of Maria, man, did I tell you about the dream I had?"

Les turned up his beer can for a swig. His voice was muffled. "Nah man. What was it?"

"Well, I'd been texting Maria for a while now, trying to get her over to my place to help me with my um—reading," he said with a goofy grin. "In my dream, she finally shows up out of the blue. No text, voice message—nothin'!"

"Ha! That's funny. So, did she come in? In your dream?" Les said, laughing and spraying beer from his lips.

"Nope. She didn't even get past the screen door."

"So, what you sayin', dawg? Did she come over or not?" he said reaching for another brew from the bottom shelf of his night table.

"Yeah, well—I mean, in the dream she showed alright, but get this! She *and* Rene arrived on the porch at the same time!"

Les made a face and fell backwards into a ratty old upholstered chair. From his expression, he was either in pain or about to push one out. "What the fuck did you say? Do you remember?"

"Things were kinda hazy, you know. Like, I didn't say nothing—any-anything! I just lo-looked at both of them through the screen, started to say something and then fell out on the floor!" Tim tried his best to look cool saying this.

Les sat up. "What! Fainted? I don't believe that shit. Come on, man!"

Tim smirked so hard it seemed that his face had turned inside out. "Aw man, I didn't really faint, dawg! I faked it—*I think*. I remember just staying on the floor, totally out of it, mumbling and shit, listening to them call out to me a few times. They tried opening the screen but it was locked. When they left, I woke up. That's it!"

Les let what Tim said sink in for about two seconds before standing up. "Uh-oh, I feel faint," he gasped and fell backwards on the bed. They screamed like a pair of birds in the rainforest.

"Wait!" Les pulled himself up from the bed. "Wow, man, like-like, that's your Eminem now!"

"My what?" Tim asked. His hands were still covering his eyes.

"Yo, Eminem, you know how they always say on TV when they find a pattern in a crime?"

"Oh, you mean M.O.? *Modus op-operandi!*" Tim said. The smirk was back.

Les made a face. "Now you going to tell me you speak Spanish?"

Tim jumped to his feet. "What? Never mind that shit—what kind of pattern? You calling me a fucking criminal?"

Les held his hands out. "Whoa. Slow down, man. Relax, dawg! S'up with you? Yeah, never mind. It's just that, if I remember correctly, faking got you out of another tight situation in the park at the beginning of the summer with that dude Maurice! Have you seen him since?"

Hearing Maurice's name surprised Tim. "N-no! But that was—I mean—yeah, I guess you can call it a pa-pattern. Real weak, huh? Why you asking about Maurice anyway?"

Les kept his eyes on his beer can. "Uh—no reason, bro, just, you know—down at the gym, sometimes we do speed drills at the bag, a little sparring here and there..."

"Oh, so like he one of your *homies* now?" Tim sneered.

Les put down his beer and held his hands up again. "Aw man, it ain't nothing like that. You, me—we *homies*. Maurice can box, but he's a chump. I could never trust that fool."

Tim let Les help him with his mitts. He really wanted to tell Les his suspicions about Darryl, to hear his friend say that his library tutor couldn't have played a part in that shit at the park. But he stayed quiet and listened to what was turning out to be a pep talk from his friend.

"Weak? Who you? Huh! Chucky didn't think so when you went up to him at the library that night. I messaged you—remember? You texted back that you didn't know how much more of this shit you could take. Remember? Look at me, Tim! Am I lying? What did the scrawny bitch say when you walked up to him and asked him if he was waiting for you?"

Tim's heart jumped in his chest when Les pronounced *asked* as *axed*—and for a moment, all he could see was red. No, Les wasn't lying, even though only half of what he'd said was true. Sweat poured down the inside of Tim's shirt and again, he had to pee *real* bad. Instead of looking at his friend, he stared at two fifty-pound plates on the floor, shifted his weight side to side and rhythmically touched his fists together. The lie metastasizing in his chest made him speak in the voice of a little boy. "Chucky said, 'I ain't waiting for no-nobody,' and then he tried to play it off like nothing happened."

"Yeah, man, it was clear that he didn't want no trouble with you. You been seriously working out and he could see that he had no chance in hell," he said, tying off Tim's right glove.

"Humph, I don't know nothin' about what that dude was thinking," Tim mumbled dreamily, watching Les slip on his own mitts. He started to help him but he liked when the dude would pull the laces tight with his teeth. *Shit, what the fuck is Les gonna say when he finds out the truth? But then, he's been holding back stuff too. Like Maurice for example! I didn't know he knew that asshole. And that glove—and now all this talk about Chucky? He'd even called him scrawny. Something must be up.*

Head down, jaw set, weaving and bobbing, Les threw punches in the air at an imaginary opponent. "I saw Spank today," he said.

Tim listened to Les' grunts swell in intensity with every combination. It was beautiful. He was the real deal, an athlete. He threw two more lightening-fast jabs and an upper cut. Glancing over his shoulder he said, "Yo, Tim. Did you hear me, boy? Where you at?"

Tim snapped back, "I got your *boy, motherf—* Yeah, I heard you. What about it? How Spank doing anyway? Where'd you see him?"

"At the gym. He's cool. Said he heard that Chucky disappeared the same night you saw him at the library." Les squeezed the words out between punches.

Tim stood up and tried to match Les' moves. "Pr-probably the boy's head exploded from being around all those books. It was some strange shit to see Chucky's ass up in there. What else did Spank say?"

Les slapped his mitts together. The sweat from the impact hit Tim in the face. "Word—ugh, word out that somebody saw you running your ass off that night. Some are saying that maybe you made him disappear." He dropped his hands and turned to face Tim. "Like, I ain't saying nothing like that, man. I know you, bro. It's just this dude Fidel—"

"Fidel! I thought you said you saw Spank?" Tim yelled in his face."

Les took a step back. "The dude was with him, dawg. They were talking right next to me. I was working out. Couldn't help hearing them."

Tim felt cold, sat down and hugged his knees. "So, what else they say? Wait! Who else was around?"

"Nobody else. Just us three," Les said with relief.

"What else did they say?" Tim asked, staring at the wall.

"Spank wasn't saying much really. Fidel was the one pushing shit. The dude tried to say maybe you did something to Chucky! Did you know they're cousins?"

In his mind, Tim saw the words *did something to Chucky* line up into a spear shape and pierce his chest. "Yeah, I-I just heard that at Spank's party. Yeah, man, where were you, dawg? Why weren't you there?"

Les leaned on the chest of drawers. Sweat rolled down his face and arms. "Aw man, I was out fishing with my pops and his boys all day. I heard there was some fine honeys present."

"You know it!" Tim sang out, sighed and looked at his gloves. "Yeah, I know they cousins. I also know Fidel is full of shit. The question is— do *you*?"

"I guess so. He's kind of strange with that jacket and shit. So—like Chucky left you alone when you walked up to him, right?"

Tim glanced at the glove hanging over the barbell. "Yeah, like I said—the dude was all fierce in the library, but then outside he was like, 'Uh—who me? I ain't looking for you.' It was almost funny!"

"Then you split?" Les said, looking Tim in the eyes.

"Yeah, bro. Like what's this? You questioning me and shit? I just got the same treatment from the cops and—"Tim stopped himself.

Les threw both hands up. "Whoa. The cops? They came for you? Oh shit!"

"It was no-nothin' like that, man. They say Chucky hadn't been home for three days and I was the last one to-to…"

"…see him."

"Yeah." *Is he trying to play me? I got to get the fuck outta here.*

"Well," Les said, throwing a couple jabs, "I told Fidel he needed to be cool, that you ain't made nobody disappear. He wanted your address, dawg!"

"What? You ga-gave it to him?!"

"Hell no! What do you think?"

Tim laughed and stood up. "This is what I think, chump," he said and threw a couple of playful jabs at his boy's nose. With the dead eyes of a shark, Les slapped both away and knocked him on his ass with a clean right cross to the jaw.

Instead of a human hand wrapped in padding and leather, it felt like Les had knocked him with a dumbbell. Tim hit the floor hard. He was so shocked at the numbness on the left side of his face, he hadn't realized that he was no longer standing. Eyes shut, he flailed his arms and legs like a puppet. When he finally opened his eyes, he saw Les' face framed in a cloud of stars.

"Aw man, Tim. I–I'm sorry, bro. I didn't know you wasn't ready. I mean, come on…give me your hand."

Tim slapped his hand away and sat up. Something smelled real bad. "Fuck you, man!"

"Tim. You alright? I'm sorry."

"Nah-nah, *ass-wipe*, I don't need your help." He tried to stand but instead stumbled and hit his head on the bench.

"Yo, Tim, be careful, bro. Slow the fuck down!" Les said, moving in to help.

Choked up with mucus, Tim screamed, "NO," and jumped to his feet. Les moved to catch him, but Tim grabbed the knife.

"So now you gonna stab me, Tim? That's so *crazy*, I can't even think about it."

Tim stumbled towards the door.

Les flipped his friend the bird. "Go ahead, *stupid*. I ain't gonna try and stop you. Get the fuck outta here!"

The violent pounding in his chest scared Tim. He didn't want to die in that stinky room.

A WAY OUT?

Sheila always liked how the chestnut brown skin of her mother's hands shone with moistness. As was often the case, those hands had been busily writing reminder notes, which usually meant something was up and soon it would be time to talk. It really didn't matter what the notes said. Nine times out of ten her mom would've forgotten or mixed them up since she never dated or threw any of them away.

But Mom had been scribbling for a while in silence. Sheila was beginning to worry. Maybe she was already *busted* for yesterday's lie—slipping over into the city with Darryl for ice cream and to watch buff boys in Washington Park go hard at the hoops. But she seriously doubted that was the problem. Mom wouldn't have been able to keep her cool for so long. She also doubted that it was about the dishes in the sink, Tim's mess from that morning. It had to be something else.

She resigned herself to wait and watch her mom—still in her work clothes—suck cigarettes and write Post-its. Sheila could make out only the one on top: *Return books to library* and wondered which books they might be. A slight curl formed at the corners of her lips as she imagined her mom meeting with Tim and Darryl to discuss grammar. Her smile faded at the sight of Julia's shaking hands and the more pronounced lines in her face these days that seem to have multiplied lately. No wonder—she hadn't been sleeping. Many a night Sheila heard her mom milling about in the kitchen, nursing her cancer sticks.

Finally Julia put down the pencil, looked her daughter in the eye and smiled big. "Well, it's official. We're moving to Chicago."

Sheila held her mom's gaze. "What? Moving? But how, when…?"

"Soon, baby. Don't you worry about a thing. With this new job, I'll be taking care of everything." Julia reached out to touch her daughter's arm.

Sheila pulled away. "Mom! What about school? Pfff—aw man, Mom—how can you do this to us?"

Taking a long drag on her butt, Julia waved her hand gently as if moving something out of the way. "School? Aw baby, I've got all the details worked out with the new school district. At least for you, your credits won't be a problem. It may be a little more complicated for your brother…but in the end, it doesn't matter 'cause…"

Sheila's eyes widened. "It does so!"

"No it doesn't, child. You'll see!"

"Yes it does. It does matter!" Sheila yelled, slapping the kitchen table.

Julia stood up and sat back down, jaw set with determination. "Look, girl," she said, pointing her finger. "This isn't a total surprise to you or Tim. I've been talking about this for quite a while now."

"Maybe, but you never said you were serious. I mean, we got friends here, and I got three more years to finish high school. A lot of these kids I went to grammar school with. So it does matter!" Sheila covered her face with her hands.

"You'll make new friends," Julia promised, stroking Sheila's forearm. Sheila made a face. "To be honest…" her mom started again.

"What? You haven't been honest up to now? You—" Sheila stopped herself. She'd crossed the line.

Julia glared at her daughter. "Don't be flip with me, girl. You know what I mean. It has been unbearable to stay in this apartment after your daddy left, but we couldn't afford to move, and it was very important to me that you and Tim were able to see him regularly without a lot of traveling. Now that he's gone, God bless him, that's no longer an issue. This new job pays much more and we'll be closer to our relatives."

"Yeah, relatives on *your* side," Sheila sneered. When she saw the look on her mom's face, she said, "Oh-oh don't get me wrong, Mom, I…"

The screen door whined and banged. "Hey y'all," Tim yelled over the boom of his headphones, turning and moonwalking into the kitchen.

At that moment, Sheila couldn't stand the sight of her brother and hoped he would go straight to his room as usual. She looked at her mom instead, who had resumed assaulting Post-it notes.

It was the expression on Sheila's face that brought Tim's little dance to a halt. "Did s-somebody else die?" he asked.

Their mother never looked up.

"Whoa—whoa, Timmy! Watch what you doing, boy!" Sheila blurted out, half yelling, half laughing. "You're such a klutz. Watch out with your backpack!"

"Wha-what-happened? Is Uncle Gentrale alright?" Tim lowered his pack to the floor.

Sheila raised a hand as if she were in school. "Mom is taking that job in Chicago," she mumbled.

Tim turned towards his mother with outstretched arms, pleading, "Nooo, Mom! Why you wanna do th-that?"

Looking up from her scratch work, Julia crossed her arms with an air of impatience. "I was just telling your sister that the job will pay a lot more and we'll be closer to *more* of our relatives."

"Hmm—what about school? I got one—no—two more years before I fi-finish and me and Rene—"

Julia smiled. "You and Rene? You and Rene what?"

"Uh—no-nothing, Mom. We was just talking and…" He stopped talking and stared at his sneakers.

"Mom says that it doesn't matter. She—"

Julia cut in. "Now, girl, I said a lot more than that! Tim, I know this is a big thing for you both and you know I love Rene—wait a minute. What's that, Timmy?"

"What's what?"

"The bruise on your jaw," said Julia, pointing at Tim's chin. "You've been rubbing it since you came in. Something happened?"

Tim looked at the floor and smiled. "Aw—nah. Just fooling around with Les. He got a lucky one in at the gym," he said, happy to not talk about Rene in front of his sis.

"Humph! He got real lucky, I'd say!" Sheila chimed in with glee.

"Shut up, Sheila." Julia held up a stiff hand like a policeman—a gesture left over from her *silent period*. "I-I know this is a big thing for y'all, but this job came up just in time. With your father gone now, I don't think that I can stand to stay around here no more."

"Anymore," Sheila pushed in.

Julia shook her head in disbelief. "What?"

"Anymore, *Mom*. You said that you can't stay around here no..."

"Shush, child! This ain't the time for that. I'm glad you're doing well enough to correct your ol' mother's English, but right now you only have to listen. Okay?"

Sheila rolled her eyes. "Okay, Mom. I'm listening," she said through a loud sigh, then took a playful swipe at her brother. At the sight of Sheila being firmly put in her place, Tim had gloated so hard he looked like a bullfrog in a hoodie.

"You too, Tim, listen now. I can't be walking these same streets, saying hello to the neighbors like nothing has changed. For me, everything has changed and without your father's support, things will get extra tough around here. I've checked into it. The schools over there start the week after they do here. So you all can say your goodbyes to everyone before coming to your new home. Uncle Gentrale says that he's not going nowh—eh-hem—*anywhere* so you can stay here with him that week. I'll have to start the new job right away. When you arrive, the new house will be ready."

Tim stood up, slapped his thighs and picked up his bag. "Well, then that's it. We're going." *Hmm...I need to get out of here anyway. Shit! Rene's going to think I knew about this all along. Okay, so, maybe I could come and stay with Uncle Gentrale weekends.*

Sheila shifted in her seat and folded her arms in front of her. "Mom, it seems like you've thought of *everything*."

"Yes, that's what I said at the beginning of this conversation. Now, never mind about *all that*, young lady, with your flip mouth! I need you to run down to the dry cleaners. Okay?"

"Yes, I remember. Uh-oh, there's the door. It's for me," Sheila said, sticking her tongue out at her brother on her way towards the front of the apartment.

IT WAS HIM AFTER ALL

On the way to his room Tim heard his sister laughing it up with someone in the living room. *What the hell is this?* he thought and took a peek to see. *Oh shit, it's Darryl!—Darryl?*

"Yo, s'up?" called out his tutor, smiling as if the world was his own. "I was just telling your sister that you're going to kick butt on that proficiency, yo!" The fingerless glove high-fived him from across the room.

Tim's voice caught in his throat. "Well, if anything good happens, it'll be th-thanks to you. I'll be with you in a minute. What's up?"

Darryl smiled, turned towards Sheila and they laughed at some inside joke. "Oh, uh, no problem, I'm actually waiting for your sis."

Tim's voice had all but disappeared. "Oh, uh-yeah man, it's all good," he said and slithered around the corner like an eel.

The familiar sound of Gentrale's voice on the other side of his bedroom door roused Tim from a deep sleep. In fact, he couldn't be sure if he was awake—the light outside his window wasn't right. *Had the entire afternoon slipped away?*

Gentrale, never late for the evening meal, answered his question. "What's for dinner?" he heard the old codger say. "Where's Tim? I need to talk to him."

Before dozing off again, Tim heard his sister say, "I think Timmy's asleep in his room."

Maurice's calloused hand feels like a piece of petrified wood. It hurts. Tim looks at the dude and starts to say something when blood pours from his lips. He wants to wipe his mouth but can't—both arms are held out from

his body by the two thugs. Their fingers dig deep into his arm pits. Maurice
is grinning like a demon. Tim looks at his face even though he knows that
he should be watching the dude's shoulders to be ready for the next punch.
Something moves behind Maurice. A partially gloved hand is scratching a
face, a face he knows. At the last fraction of a second he sees the next blow
coming. He moves, the ring glances off his cheek. As if adhering to some kind
of planned rationing, the chumps holding him punch him in the gut two
times each with their free hands. The name of the gloved guy comes to him as
he doubles over and is dropped to the ground. They are kicking him now.

He opens his eyes, but Darryl is gone.

The dream left Tim to roll off his mattress head first onto the floor
where he remained for a good while, staring at the ceiling. Now the
ache in his jaw had competition from a pain on the top of his head. Les
had gotten him good, and he deserved it.

The dude didn't mean any harm. With those questions, he was
actually looking out for him. Tim's heart sank when he imagined what
Les would say after everything came out about Chucky. Darryl, his fake
friend, was altogether another matter. That had to be him at the park.
That's why he could never get the punk to be straight about the glove.

Could his sister have known? It didn't matter. Time was running
out. He would have to deal with Darryl's ass soon, special friend of
Sheila's or not.

And he had to make that chump Maurice pay somehow.

R-E-S-P-E-C-T

The next morning Tim watched his mom wait by the stove for her coffee to bubble up in the pot. Like the atmosphere in the apartment, she had changed since his dad died. As far he could tell, most of the Post-its had disappeared. Same for the sundry coffee cups, pens, paperclips, hairclips, gum wrappers, business cards, lipsticks, eye shadow, earrings, beads, and bangles that seemed to have staked out permanent settlements. Pillows on the chairs in the living room had new covers and the dust bunnies underneath had scurried away. Even the light coming through the front windows seemed brighter.

Julia hummed as she waited. Tim recognized the tune as a hymn she would sing Sunday mornings while getting ready for church.

She doesn't miss him.

It had been barely five days since they buried his dad and the world had already begun to fill in the hole that he left.

The bad ol' days may have finally passed.

"Good morning, Timmy. You're up and awake?"

"Good morning. *Mom!* I told you not to call me that. What you doing home on a Friday morning? You sick? Something happened at work?"

"I'm fine, *Tim*. And no, nothing happened at work except that I'm done over there, and I don't want to see inside of *even the outside* of that place again. I'll be taking the train for Chicago soon. Don't you remember? But never mind all that for now." She placed two bowls, spoons, milk, bananas and a box of cornflakes on the table. They sat opposite one another. "How you doin', baby?" She sang it so sweetly, his teeth hurt.

"I'm alright—I guess," Tim said through a yawn.

"You guess? I knew something was bothering you. Now tell me the truth—about that bruise for one thing! I know I've been kind of—distracted lately and, uh—it's not that Maurice boy, is it? Is he bothering you again?"

"Distracted? That's what you call it? Dag, Mom! Ugh! No, I ain't seen Maurice!" Tim sat down at the table.

"Well, that's a relief! Yes, I know I haven't been paying enough attention to y'all. With the divorce, money problems, Gentrale, the funeral…it's been rough. I'm so glad you two turned out to be such good kids. I'm so proud of y'all. You know that, don't you?"

Tim hung his head at hearing the word *proud*.

Julia sipped her coffee and watched him. "You listening to me or what?"

"Yea-eh-hem—um, yeah I'm listening. Hey, uhm…do you remember me telling you—I'm back with Rene!?"

"I thought that's what you were trying to say yesterday! She's a good girl. I was so sad to hear that y'all broke up. Have you talked with her? About the move, I mean?"

"Uh…not exactly, no."

"Maybe we could make it work if you stay here with Gentrale? What do you think?"

Oh shit, he thought. "Uh…let me think a-about th-that, Mom. I'm thinking this mo-move may not be a ba-bad idea. There's some cool sp-spots over there and whatnot."

"Hmm…okay, you think about it. So, um…what exactly happened with you and Rene?" She watched her son blush, yawn and extend his arms above his head.

Julia put her hands on her hips and looked straight at him. "'Cause, I'm too young to be a grandmother. You get me, boy?"

"Yeah, Mom, I get it! Geez!" Tim wiped his forehead as he walked across the kitchen.

Julia sat erect in her chair and pointed a finger at him. "Are you calling the Lord's name in vain, my man?"

"No!" He jutted out his jaw like his uncle. "No-I-ain't-calling-the-Lord's-name-in-vain. Okay? Mom, let me ask you a question." He turned away from her to put some bread in the toaster.

"Hmm…what's that?"

"What happened between you and Daddy? I-I mean, last time I saw him he was going on and on about still loving you and stuff. If that's true, why did he leave us?" Behind him Tim heard a sigh, a scrape, a click of the tongue. For a moment, he thought she would let the question hang in the air forever. Finally, he turned around. Julia seemed to take it as a cue.

"No, boy! He didn't leave us. We just couldn't stay together anymore—with his drinking all the time. And his friends! Oh Lord!" She picked up a cigarette, held it between her lips.

"Haaaa! Yeah! Good ol' Ba-Baggy! You couldn't stand-him, I could tell."

"Well, it wasn't exactly a secret. I wasn't trying to hide anything. The man gave me the creeps, with his raccoon-eyes!" Her laugh catapulted the cigarette from her mouth. She caught it midair.

"Whoa, that's cold, Mom. Even for you! But, but…hmm…I get you. Must have been tough. Dad could get pretty drunk, huh?"

"Yes, he had a real problem."

"But Uncle Gentrale said that he wasn't no alcoholic. Said that he just liked to drink."

Julia turned her nose up at that one. "Humph. Well, if he wasn't an alkee, he was certainly close enough!" she said, pulling at the back of her bathrobe as she got up. "You want some?" She turned toward the stove. "What else y'all talked about?"

"Nah, you know I don't like coffee. Who? Me and *Unk*?"

"*Yes*, Timmy! You and your uncle." At that moment standing at the stove, she reminded him of his dad, his dad who never had a chance—not a real one. After all he'd been through, it didn't seem right that he lay in the ground being eaten by worms. Tim felt dizzy as he imagined them crawling out of his dad's eyes. He rested his head onto his forearms. His mom, still talking away, hadn't even noticed. *No, she didn't miss him. She was happy—happy to be making plans for them all.*

He finally asked the question that had been on his mind. "Do you have a boyfriend in Chicago?" And watched the saucer in her hand hit the floor.

"Is that what he said about me?" she yelled, hands splayed to her sides. Since she hadn't turned around, she appeared to be talking to the stove.

The shards scattered everywhere. Tim stared at his mother's back. "Well, do you, Mom?" he insisted. As he waited, a shiver ran up and down his spine. Whether she was about to lie to him or not, he couldn't tell—he never could. But he doubted it. He had her now. She had to tell him the truth. "I mean, it's not that dude who went to jail, is it?"

"*Child*, where you get off asking me something like that?" she said, finally turning to face him. "*Firstly*, it ain't none of yo-your—beeswax. Now-now, I made some mistakes, yeah, but all that's behind us, Timmy—*Tim!* And I ain't about to go listing them to you. I told y'all how sorry I am for all the stuff we had to deal with because of my silly…Oh God! I'm real, real sorry, baby. I've asked the Lord to forgive and keep me strong so that I'll be able to make it up to y'all, to myself. Read my lips—they are very large, there-ain't-no-boyfriend. For your in-for-ma-TION!"

"And se-secondly?" Tim asked coolly. Secretly relieved, he wanted to tell her that it was okay, but he didn't.

Julia shook her head. "*What* secondly?"

"You said firstly, so there must be a secondly coming," he said, reflexively cocking an ear towards a noise at the front door.

"There ain't no *secondly* for you right now. You don't deserve…uh-uh…*secondly*, Mr-Mr Prosecutor!"

From the way she'd snatched up the broom and said *Mr. Prosecutor*, Tim relaxed. The corners of her mouth turned up and her eyes flashed as she spoke. He didn't want the moment to end. "But *Moooom*…" he whined, trying to get back to those days when they were all together, all so young. The time of smiles and hugs when only friendly cussing and social drinking went on between the adults. A time when they spoke about everything because everything was new—way before the looks, the silences, the hollering and screaming, the absences, the secrets, the alcohol-laced BO hanging in the air, the anger, shame and the, the—*killing*.

"Enough of that foolishness. You hear me? Now, what did you talk about with Gentrale?" She left the shattered saucer in a little pile by the stove and sat down next to him. She stroked the top of his head, but when she got too close to his bruise, he pushed her hand away.

"Yeah, Mom, like—what happened? Unk went on and on about respecting a person's place in the world and stuff like that. Seems-to me that something big went down between them."

"Darling—my sweet boy, don't you worry your head about all that. That's some seriously old news. Sometimes people get themselves so tangled up in the disappointments of life that they miss out on what matters. Your daddy carried some big guilt around and was always trying to offload it in a bottle. The important thing is that your uncle was right about respect and all."

Fighting back tears, Tim surrendered to her caress and leaned into her shoulder.

I just wanted the dude to leave me alone. But he dissed me every chance he got. He thought he really had something on me with Maria. Yeah, she's fine, but she never could be Rene. Then he's standing over me laughing his ass off while I'm down with my face in the dirt. I guess it was true, I couldn't take it no more and when I heard that fucking ringtone again—ugh! Damn, why did the scrawny bitch have to die?

"Yeah, but what is it, Mom?" Tim said. His phone buzzed. He fished his cell out of his back pocket.

"What?"

"Respect, Mom!" He scrolled through a couple texts that had

come in, then looked up at her. "What is it? Even my teacher was talking about it the last day of school." At the mention of school, his voice caught. His heart raced fast and hard in his chest. *Had she heard something about Jones?*

"Hmm, an example of showing respect is—to give your full attention when somebody's talking to you! Now put that darn phone in your pocket. Don't be texting while I'm talking to you, boy!" she said, slapping him with a dishtowel.

Tim sat up in his chair and put his phone facedown but kept a hand on it. "I'm sorry, Mom. But that's it? Paying attention?"

"No, there's more to it than that, Timmy. *Tim*! But that's a good place to start because if you're paying attention, full attention, to a person or a situation, you'll have a pretty good chance to do some good."

"So, like—what kind of good am I doing by not texting somebody right now?" He slowly flipped the phone from one side to the other as he spoke.

"For one thing, you're giving yourself a better chance to learn something from your mama. That's pretty good in my book," she said with a sweet smile.

"Alright, but…?"

"If you're texting somebody while sitting here pretending to talk to me, you're not really with either one of us, me or your friend on the phone. In a way, you're only with yourself. It's like saying we don't deserve your full attention. It's like saying my place in your life isn't important enough to get the whole you, the whole Tim. In the end, you risk missing out big time, missing out on what I may have been trying to say to you. Or maybe you miss out on helping someone. Listening to someone alone often gives more help than you can imagine. What you do and say matters, Tim!"

Hearing that, Tim's eyes widened in surprise. "Huh?" *Oh shit, I knew it! She's talked to Jones!*

Julia noticed. "You surprised by all this, Tim?" she said sipping her coffee.

"Huh? Uh—no. I'm just listening to you. That's all. Wha-what about paying attention to uh—a situation? What's that got to do with…"

Julia held both hands up and did a little dance in her seat. "*R-E-S-P-E-C-T*! Usually when you aren't paying enough attention to a situation, you end up disrespecting your *own* self more than anybody else."

"Aw, get outta here. Ha!" he said, balling up the dishtowel to shoot it into the sink.

"Don't be so quick to dismiss what your ol' mom is trying to teach you. Let me ask you this—when that hoodlum Maurice found you in the park that day. Why didn't you run away? I know you can run, boy."

"*Mom*!" he exclaimed. "My sneaker was stuck. I told you! And besides, I didn't think…" He slapped, then pushed the table hard. A salt shaker fell to the floor. Tim went to retrieve it.

"Never mind, boy. Just leave it, calm down and listen. Yes, you didn't think…and well, that's not good at any time. Maybe you thought you could fight off three people? What if one of them had a gun? Or maybe you wanted to talk them out of beating you? Nah, Timmy. You didn't pay enough attention to the situation and therefore disrespected your own God-given sense. And got the poop kicked out of you!"

"Aw, come on, Mom! That can't be all there is to it. Can it? Just be alert and everything'll be alright?"

"Yes, you will be able to—*look, Tim*! Your hands, they're shaking, boy! Oh, I know this is hard to hear, sweetheart, but you've got to sit still for it anyway," Julia said, silently willing herself to stay cool. "Well, yes, it's true, you *will* be able to avoid a lot of problems and problem people—and survive—if you stay attentive to your surroundings. And while we're on the subject of survival, let me remind you that as a young black boy on the streets, whenever you run into the police—and you *will* from time to time—please, please be polite and low key at all costs. Just answer their questions and don't run away from them."

"Humph…low key, huh? So, like you sayin' that it was Trayvon's fault he got killed because he wasn't *polite* enough to that fool Zimmerman? Huh? Dag, Mom! The dude was walking down the street eating a bag of *Skittles*! Still, that wasn't low key enough for that nutjob who was playin' police."

"Now, uh-uh—you know I'm not saying it was Trayvon's fault! You know that, boy! I…" Julia stopped talking when Tim closed his eyes and rubbed his temples with his fingers.

"Okay, okay, I'm sorry, Mom. I know you ain't saying nothing like that. Sorry. I getchu. Honest."

They sat still and quiet, caressing each other with their eyes and let the tension subside naturally.

Julia scratched her chin, "Hmm—I'm thinking about you and Sheila now." She stood up and grabbed the broom again.

"Uh-huh."

"Maybe the situation between you and your sister is about paying attention in a different way. You know that she has a weight problem. You also know that she's trying to do something about it. Not *enough* mind you, but she's trying. Right?"

"Yeah, I guess." Tim slumped in his chair.

"I know kids tease each other. Lord knows we did. But if you only tease her about her weight, it could have a bad effect on her. She could get the idea that you only see her as a fat girl…which she is, but that's not all she is!"

"Well then, what else can I tease her about?" Tim said with a sly smile, pulling himself erect.

"Humph. You're a real piece-a-work, boy. You know that, Tim! No, what I'm saying is that if her fatness…"

"Ahhhh HA! Her Fatness!—Ow! Ouch! Stop it, Mom! That broom hurts! I'm serious!" Tim screamed. Trying to avoid the next blow, he fell off the chair onto one knee.

Something solid hit the floor. Julia's broom froze in midair, just over her son's head. "Oh! Wait—what's that? Whose phone is that, Timmy? It isn't yours."

"Uh—oh, no-nothin', it's n-not mine. Les left it on the bench at the gym. I have to give it back to him. He-he's been trying to catch up with me. So—you was saying something about her *fatness?*" Tim said with a twinkle in his eye. He hoped it would be enough to distract her.

"Shush, boy. Unless you want some more of this!" She shook the broom at him. "Now wait. You listening? Good! If her weight is all you can talk about, she could feel that her brother doesn't know her or maybe, doesn't want to know her."

Tim slapped his leg and leaned back in his chair. "Oh, so you sayin' I can't tease her now. She teases me all the time, I…"

"*Yeah*, but she teases you about your knobby knees, or how you stutter when you get nervous, your BO—sorry about that, honey—your sudden interest in yoga—many things! She really pays attention to you and what you're up to in your life. She also encourages you and tries to help you." Julia swept up the broken saucer pieces as she spoke.

Tim couldn't believe what he'd heard. "Help me? Yeah, if getting me beat up is some kind of help!"

"Child, we just went over that, Tim! You could've gotten away if you were—"

"Paying attention," Tim agreed with a heavy sigh that sounded more like a surrender.

"Right! All I'm saying is that there is a lot more to your sister." Julia punctuated her words by hitting the side of the trashcan with the dustpan.

"Oh, so you saying that I can find other things to bust on her about?" he said leaning forward, arming up for the next opportunity.

"If it means you're busting on your sister in more detail, being more creative about it—well, yes I-I suppose," Julia said.

Tim studied the faint frown on his mother's face. "Ha, like the way she acts wh-whenever—Darryl comes around." *The chump.* "Or the fact that even though she's smart, sh-she's nerdy. I mean it's not li-like you got to be a geek to get go-good grades!"

The knocking on the trashcan stopped suddenly. "And, how would you know that?" Julia said sternly.

"Huh? Aw, man!" Tim slapped the table. "Mom! Now it's you who's getting on my case!"

Julia leaned the broom into the corner and folded her arms. "Uh-huh, think about it. Ok? I was just saying." At that moment his mother looked like all she needed was some kind of victory banner stretched out behind her.

"Yeah, yeah, I'm thinking about it, I got you. Uh-oh, shh—here she comes now."

Sheila slipped through the kitchen doorway studying their faces as if she may have missed something. "Good morning! Y'all didn't make any more big decisions, did you? So, are we still going to Chi-Town or what? I heard that's how some people say it over there."

"Yes, we're still going, sweetheart, but no more big decisions for now," Julia said, watching Tim as she spoke.

Tim pushed Chucky's phone deep into his pocket. "Yeah, we just talking about school and stuff."

"So then, Timmy—what about that proficiency?" Sheila asked.

Tim's eyes widened at the mention of the proficiency. He sat still in his chair and studied his hands that were folded in his lap.

Sheila smiled. "Tim, *Timmmmmy*! Didn't you hear me? What's the matter with you?"

"You heard Darryl, your chump *boyfriend*, say that I'm going to kick butt on that thing!"

"Timmy!" Julia chided.

"He ain't my boyfriend, he's my friend. And, where you get off calling him names?" Sheila demanded.

Tim stood and turned to leave. His mother's voice stopped him.

"Don't go anywhere, sweetheart. Sit down and talk to us!" She spoke as calmly as she could.

"Yes, Timmy, what's this all about?"

All went quiet except for the sounds of kids playing in the street. As Tim struggled to put together the next lie, his face felt like it would fall off the front of his head. "Uh, nothing, Mom. I'm s-sorry Sheila, Mom. I didn't mean nothing. Really! I don't know why I-I s-said that. Darryl's okay, I-I guess."

Julia gulped down the last drop of coffee in her cup and sat down at the table. "Sheila baby, it sounds to me like your brother's a little jealous. Ha!"

"Ma, I ain't jealous of nobody! Why you wanna s-say s-something like that?"

Still standing, Sheila folded her arms and leaned on the wall. "Could be!"

Julia eyed her daughter as if to say *put a cork in it*. "Okay, Tim, I didn't mean to say you're jealous of the boy. But he has helped you! Right?"

Tim couldn't look at them as he answered. "Yeah. But…"

"Yeah, but what? He helped you and you're going to *pass* that test. And that's it."

Secretly disturbed now, Tim imagined himself trashing the kitchen, taking his sister by the hair and throwing her out of the back door into the yard. Instead, he sat quietly, hung his head a little and smiled—hoping to chill out his mom. He wanted out of the conversation, out of the entire situation. Yes, he wanted to escape. Suddenly, he couldn't wait for his mom to move them to Chicago.

But Sheila gave him the easiest out possible: "Wa-wanna-b-bet on that test? How much you got to loo-loo-lose, big *brother?*"

Without dropping a beat, Tim leaped into the moment with both feet: "Sure, girl! How about one of those *gazillion* Italian sausages with extra mayo you like so much? I-I think it won't hurt if you mi-miss one this week!"

"Oh no! I *know* you didn't say what I thought you said!" his sister yelled and nailed him on the forehead with a potholder thrown from across the room. Julia screamed for them to be careful—something about glass on the floor, but it didn't matter. For the moment at least, everything was okay, but letting Sheila catch him couldn't be an option. Arrested by a severe case of the giggles and having made it around the kitchen table twice, Tim bolted out of the back door with *Her Fatness* on his heels.

A LONG TIME TO WAIT FOR SOMEONE

The morning family drama left Julia suddenly fatigued. She took a final sip of coffee, returned to her bedroom and lay down wearily upon her flowered sheets. She hoped that all of her talk about respect would help to guide her son who seemed to her to be in danger of veering off the *righteous* path.

Tim's questions disturbed her more than she was willing to admit though—especially the one about Trayvon Martin. The shock of the moment had left Julia with neither the heart or strength to question him about it. Her only hope was that his consciousness of the situation would help him to be more careful in his movements out on the street. She shuddered at the realization that her days of protecting him were coming to a close. *Lord, how many boys like Trayvon and my own son will have to die at the hands of the police before this ends?*

Although she was glad to have been able to answer him more or less honestly about a boyfriend in Chicago, his question reminded her that she was not so happy to be sleeping alone. She missed her husband. Yes, Victor was a drunk, eleven years older than she was and snored like a wild boar, but she loved him, loved the physical closeness they'd enjoyed. All of that ended long before he'd actually moved out. As far as she was concerned, the Lord would take care of her and the kids now. At the thought of her Savior, she rolled her slight frame over the side of the bed onto her knees to give thanks to Christ for her health, her children, life and new job, no matter how humble. She declared her devotion and promised again to walk the straight and narrow.

As she expressed regret for her transgressions, particularly those related to the court case, she couldn't help but wonder about Al, her special friend. That's what they called themselves, *special friends*. When a strong thirst hit her, she padded her way to the fridge for a glass of water. It turned out to be warm but still cooler than the air of the morning. It wasn't even 10:30. She reckoned that it had already hit eighty-five degrees. She gulped down the water and slammed the door. *How is Al managing in prison? Lord knows, he's not a tough guy.* There was good reason to worry. A sly smile moved onto her lips as she remembered the time when they were *trapped* in a motel room by a door stuck from humidity. Instead of calling management, Al had insisted upon opening it himself. The only thing he accomplished was spraining his neck and shoulder. They laughed about that for weeks.

She wanted to see him so badly. But what could she do? By a mere technicality she was spared having to do time herself. Going to visit him would serve only to raise suspicions once again. Or so she thought. Anyway, they'd agreed that however things turned out, he'd do the time and they would hook up later. Five years was a long time to wait for someone though. Deeply she knew it was over and gave thanks for the comfort that the relationship afforded her. After facing the shocking certainty of her marriage having finally failed, the story with Al helped her to keep it together for her children.

Instead of getting started with the day, Julia went to the closet where she kept the the family photo album. The door was open and as usual it leaned dangerously to the right, threatening to collapse. Such things didn't bother her at the moment. She needed distraction, to move her thinking towards more hopeful thoughts. The stiff yellow pages of the binder made loud cracking noises with every turn. Inside there were too many memories to count: Tim in kindergarten, Sheila at three years, digging her fingers in the soil of the backyard garden, Tim, eight-years old, sitting in the family recliner holding a pipe in his mouth and a newspaper in his hands. He'd gotten a good laugh out of them, of course.

There was Sheila squashing a Raggedy Ann, family trips to Wildwood Beach, the Pocanos, Atlantic City, Tim's graduation from elementary school. Then came the elders: her own mother and father, Aunt Tissie, Uncle Joe.

Something fell out of a page onto the throw rug—an old Polaroid of Victor and her with the kids. They were quite small at the time, maybe five and seven years. It was their only trip to Atlantic City as a family. They were on the boardwalk in front of a tacky concession stand, full of amusements for the kids, maps and every kind of souvenir available at the time. Dressed in bathing suits, goggles and flippers, they were set for a day on the beach.

The memory descended upon her like a fever. She let the binder slide to the floor and collapsed onto the bed. A gentle breeze pushed the curtains across her face.

The sun was so bright it was impossible to see without sunglasses. And even then, it was near impossible. However, she could see Victor and the kids playing in the water, just at the edge. Families and couples were sprawled on colorful towels in every direction. A sea of umbrellas stood in loose rows ten deep along the shore. Vendors stepped carefully as they shouted the contents of their coolers: Coke, Fanta, Sprite but no beer. Alcohol on the beach was prohibited. The magazine by her side had taken on the role of a prop, merely something to complete the picture. She remembered thinking life was good before apparently nodding off. At the sound of a scream, her eyes snapped open to see the fat lady under the next umbrella holding her hands to her mouth. People were jumping up and running towards the water. Alarmed, Julia searched the shore for—Oh my God, where are they? She stood and surged for the water line, knocking over her umbrella. A standing crowd of bathers encircled something, someone. She broke through, somehow knowing that it was her boy.

Awake, Tim lay still on a stretcher. A medic kneeling beside him spoke softly. The oxygen mask had been removed. Dumbfounded and blind with dread, Julia ran and tripped over someone's foot and fell upon her elbows.

She was getting up when the medic turned and asked if she was all right. Nodding yes, she heard Victor's drunken voice behind her. Where the hell had he been hiding the bottle? she thought. She felt his hand upon her shoulder. "Julia, you ok? We don't need no more accidents, I mean—" That's when she cold cocked him in the eye.

The memory of punching Victor in the face snapped her to full consciousness, but she hardly moved as she relived the excitement of the melee and the feeling of her own power. There was the flash of red at Victor's eye socket, the distress in his voice as he cursed at the pain, the shock and awe of the crowd, the grip of someone holding onto her arm, the sound of her son and daughter crying out to her, the way she broke free and dived down next to the stretcher, next to her boy.

From that day onwards, Tim had developed a stutter.

SUSPECT

Tim liked the no bullshit feel of Omar's Gym. Everything was close at hand, no wasted space or materials could be found and there were only two colors in the whole joint: light and dark grey. No sissy step or elliptical machines around—hardly any machines, in fact. If you wanted cardio, you ran laps around the boxing ring or used the solitary stationary cycle that had two settings: hard and real hard. Another feature that endeared him to the funky space: almost everything was bolted down. Even the floor, completely covered by two-inch interlocking rubber mats, gave him a sense of security. He loved how the dumbbells were kept in strict order by weight: single pounders in the first slots of the rack, sixty-five pounders at the other end. Plate weights hung in layers around the perimeter near the benches.

Lying on a bench press, he pondered the hundred-pound plates hanging on the bar and decided to leave that notion alone for now. Instead, he headed for the heavy bag that begged for his attention. Yes, to quote his best friend Les, *nothing bullshit about a punching bag*.

As far as he could tell, there were only two exceptions to the no-nonsense rule at Omar's: the ceiling lamps that bathed the place in a mysterious yellowish light. From the bench, if you squinted just right, you could imagine them to be evenly spaced suns in a dark sky. The other exception came in the form of two full-sized porn star posters in the locker room. But then, he thought, biting down on his glove laces, *they have their uses as well*.

It took only ten seconds with the bag for him to break a sweat. As the padded cylinder swayed from his exertions, his grin widened with every blow. He remembered when hitting the bag had felt like punching a wall. He reveled in his own power.

Spank and Fidel walked in.

"Whoa-whoa-whoa, Tim. Man! S'up, brother? You got it on, yo!" Spank said.

Tim ignored them as long as he could. Something about Spank didn't look right.

Fidel slapped Spank on the shoulder, "Man, leave the dude to his activities. Can't you see that you're breaking his concentration?"

Spank laughed. "Yeah, but you need a brain to concentr…"

Tim stood straight up and turned towards them. "Yeah, listen to Fidel and leave me alone. I'll get with you later, alright?" he said, giving Fidel a less-than-friendly look.

The duo sat on the floor. He didn't think that they'd go away—it would've looked like he had punked them. He got back to work. The red bag shined with sweat, whined like a demon on its chain as he loaded up combinations, grunting with the best animalistic sounds he could muster. He liked those sounds.

Finally it was over. His hecklers—who hadn't noticed—were in deep conversation.

Fidel spoke in a harsh whisper. "Aw, man. I don't believe it. What I know is that a week, ten days ago he was at the library that night—arguing with them! At least that's how I heard it." He used his hands a lot as he spoke. His loose-fitting jacket seemed to move on his shoulders with a life of its own.

Spank shook his head no. "Well, I didn't hear it like that."

"Oh yeah? What'd you hear? Tell me again." Fidel punched one hand into the other.

"Spank, y'all still talking about that shit at Rasheed's?" Tim broke in. "Still trying to blame the shit on me? Well, you can forget that shit!" he said waving them off with a gloved hand. Sweat flew off in all directions. Fidel inspected his jacket for moisture.

Spank, half laughing at Fidel's concern for his jacket, tried to diffuse the situation. "Nah, nah, my brother. We know that was no set up. You was *trapped*, man! You had to get yo' ass out quick."

Fidel spoke without looking at Tim. "Have you seen Chucky around lately?"

Even though he'd sort of expected it, Fidel's question hit Tim like a pipe in the balls. "N-no, I ain't seen him," he stuttered. His defect served him well this time because it made him angry. "Didn't we fucking talk about this already?"

"Shit, Fidel, he ain't got nothin' to do with that," Spank said standing up and hunching his shoulders. He turned a 360 on the ball of one foot and shot a phantom three-pointer—*all net.*

Fidel stayed on the floor. He whistled through his teeth and spoke as if Tim wasn't there. "On the contrary, my brother, I think maybe he in fact did have something to do with it."

"Yeah, man, you done told me a hundred times and I told you—I heard they was just fooling around." Spank spoke softly as if they might be overheard. No one else was there.

Fidel glanced at Tim. "Hmm…as I was saying—the same night? That's too much of a coincidence for me, brother. *Something* went down and mark my word, I *will* find out exactly what happened."

"And so?" Tim said. "You know how your cousin is—always getting up in people's face. Never alone though—somebody's always there to take his back. I ignored his ass for the most part."

Fidel held a hand up, still looking directly at Tim. "Please, shut up, Spank! Well, Tim, I heard that you all were supposed to meet outside to settle things and no one has seen Chucky since."

Fidel stood up, looked towards the floor for a second then back at Tim. "All I'm seeing these days is you everywhere I go."

"And so? You see me. Who do I look like to you? You need information? Go online, *mother*—"Tim stopped himself midsentence, held up a hand and turned towards the locker room. "Spank—I'll catch you later," he said and walked away. Something made him glance over his shoulder. He turned and paused. Fidel was smiling.

He unbuttoned his jacket. "Aw, don't go away angry like that, my brother." His voice sounded like a snake choking on cornflakes.

"What? You going to miss me, *Fido?*"

Spank jumped like he would explode at any minute. "Oh shit! Fidel, *did you hear...?*"

"Shut the fuck up, Spank!" Fidel barked. "I'm not asking this time."

"Okay, I ain't got nothin' else to say to y'all." Tim smiled this time and turned away again.

Fidel buttoned his jacket. "Yeah easy, Tim. I will catch you later."

CONFESSION

Tim didn't want to admit it, but what Fidel had said in the gym really fucked with him even though he knew in his heart that the boy couldn't *know* anything. He had stayed and worked out as late as he could in the cool of Omar's, hoping to burn off some stress. Now sweat ran down his back as he waited for Darryl just outside of the library exit.

The thing with the glove was still a mystery. Going to Sheila about it was out. He wouldn't have gotten a straight answer out of her anyway. Besides, he didn't want to tell her that Darryl was probably there when Maurice jumped him in the park. He had to confront the dude, he had to do something.

The library doors swung open.

Darryl emerged with his fist extended. He carried a huge gym bag over his shoulder. "Hey, Tim! S'up, cuz? What are you doing here? Didn't think I'd see you today."

Tim gave up the bump. "'S'up, Darryl—just passing through. It's crazy hot out here, yo! What you doing tonight? I know you ain't hanging with my sis. She's out with her homegirls."

"Ha, now you're keeping tabs on me, man? There's a night game in the park. Want to hang?" he said, walking down the path toward the curb. Tim followed.

"It's nine o'clock, man. Ain't it kind of late for a game?" he said, worried that they wouldn't get a chance to talk about Maurice.

"Where have you been, dude?" he said, smacking Tim on the shoulder. "All summer the lights have been coming on at eight and stay on 'till midnight. So, are you in or what?"

"Hell yeah, you know it."

As usual, traffic was heavy. After dodging a couple cars, they stood on the very same island he'd escaped to the night when Chucky and his boys had chased him. The memory made him mad and more certain that he had to set things straight with this bullshit Darryl fuck-head.

Waiting in line at the local D & D for a couple smoothies, Tim stole another look at the glove and it pissed him off even more. Now he clearly remembered seeing Darryl in the park, standing off to the side as Maurice unloaded on him. The slick cool of Les' knife in his pocket calmed him. He'd almost forgotten the thing was there.

They stepped out onto the pavement. Darryl turned down King— the same street where Tim had run for his life over a week ago. "Yo, Tim, come on, bro! Quit dragging your feet—we're late, man."

Kids played on the sidewalk, on porches, in front yards and in the street. Tim wondered how he'd missed all of this that night. Then he spotted the house. The same dudes who'd chased after him through the alley were hanging on the porch as if they had never moved.

Fearing to be recognized, Tim stepped to the curbside of the sidewalk when he caught up with Darryl. "Who's going to be there tonight?" he said, keeping an eye on the boys on the porch.

"Aw man, you know—the same dudes as usual: Hank, Junkie Spliff. Even your girl, Lucy. *Word* is she took you to the hoop recently." Darryl said with a sly smile.

"*Man*, if you believe that shit, I wanna sell you—"

Tim stopped talking when Darryl turned and continued backwards half running, half skipping down the sidewalk. "Aw man, Tim! I almost forgot to tell you. The police came to the library again."

"Oh yeah?" Tim said, having to jog to keep up.

"Yeah, was asking everybody a lot of the same questions about the night Chucky disappeared. Afterwards, Mrs. Shepard was a nervous wreck."

Tim thought it funny to imagine Mrs. Shepard nervous. "Ha! What was that like? She always be—hey. Darryl, *watch out!*"

The Doberman came like a bullet, hit the fence full force and grabbed a handle of Darryl's bag in its teeth. Screaming, Darryl held onto the other handle with one hand while Tim held onto his free arm. Tim watched the dog the entire time and swore to himself that the pooch had given him a look when his owners pulled him back.

"Shit, man—y'all need to control that bitch!" Darryl yelled, inspecting his bag.

The hoods, laughing, exchanging fist bumps, said nothing and returned to their perches.

"You alright, bro?" Tim said, words dripping with guilt.

"Yeah, I'm good, but I have to get out of here," Darryl said and jogged away towards the park entrance with Tim bringing up the rear.

He listened to the boy jabber on about the dog: the bitch had bitten nearly clean through the handle of his gym bag, how good he usually is with animals, the dog didn't appear to be after him, how he wasn't afraid, what he was about to do if those hoods hadn't shown up. Tim didn't care. Happy to finally be in the park, he could think about what was next. The basketball courts were on the opposite side of the park from...

Say it, motherfucker!...from where you left fuckin' Chucky. Shit!

What exactly he had to say to Darryl, he didn't know. But Darryl had to know that the game, this game with him was over. *Who does he think he is? I mean, does he think that giving me some English lessons could make up for that shit? Nah-nah. He stood by and watched them beat the shit out of me. What does he think? Hooking up with my sister excuses him? Nah-nah, buddy.*

When they arrived at the fence, a group of white boys were playing four-on-four full-court.

Tim smiled at the sight. "Man, you sure this is the right place?"

Darryl just stood there and watched the action for a minute before saying, "Yeah-yeah, I don't get it. The game was for tonight at eight. Oh-ho-ho! Hey, Lucy!"

"Yo, Darryl. How's it hangin', baby, to the left? Ha! S'up, Tim!" Lucy said, dribbling a ball as she spoke. "*Me seems* you done healed up from our last meeting," she quipped, grinning from ear to ear.

Darryl tried and failed to snatch the ball. "Yo, Lucy, what's going on? No game tonight?"

"Tru-dat, dawg. These dudes was here when I came up before. Ain't seen nobody else," she said, bouncing the ball from one hand to the other.

"Shit, man, this is a waste of time," Tim said and turned to leave.

"Yeah, Tim, I feel you! You got some stocks and shit to trade or something?"

Tim pulled on Darryl's gym bag. "Aw man, Darryl. Let's get the hell outta here. See you, Lucy-Lu."

Weaving side to side, passing the ball between her legs twice, the girl looked wicked fresh. It would have been a great game. "Yeah easy, Tim. Remember, I'm good for a rematch anytime, yo."

They walked in silence. Tim waited for Darryl to speak first. After a winding descent, the path led them to a long stone tunnel. Their footsteps produced a repartee of syncopated percussion sounds on the walls.

Tim couldn't wait any longer. "Darryl. You had that glove for the entire summer, right?"

"Yeah. I think it's about time to get another one," Darryl mumbled, looking at it.

"You had it on the last day of school too. Right?"

Darryl frowned and snapped back. "That's right. What about it, homie? Didn't we cover this some time ago? For real, why are you so interested?"

Tim stopped, tugged on Darryl's bag to make him turn around. They were in the middle of the tunnel now. Long sinuous echoes followed every scrape and syllable. Tim spoke slowly.

"Well, on the next to last day of school, I got jumped by Maurice Rice and his boys. They messed me up, man, for nothing—some bullshit 'bout my sister. They didn't want money. Seemed to me they just wanted some entertainment."

Darryl listened, but kept his gaze towards the opening in the tunnel. "I'm sorry to hear that, bro, but what does that have to do with my glove? I mean…"

Tim pushed Darryl into the wall hard. Darryl slipped, hit his head and fell into a puddle. When he tried to get up, Tim took out Les' knife and kicked the boy in the shoulder. "Stay down, motherfucker. I'm not telling you again," he yelled. The sound of his voice boomed.

"Ugh, what the fuck are you doing, Tim? It's wet down here. Enough of this shit, I'm getting up," he said and pushed away from the wall.

"No you're not," Tim yelled, kicking him again, making sure that he saw the knife.

"Oh, so you're going to cut me now? Damn! So, it is true! You did do something to Chucky! Man, you won't believe how I've been defending your ass all this time!" He lay on his back holding his upper-body from the floor with his elbows.

Tim placed his foot in the center of Darryl's chest, leaned in, and pointed the knife at the zipper of his jeans. Darryl, completely wet from bottom to his shoulder blades, sat between the curve of the wall and the floor of the tunnel. "Stay still and shut up, *pussy*! Who says I got s-something to do with that? You don't know what you're talkin' about, *stupid*. Now say it! You were th-there with Maurice that day. *Say it, bitch!*"

Darryl's voice squeaked a little from Tim's weight on his chest. "Aw man, Tim, get off me. You wrong, cuz. Why would I…"

The knife sliced through the leg of Darryl's baggy jeans so easily it surprised them both. "I-I ain't your cu-cuz. You sure you wanna tell me that, bitch?" he whispered *bitch* for no reason.

"Tim, bro. You've gone crazy or what?" Darryl pleaded, through tears. "Okay, okay, I was there but I hardly even knew you, man. And I didn't touch you. Remember? *I didn't touch you!* When you went down on the ground, I split. You saw me—*I thought*. But since you were meeting me at the library all summer, I figured that you hadn't remembered. *Ahhhh!* Let me up and put that shit away, you're going to cut me for real. This isn't you, Tim. It ain't you. I don't hang with those dudes anymore."

Darryl started to really scream when Tim put his hand in his pocket. "I'm sorry, I'm sorry, man!" A message beeped in on Chucky's phone just as Tim fished it out. The screen read:

`Call me!` **Fidel**

He pointed the phone at Darryl, who shook his head side to side saying, "Oh, so now you going to make a photo of this? Nah-nah, it's not going to happ…"

"Shut the fuck up, fool, and stay down!" Tim said, swinging the knife.

"Come on, Tim-bro, get off me!" Darryl cried, trying to push up to his feet. Tim kicked the boy back into the puddle, hit the shutter button and ran off. Blinded by the flash, Darryl listened to Tim's splashy footsteps retreat into the darkness.

NUGGETS

The four o'clock swelter had set in. Tim sat on his stoop. Sweat ran down his arms, soaking the paper bag he held in his lap.

Across the street, on the far end of a parking lot, air conditioners roared from a line of dilapidated structures that looked like broken teeth. He considered waiting in the barbeque takeout for some relief, but then thought again. *I better stay my ass right here on the step as planned. If Les don't see me right 'way, he might turn around and go back home. He could be a real dufus sometimes.*

It had been about nine days since *the killing*—as he started to refer to it in his mind—and there had been nothing on the news about a body or a missing person. *Damn, somebody or some dog has got to find him any day now. He must be smelling pretty bad,* he thought. He chuckled sadly at the thought that the last time he'd seen Darryl, he had a pretty bad stink going on too and wondered if the boy had actually shit himself. Sitting on the steps in the heat, going into a panic at the sight of every passing police cruiser, sent him so deep within himself, pressed upon him so hard, that at one point he almost lost consciousness. He held onto the banister, looking up and down the street again for his friend.

Where is Les? That boy is always late. Strong as he is, you'd think he'd be able to jump up and bounce over here.

Aw man! Nobody's going to believe it was an accident, nobody! I'm sure he had Maria make that ringtone just to fuck with me. I didn't mean that shit. Now what am I going to do? Everybody's looking for the punk, I know the police haven't given up on my ass, and I ain't got no money to go nowhere. Maybe if we go to Chicago? They still will get me eventually. Damn, this is gonna mess up Mom good. With Dad finishing up like he did and now

me? Dad didn't mean for his brother to go and get himself killed—it just
happened. I mean, if things wasn't all fucked up back on the farm and shit,
Dad wouldn't have had to steal to get outta there.

I don't blame him, I would've done the same. So now what? Am I
supposed to go and steal some cash to get away? Oh shit, another message?

Unknown number

Wonder what's that about?

Tim jerked around at the sound of someone walking towards him.

"S'up, Tim?" Les said. He looked like a boulder in a tee shirt.

"Oh shit! You scared the shit out of me, boy! What up, Les?"

"Come on, let's get outta this heat." Les said it like an order and
headed for his favorite restaurant.

"So it's true! You only agreed to come over here 'cause you wanted
to go to the Chicken Shack! Anyway, have you heard how they make
those nuggets you like so much?"

"Nah—I ain't worried 'bout that shit, homie. I'm ready to eat. Come
on, let's go!" Les said, continuing on without looking back.

The joint was crowded with hungry teenagers. They stood around
holding their trays for a minute before a table opened up. Seated now,
Les spoke through greasy lips. "Mmm—damn, they're good, Timmy!
Sure you don't want none? What's in the bag? You on some kind'a
mission?"

"Yo, I told you not to call me that!"

Les wiped his mouth and hands and sat up straight at the tiny
table. "Alright, dude, chill okay? Just don't go all *Van Damme* on me
again. I might have to fuck you up for real. So how's it goin' at the
library with Darryl? Tim…you okay, man?"

At mention of his tutor's name, Tim went deaf for a second. All he
could hear were Darryl's pleas to be released. Once again, he had tucked
the entire episode away in a place as dark as the tunnel where he left
the crybaby. From the way his hands had jerked and almost cleared the
table, he must have gone a little blind as well.

"Oh shit, Tim! Watch what you doin', dude!" Les yelled, using his hand like a squeegee to keep the liquid from his lap.

"Aw man! Sorry, Les. I'll get you another one," he said, and grabbed a roll of paper towels sitting on the counter next to them.

Les patted himself down with a huge wad of napkins. He studied his friend. That made Tim nervous. He moved around in a herky-jerky manner and mumbled curses to himself, apologizing as he cleaned up the mess.

Les couldn't watch him anymore. "No problem, homie. Get up off the floor, man! You even got yourself all wet in shit. You nervous or something?"

"I'm not all that w-wet, man. It's cool," Tim said continuing to mop up the mess. "Sorry about that, y'all," he yelled across the small space at the Hispanic dudes working behind the bulletproof Plexiglass.

Tim sat down and inspected his bag as he spoke. "Yeah, it's been going pretty smooth. I told you it was my uncle who got me started goin' over to the library, right?"

"Yeah—that was funny. So...you gonna pass that test or what?" Les asked quietly.

"*I* don't know, man!" Tim slumped in his seat. "Shit's changing all around so fast. Couple days ago my mom said she got a new job and we're moving to Chicago. I can't even think about that right now. I got other shit on my mind like that fucking Fidel at the gym the other day."

Les put down his fork. "Oh shit! Yeah, just yesterday I saw that foul dude again. Told me to tell you that he would be in touch with you soon. Better watch your back. I couldn't believe what I heard about Rasheed's. Man, what the *hell* were you doin' with those fools?" Les said, working hard to hold his voice down. The place had suddenly become crowded with nugget lovers.

"Aw man. Wasn't nothin'. They wanted to get some..."

"Some what? I heard y'all went over there to *rob* the place!" Les whispered.

"Well, I don't know—I was in the car the whole time and..."

"And what? You was the lookout man? Shit, Tim! Fidel said something about you leaving them when the police showed up." Les leaned forward with both hands on the table.

"I-I *told* them that I was le-leaving!" Tim said, with a wave of his hand.

Les dialed back his tone a bit. "Now take it easy, man. Let me tell you this. That thug Fido thinks you got something to do with Chucky disappearing. It's true nobody has seen the dude for a while now."

"And so?" Tim said, looking around the room. They were now surrounded by a crowd of chewing teens, hunched over Styrofoam tubs of nuggets and fries.

"And so? So tell me. Why does Fidel think—?"

"Man, I don't know wh-what or why that fo-fool thinks anything. At the gym, he was saying the same shit. I told him to leave me the fuck alone. You know he's crazy? Right?"

"Dangerous too. Don't you forget it. Come on! Try to tell me, man, without gettin' all wild and shit. That night when I called you at the library, Chucky was hassling you. What went down for real?" Holding onto his last nugget as he spoke, Les looked like a dog with a bone. He wasn't letting go of this one.

Tim hesitated. "Ye-yeah like, I told you…"

Les tossed his bag and napkins in a huge trash receptacle next to them. "Don't give me that shit, boy! What the fuck happened?"

"I told you, Les! Damn! They left me at the table laughing and shit."

"Who's they?

"Chucky was with some dude I never saw before. When I came out, I walked up to him and his boys."

"Yeah-yeah, I remember all that now. You punked the dude in the parking lot. Watch your back, homie. You said it yourself, that dude Fidel is crazy."

"Hmm, no shit. Yo. I-I'm sorry for going crazy on you that day. L-let me give this back to you." He slid Les' knife across the table.

Les pocketed it real fast. "Oh shit. What are you doing? Numb brains! Why you bringing *that* in here? Yeah, that was some lame shit you pulled at my house, *dawg*. If you wasn't my boy, I would've broke your ass right then and there. Like what the fuck is goin' on, Tim?"

Tim shook his head, reached in the bag again and pulled out his baseball glove and placed it on the table between them. "Take this too."

"What? Na-nah, man. Now I know *something* is up!" Les said, sliding the glove towards Tim.

"Just take it, bro. We moving in about a week or so. I don't use it, and I know you still play sometimes."

"Yeah, but didn't your pops give that to you?"

"He wanted me to have it. Now I want you to have it. Can you for once just say *okay* and shut the fuck up?" Tim said. Something buzzed.

"That must be yours, man, mine is off. You not gonna get it?"

"Oh, that's Sheila texting me," he said. "Oh wow, look who just came in! Now be *cool*, Les. Alright?"

Les turned. "What? Oh! Yo, Rene baby, how you be?"

"I'm fine, Mr. Les. Tim, what up with you?" she said, touching him on the shoulder.

"Hey, Boo," he crooned. "S'up?"

"Apparently nothing much. Haven't seen you since uh—*the funeral*." She paused, giving him a certain look. "How's your mother holding up? I'm going over there right now to see them."

"She's alright, making plans and cleaning the house. She's good. Sheila's home too. You can—"

"Yes, *Timmy*, I know what I can and can't do. Don't need your advice, brother," she teased.

Les cracked up, "Oooh-wee, Tim, you done stepped in it—"

"Shut up, Mr. Les," Rene said, sweetly.

Tim always wondered about that *Mr. Les* business. "Ha, Les, I know you heard the lady. Hey, Boo, I know I'll see you at the music fest tomorrow. Right?"

"Really? *You know it?* That's strange because I don't even know it. Anyway, check y'all later. *MAYBE*." She waved and headed for the door. Tim and Les weren't the only customers watching her exit.

"Yo," Les said almost turning over the table in the process. "I'm goin' over to the gym. You coming?"

"Nah, I'll have to check you later," Tim said over his shoulder, already up and running out the door after Boo. "Yo, Rene, wait up!" he yelled across the parking lot.

Like loose bones vibrating in his pocket, Chucky's phone buzzed again. There were two unknown numbers and two texts:

Where are you? Call me! **Maria**

Charles baby, this your mama! I hope to God you're okay. Where are you, honey? It's been too long. Call me tonight or I'm going to the police. **Mom**

APOLOGY

That night at the dinner table Tim kept his head down as he tucked into a plate of green beans, potatoes and ham. His uncle watched him closely from across the table as his mom chattered on about her new job and how much better life would be for them in Chicago. Sheila chewed her food, scanned a magazine and pretended to listen to her, being sure to make the right sounds at the right times.

"I've written everything down and made copies for everybody. Here…" Julia placed a single sheet of paper in front of each of them. "Go ahead, check it out. I've listed all the things we're giving away, what we'll be shipping to Chicago and what I'm leaving with you, Gentrale. Sheila, Tim—y'all will be coming after the first week of school. All the flight information stuff is at the bottom of the page. The new address in Chicago is at the top. Actually, it's a suburb north of the city called Skokie."

Sheila frowned. "Skokie? Dag, what kind of name is that?"

"Yeah, it sounds like anotha' word for crazy, like, 'That dude is seriously *skokie!*'" Tim crossed his eyes and moved like a bobblehead doll in his chair. Sheila joined in almost immediately saying, "Hey, we could invent a new dance."

"You all gonna make me dizzy if you keep that stuff up," Gentrale said with a smile.

Julia managed to frown and laugh at the same time. "*Neva-mind* about all that, Timmy—*Mr. Poet.* That's where we're going. I've already reserved the taxi for tomorrow morning. I'm bringing four suitcases with me—Lord, have mercy! It's gonna cost a bunch, but it'll be worth it in the end. You'll see. *Word* on that! Like you kids like to say."

"Whoa! Check out Mom with the *word, yo!*" Tim said, fist bumping with his sis.

Julia came back quick on him. "Yes, you heard right young man. I..."

Gentrale interrupted her. "Excuse me, Julia, but since you're leaving in the morning, I must ask something right here and now while we're all together at the table."

"Oh! Okay, Gentrale. What is it?" Julia asked real sober-like.

Gentrale looked at his nephew. "Eh-hem, let me get this straight. Tim, that boy Chucky—did you know him?"

"Yeah, Unk, I *know* him—he *tries* to be a bully."

Julia frowned and put her fork down. "Now, Tim, you're not going to sit here at my table and disparage somebody who may be in trouble, hurt or worse, no matter their faults!"

Tim rubbed an eye with the back of his hand—the one that held his fork. When he spoke, he yawned and his voice came out in a kind of whine. "Sorry, Mom. I just never liked the dude..."

"He's always up in somebody's face, Mom, and he keeps his silly boys with him for protection," volunteered Sheila.

"Well...when we were kids back on the farm, your daddy and me had a word for that type of nig—"

"*GEN-TRALE!*" chided Julia. She balled up a napkin and threw it at him.

The old man batted it away. "Sorry, Julia, and y'all too," he said, nodding at Tim and Sheila. Arms folded, Julia rolled her eyes. "I'm *not* having such language in this house," she said. She took a deep breath and turned toward her son. "Tim, it looked like you wanted to say something?" Her voice had a renewed calm. She took a sip of water. Sheila picked up the napkin from the floor.

"Ha! Yeah, Unk, I'm sure y'all did have some funny names for those kinda fools. Oh-oh, like one night at the library that *fool* Chucky and some other dude was messin' with me at the table. I tried to ignore him, but—"Tim suddenly stopped talking when his mom, glaring at him, sat up in her chair and folded her arms for the second time in five minutes. *Oh shit!* he thought.

"But what, Tim?" asked Julia.

"Mom, he probably got himself beat up *again*," taunted his sister.

With both elbows on the table, Tim covered his eyes. "You shut up, *Tubby*. I'll take you and…"

"TIMMY! You'll take her and do WHAT, exactly? What's wrong with you, boy?" Julia, suddenly breathing hard, visibly shook in her seat and glared at him. "That's no way for a young man to talk to his sister. No way indeed, Tim…wait, are you *crying*, Timmy?"

"Na-nah—I ain't cryin'." His voice was husky and wet. "Sorry, I'm sorry, Uncle Gentrale."

"And to your sister, young man! What did we talk about just recently?"

"S-sorry, Sheila," he stuttered out. He started to get up, but his uncle held onto his forearm and gestured for him to stay where he was.

After a pause, Gentrale cleared his throat and spoke up. "There must be something heavy going on. Uh—I wasn't going to say anything, Julia, but on the day of Victor's wake, some bad dudes stopped us on the street. Since the police were here yesterday asking to talk with your boy here, *Mr. Fierce*, I think we need to hear from him right about now." Everyone looked at Tim who sat with his head down, hands in his lap.

Julia slapped the table and stood up. "TIMMY! Why in heaven's name would the police want to speak with you? Is it about that boy Chucky?"

"*Mom*! I don't know, I-I don't think—"

"Tim, don't lie to us," Julia continued. "A minute ago you said that you had something to do with that child. Now spill it! What happened?" Julia had moved to Tim's side of the table and stood over him.

"Dag, I don't like the way y'all lookin' at me, like I'm a criminal or something. Ok, before running out of there—"

"From the library?" Sheila asked.

"Yes, from the library—Chucky was saying stuff—like, he wanted to kick my—*you know what*—outside in the parking lot."

"So, child, you left right away through the front door. Right?" Julia demanded.

"Mom, I uh…"

"THROUGH THE FRONT DOOR! RIGHT, TIMMY?" she yelled.

"Oh—uh, n-nah, I waited the fifteen minutes 'till the library closed—and by then, those dudes had been gone for ten or more. You know what I mean? When the bell rang, I left out the back with everybody else and got out quick. I didn't see nobody. Later that night, I went to Dad's place."

"Uh, Tim," broke in Gentrale, "so why are the cops coming here asking for you? Your daddy may have had his troubles, but never with the police." He sat up straight and touched his bowtie. "No *Thornton* has!"

"And what are you trying to say, Gentrale?" Julia asked.

Gentrale realized he had stepped in it again. "Aw darlin', absolutely nothing in particular."

"Yeah, Tim." Sheila said, clearing off the table. "The police did say specifically that you were the *last person* seen with Chucky that night."

"Way-way-wait a minute, y'all. Maybe I was *one* of the last people, but not *the* last one. Like I said, he was with another boy I didn't know."

"Timmy! You're not going to get your phone? It's been buzzing for awhile now," Sheila said.

"Oh!" He took a quick glance at the screen of Chucky's cell."

<code>Call me, Charles: Mom</code>

Sheila leaned towards him to see. "Who's that, big brother?" she said laughing.

"It-it's a missed call. It's no-nothing."

"There it goes again, boy. Why you putting it away?" His mom glared at him.

"I to-told you it's nothing!"

Julia moved back to her chair and sat down. She held her right hand over her heart. "Lord, Tim. What have you done, child?"

"*Nothin'*, Mom." Tim's voice cracked this time. The tears were on their way. "That's it. You kn-know the police have to fi-find anybody to put the bl-blame on. What y'all think anyway?"

"Boy, it ain't what we think, it's what the police thinks now!" Gentrale said.

Julia touched his arm. "Don't scare him. It's obvious he hasn't done anything. Just in the wrong place at the wrong time." When she turned and spoke to her son, her voice was stern yet laden with concern. "Now, Timmy, I want to leave here tomorrow morning not having to worry. Do I have *anything* to worry about, son?"

"Ye-yeah, I mean—no, Mom."

Julia punched him in the shoulder. "*What?* Say it where I can hear you—so we *all* can hear you!"

Instead of looking at Julia, Tim stared straight ahead at the wall, rubbed his shoulder and spoke through a pout. "*Nooo*, Mom, you don't have to worry about me."

Gentrale groaned, like he was nursing an old wound. "What's obvious is that they don't have any evidence yet. Otherwise, they'd be on him like white on rice."

It was 10:30 at night when the thump of Gentrale's cane told Tim that the old man had finally shuffled into his bedroom.

He scooted down the hall to Sheila's door.

"Who is it?"

"It's me."

"What do you want?"

"I have to talk to you."

"This better be good."

As soon as he opened the door a heavy scent of nail polish remover combined with peppermint candy hit him in the face. Something silly played on YouTube. Before he could speak, Sheila held up a mighty hand while she finished her text.

Tim craned his neck to see the screen, "Who-who you texting now? The police? Ha!"

Sheila pursed her lips and looked at her brother over her glasses. "What are you talking about? Forget that. Did you know that the net is blowing up about that dude Chucky? Seems that he's been missing more than a week now. Anyway, what do you want? And what's with the camera. I know you aren't planning on taking photos! Well, you better not be!"

Tim stepped over clothes and hair stuff that lay on the floor. He looked his sister in the eyes. "H-hey, I re-really am sorry for calling you *tubby* at the table."

"So, why do you have that little grin on your face? What's so funny, *clown-boy?*" she said with a smirk.

"Hey—uh, it's not funny. Okay? And I'm sorry, that's all," he said, sans smile.

"Fine. Apology accepted." She put down her phone and sat up on the bed. "But what's so important that you had to come in here to tell me?"

"I–I want you to have this." Tim placed the SLR in her lap.

"What am I going to do with this big ol' thing? Besides, Daddy gave it to you. Do you remember how jealous I was?" she said, turning it over in her hands.

"Ye-yeah, but I don't need it now—thought maybe you'd like it. If you don't want to take it as a gift, just hold onto it for me." Tim moved side to side, shifting his weight from one foot to the other.

"What? But why? Are you going somewhere, Timmy?" She slapped her thigh. "*You are* in trouble! Aren't you! Now don't lie! Tell me!" she demanded, trying to give the camera back to him.

"Shh—chill, Sheila. Keep it for me, okay? And don't tell Mom. I'm thinking, just thinking about staying here with Uncle Gentrale. You *used* to be able to ke-keep a secret," he said, pushing it back into her hands.

"So, it-it's like a se-secret? What ki-kind-a—waaaiit, Timmy! Aw man, I was only kidding. I—ugh—wait up." She jumped off the bed. "Don't go, don't close the door!"

Tim shot his voice over his shoulder as he left. "I'm out. We're done. Do what you want with the camera."

The sudden sharp beep from Chucky's phone sounded like a smoke alarm in the narrow hallway. *Shit!* Tim fumbled for the thing in his pocket and bolted to his room.

As if dazed, he leaned heavily on his door and stared at the backlit words until his hand went limp. The cell hit the floor with a loud crack and bounced out of sight as if even it couldn't bear the shame. Sweat poured out of him like a broken water main as he reached underneath the bed frame to retrieve it. Dust balls stuck to his skin like furry gauze.

Got it.

Lying on the floor, mouthing the words, Tim read the text on the tiny screen several times before dozing off.

> Chucky, call me when you get this.
> Your pop's been calling every day
> asking about you. **Fidel**

His last thought before dozing off was to answer it.

TEA PARTY

Tim got off the bus at Central and Oakwood, the corner entrance to Orange Park, and for a moment, didn't recognize the place. It had been a while since he'd come here, when chip bags, beer cans and pizza boxes lay strewn everywhere. Now only plastic-lined trashcans stood guard.

He joined a thick line of happy music lovers on their way to the other side of the park where the stages stood. People who knew the score moved quickest in order to claim a good spot on the grass. The scent of hot dogs, burgers, fries and barbecued ribs wafted through the air, as did the sound check of guitars, drums and microphones in the distance. But he didn't care about any of that shit. He only wanted to find Rene.

She has to be here, I know it, Tim thought as he peered through the dense crowd. Colorful blankets covered the grassy clearing in front of the main stage. Kids chasing balloons ran wild, adults fanned newly lit coals in their grills while vendors, moving cheerfully among the public, sang their songs of cheap thrills.

Tim made his way over to the concession stands where he found Les trying to hold onto six hot dogs and a couple Big Gulps. "Dag, Les! I guess those nuggets from yesterday left you hungry. Did you leave any for me?"

"You better hurry up, dawg. You know how it goes. Soon the lines will stretch back to the gate. So I'm gettin' mine now," he burped out through a mouth full of dog. Tim wondered how the boy could eat, talk and twirl a toothpick between his teeth at the same time.

"Yo, Les," Tim said, pulling him over to the side. "Have you seen Fidel? I swear I saw so-some du-dude with a leather jacket ha-hanging around, looking evil as shit."

"Well, if you saw a leather jacket in this weather, it's gotta be that fool. Maybe you should go home, Tim. You know he's saying he wants to talk to you." Les pulled his cell from his pocket. "Yo, man, you know it's all over Facebook about his cousin. Some fool's done picked up on the rumor about you, dawg. Check it out." He pointed the screen at Tim's face.

Tim pushed the phone away. "Yeah-yeah, his cousin Chucky. Yeah, man, I know. Soon as I hook up with Rene, I'm outta here. Watch my back, homie." He looked around. He would have to move fast before the grounds got crazy crowded.

"Yeah, cool. I got you. Hey, let's get a couple of burgers before the line gets too long. I'll pay. My pops gave up some extra cash this morning. Oh shit, look who's coming."

"Yo, Les, s'up? Tim, my man!" Spank spoke through a big grin.

"Hey, Spank," Tim said, throwing back a stiff smile. "So, you still talking, huh? Not holding that Rasheed shit against me?"

"What? Sh—nah, man! With me, what's done is done. Fidel might see it another way—you know! Anyway, we got out all right. You wasn't wrong to split. If the cops had seen you, man, you'd be in even more trouble."

Tim frowned and moved toward Spank. "Man, whatchu talking about. Last time I saw you and Fido, I thought we closed on that shit."

Les, with an arm like a tree limb, pulled on Tim's shoulder until he had to take a step back.

Tim didn't push his hand away. "So, just *say* it, Spank. What the fuck's on your mind?"

"Yo, man, like I know what you said then," Spank said, bringing his hands together at his chest as if in prayer. "But the word on the street and the net is that you had something with Chucky the night before he uh, like—you know, disappeared."

"That's some *bullshit*," Les told him, glaring. Tim watched his friend defend him and had to look away for feeling so shitty.

Spank looked Les squarely in the eyes and continued to speak. "Fidel say the cops been askin' questions around the hood about *you*." He pointed at Tim. "Everybody say, you been hiding out big-time." Before Tim could respond, Les did it again. "I told y'all on the street the other day to mind y'all's business, Spank-a-Lank. Tim ain't got nothin' to do with that fuck-face Chucky. The boy probably got his ass in deep with those Weequahic dudes."

"Yeah, Les, I-I know. But—" Spank stopped talking midsentence.

Tim couldn't hold his tongue any longer and took a step towards Spank. "No buts, Sp-Spank. Now I'm te-te-telling you. Don't be going around ta-talking about me, especially in connec-connection with that scrawny pu-punk Chucky. We c-cool?"

"Yeah, Tim, we cool. Now I think you better back the fuck off," Spank said, staring straight into Tim's eyes.

"Nah-nah, you the one that's going to back off! Don't touch me, Les!" he said, batting away his hand.

Les pointed over the crowd and said. "Oo-wee! Is that Rene in the pink hotpants coming this way? Y'all chill now. Okay?"

"Nice eye, Les!" Tim said, taking a step back. "Later, Spank. You still cool with me, man." He squeezed out a fake smile.

Spank smiled slowly. "Yeah I'm feelin' you, Tim. Like I said before, no worries."

Tim cupped his hands and called out to Rene over the wall of sound coming from the stages.

Finally she turned around. "Hey, *Timmy*—Tim! I thought that was you over there."

"So you remember my voice, huh?" he said, sidling up to her.

"I think the question be, *do you remember me?*" she said, gently pushing away.

Tim laced his fingers on top of his head, looked at the sky and on one foot, spun around like a top. "Aw man, Boo, it hasn't been that long!" He reached out to hug her.

Laughing, Rene stepped back, just out of his reach. "Not really. I'm just playing with you, *silly boy*! But, Tim! What's all of this talk about you and Chucky Black? I thought you all didn't hang."

His head throbbed at the mention of Chucky. Reflexively, he looked over his shoulder and scanned the crowd for Fidel. "Yo, I came here to see you, Boo, not for some gossip," he whispered, moving in close again.

Rene pushed him back—hard this time. "So, what's going on, Tim. Why are you so serious? Did something happen? Sheila said—"

"Never mind what Sheila said. Okay? I just wanted to give you this." He extended his open palm towards her.

Rene shook her head side to side and pushed it away. "Whoa! Now I'm sure something is wrong. Your middle school baseball ring? Come on, Timmy, I remember when you got that. We…"

"Yeah, I know. That's why I want you to hold onto it for me."

Rene heard the huskiness in his voice, hugged him and spoke into his ear. "What are you talking about? *Hold on to it?* Where are you going?"

"I ain't going nowhere, Boo. It's simple, if we're really together, I want you to have it. That's all," he said, still holding her close.

Rene smiled. "Well, okay then," she said and kissed him on the cheek.

"So, can I see you later?" he asked, looking into her eyes.

"I'll have to talk to you later on that one, *homeboy*. Hey, is that Maria over there? Ha! I got your ass good, *Timmy*! Oh, hey Mr. Les. Hey, Spank. What's up?" she called out, waving at the gawking duo. "See you later, Tim. I came early and got a good spot on the other side. You can come over there if you want. Bye!"

Les rubbed his hands together. "Looks like progress to me, dude!"

Tim shook his head side to side. "Remember, bro, looks are deceiving." They watched Rene push through the crowd. "Hey, we still down for Monday night at the gym?"

At the mention of the gym, Les flexed his pecs. "Yeah, like I said, I can't swing by before nine, after closin' time. Will you still be there?"

"Yeah, man, you know the dude lets me close up when I stay late. I'll leave the door cracked so you can let yourself in. Cool?" Tim said, giving up a bump.

"Yeah—cool. Now you, Tim Thornton, has got to get the fuck out of here! I saw that dude Fidel standin' around just now, hands in his pockets as usual—not talkin' to nobody. Tell him, Spank, you his boy and shit," Les said, slapping Spank on the shoulder.

"I'm not telling him that and I ain't nobody's boy. But I will tell you this, Tim—he wants you *bad*, bro," Spank said, nodding and swaying side to side to the music.

Tim waved his hand. "Man, I don't give a shit about Fido—Oh, hey, Sheila! Did you just get here?"

"Timmy, I've been looking everywhere for you. That foul dude Fidel…"

"Yeah, I heard. He's got some problem about his cousin," Tim said, trying to sound bored.

"Well, you and Les didn't see, but he was standing right behind you two while you were talking. For a minute, it looked like he was with you guys, until you turned around." She clapped and made a swooping move with her hands. "That's when he took off real quick."

Tim turned to look around. "What? He was here? Les, did you see?"

"Nope. Didn't see nothin'. Told you, bro, you have to be careful. Sheila, tell your brother to go home, please," he said, making a painful face.

"You heard him. Go home, Timmy. He's the only fool I know that can wear a leather jacket today without breaking a sweat. Chucky is probably hiding out from some bad dudes. I wouldn't know. But that dude Fidel is cold, man! I'll check with you later." She gave a little wave and turned to leave.

"Wait Sheila! Hold up a minute," Tim said, staring over her shoulder. "Don't turn around—here comes Maurice."

"What up, Tim?" the tattooed thug sang. "Oh–ho-ho, everybody's here today," he said, winking at Sheila. "S'up, girl? Hey, big Les."

Les was quick to speak up. "Maurice, you need to move on. I'll catch up with you later, okay?"

"Move on? Move on? Since when you the police, big man?" He did a little side-to-side dance as he spoke. "I gotta right to be here like everybody else. Word on that! So, Tim, you ain't got nothin' to say? Oh yeah! Maybe we need Mr. Jones here to speak for you?"

No one could say when it became airborne, but everybody saw when Tim brought the ten-gallon iced tea dispenser down into the middle of Maurice's chest. And no one missed how the thing followed the thug all the way to the ground, cracked open and left the boy tea-colored from head to toe. The crowd screamed with shameless delight.

"Maurice, Maurice!" Les yelled over the noise. The dude didn't move, didn't make a sound—not even when Tim stuttered out, "WAKE UP, WAKE UP ASSPHA–HOLE!"

STOP AND FRISK

In the confusion, no one noticed when Tim had split the scene. He needed time to decompress. Not being able to lift that cooler high enough to hit Maurice up side the head bothered him. And the sight of the dude lying lifeless on the ground had resurrected a half-buried memory. On top of it all, he'd spied Fidel standing nearby in the shade of a tree. The creep had finally slung that stupid leather over his shoulder, proving his humanity. However, instead of cracking up at the scene like everyone else, he had simply stood by and stared with a little smile on his lips. If nothing else, that prompted Tim to get a hustle on, having to make several detours to avoid the police.

He headed straight for Les' house and sat on the stoop. He couldn't go home. Sheila would light into his ass about what just happened and he didn't want to fight with her. Dealing with his uncle was out—those eyes could sweat an onion.

Tim stood and peered down the street in both directions, hoping to God that Fidel hadn't followed him. Les was right—that dude was dangerous—he would have to watch his back for a minute.

A black and white cruiser approached from down the street. Patting his pockets as inconspicuously as possible he thought, *Oh shit! The phone! Did I drop…? Where in the hell? It's not here! But how could I? Oh well, it don't matter no how—it must be home—yeah, and the ringer is on silent.*

I think.

Two giant cops emerged from the car and stepped onto the sidewalk. The black one had his hand on his Taser, the white one his Glock.

The black one smiled before speaking. "Timothy Thornton?"

"Yeah?" Tim stared at the ground.

"My name is Officer Brown, this is Officer Sweeney. Stand up, please, and come down to the sidewalk," he said, smiling.

Tim looked at each of them before speaking. "What's this about?"

It was the white one's turn now. "Son, stand up and come down to the sidewalk," he said. There was no smile in sight.

Tim frowned. "What? I ain't your son!"

"We're not going to tell you again, young man," said the black cop, Taser hand twitching.

Tim stood up. "Alright, I'm coming down, but tell your boy to take his hand off his piece and shit. Look around, people are looking, somebody's even taking video over there. See? For the record, you know my name and I ain't being violent. What's this?"

The cops grabbed his arms and turned him around. "Put your hands on the car, please," said the black one taking hold of Tim's wrist.

"Aw man, ow! Wait, man. So ya'll not going to read me my rights?" he yelled.

The two officers looked at each other. They appeared amused. One of them said, "You're not being arrested, Tim, you're being searched."

"For what?"

"Contraband. Suspicious materials," the white one said, patting him down.

"What? Suspicious materi…?"

"Open your mouth," one of them said, cutting Tim off.

Tim turned his head towards them to speak. "Man, I ain't…" The cop grabbed his cheeks and squeezed. "Okay–okay. Ahhhh. Damn, I see y'all laughin'. I hope y'all having a good time," Tim said, pulling away as the cop released pressure on his face.

The black cop tipped his hat and smiled. "Thank you, Mr. Thornton. Have a good day." The white cop had already gotten back in the car.

Tim climbed back up the few stairs and sat down. "Yeah, *right*," he said, as the cruiser sped off.

People on the street stared at Tim. Others peered from behind curtains. Les walked up still aiming his phone at him. His face didn't seem right, like a familiar photo hung askew. But then, in another way his expression was perfect. Tim had recognized it as similar to what he had been seeing in the mirror lately. Recently at the library, he had read something about friends representing different aspects of one's self. Here Les was showing him with a certain look in his eye that his entire life had somehow gone off.

Reading made him think of Darryl on the ground, wet and dirty. How easily the knife had sliced through his jeans—the sudden chill/thrill he felt at the sound of the boy's scream and how he continued with his improvised revenge not giving a damn that anyone at either end of the tunnel might hear the whole thing. He had to see it to the end, had to hear the boy say the truth. Darryl's fingerless glove held up like some kind of sacrifice, his cries echoing off the walls, his resemblance to Chucky on the ground, one eye submerged in red muck—nothing could deter him.

His best bud's voice broke his spell. "Yo, Tim! You hear me, *dawg?* What were they searchin' for?"

He couldn't say.

Why him?

He didn't know.

Why did they look in his mouth?

He hadn't a clue.

Did they ask about him, about Les?

No, they didn't ask about anybody. It was just a stop and frisk.

Tim wondered: *Les knew the deal, so why all the questions?* While he remained bent over the hood of the car, the cops checked out his cell for a long time, scrolling through the contacts. Maybe they knew about Chucky's phone? Les said that it probably had something to do with Rasheed's. Tim let that ride as a possibility, although he doubted it. As far as he knew, they'd all gotten away. Rasheed hadn't even filed a report.

"Tim! You listening, bro?" Les said, poking him in the chest.

"Yeah, yeah," he said, a little annoyed. "I'm listening, man. S'up?"

"Seemed like you went off somewhere for a minute. I'm just glad nothin' happened with those cops. What do you think about that shit? You don't seem too upset, man. You know they be killing motherfuckers up in here every week! Think they will come after you again?" Les sat next to him on the steps.

"Shit, man," Tim said, groaning as he stood up. "I don't know—was thinking about Jones, that's all."

"Jones? Yeah, what was Maurice talking about? Ha! Before the tea party that is!"

"Hee—*tea party*, yeah that's what it was alright," Tim said, holding up his hand for a high five.

"Yo, uh, so what about Mr. Jones? I did hear something about some kind of *thing* y'all had," Les asked, being careful.

Tim looked out into the street as he spoke. "I fi-figured you'd heard and was just n-not saying nothin', *dawg*."

"Heard what?" He turned around to look at him.

Tim spoke almost at a whisper. "Last d-day of school, I had a fi-fight with Mr. Jones."

"*Shit*! Really? Get outta here!" Les said, punching Tim on the shoulder. "Where? How? Look at me, bro!"

"Ain't nothin' to it now, man, I deserved it—*I guess*. The dude got sick of my shit and jumped me after class." Tim shrugged his shoulders.

Les jumped to his feet. "In the fuckin' school, Tim? Did you report his ass?"

"Nah, man, I didn't report nobody. You know the dude—he's alright. And he wasn't wrong. He been trying help me for a while and I ju-just…" Tim leaned his head on his knees.

"Blew it," Les said.

Tim sighed, leaned back now, and punched the palm of his hand. "Yeah, man. I blew it, big time, yo."

"So, how did it go? Did you get some good licks in?" Les asked, smiling mischievously.

"Nah, man, it wasn't like that, yo. It was more like a wrestling match. But I tell you—that dude is strong. I would've been in trouble if it was fo' real."

"Humph, yeah, it don't sound like a real fight. What? Where you goin'?"

Tim jumped down to the sidewalk. "You still got those weights in the basement?" Tim said, already heading down the alley towards the back of the house. "Let's go. I feel like throwin' some iron. You?"

"Yeah, you know it. But, where you goin'? The door's over this way. Come on, *potato-head.*"

A SECRET NO MORE

That evening—Sheila well into her third hour—blasted out tweets, emails and chat lines to six friends at once. When everything that could be said about the music fest had been covered, she closed her eyes and sprawled across her bed like a sated lioness.

If it weren't for the quiet of the afternoon, she wouldn't have heard it at all—a whiny singsong chatter that repeated like a ringtone. It couldn't have been Timmy's phone—he would never leave it behind.

She had to check this out.

Pausing by the door, it occurred to her that this was Tim's room that she was about to enter—stinky and full of *boy's* stuff: games, comics, dirty socks and jock straps—*ew*. There might even be some porn buried somewhere—hmm…*but there's no time for that*! If he caught her, there would be hell to pay. If she was going to find whatever it was, she had to move quickly. Its voice called out to her, like a secret.

Fuck it.

In the dark, an orange light glowed from the top drawer of the bureau that had been left open a crack for a power cord that was plugged into the wall. She could hear it clearly now.

♪ *Chuck-keeee, Chuck-keee, pick-up swee-teee…* ♪

Even though the ringtone had stopped just as she reached into the drawer, the voice, so familiar, replayed over and over in her head. Swallowing hard, she stared at the screen.

MISSED CALL: **SPANK**

She laughed when she saw Spank's name, maybe the craziest of

Tim's friends—if you didn't count that weirdo Lucy girl who always stood a little too close for her taste. At the music fest, way before Tim went off on Maurice, Lucy spent most of her time losing a bet: trying to hold a handstand on the grass for a full minute.

Her hands shook as she searched through the contacts and text messages. Most were unknown to her. All of the texts were pretty straight ahead: Call me. **Fidel**. Lemme hear from you soon: **Maria**. Where are you homie? **Spank**. Etc. There were a lot of unknown callers. A couple messages from the mother of someone the person referred to as Charles? Something about the police?

"Oh shit!" She watched her finger touch *Photos* as if it had a mind of its own. A dark image popped up. The subject's hand, upturned and defensive, partially covered his face.

Sheila sat on the bed in the dark room and considered the curtains that were completely drawn. She thought to open them, but then decided against it. She listened to water gurgle in their gimpy toilet. Outside, some kids argued about a basketball game. She stared at the photo. The hand wore a fingerless glove that dominated the frame. In the background, Darryl's pained face stared into the camera.

Her fingers swiped the screen to the right. Something broken and bloodied like a large doll, its legs in an impossible position, its head turned to the side, lay on the ground. Like Darryl in the previous photo, it appeared to stare into the lens.

At that moment, two things went down at the same time: from her room a new chat message beeped in on the laptop and the damned phone slipped out of her hands. She caught it in mid-air.

It was Darryl waiting for her online.

saggindaddy: S'up?
Im>U: S'up? That's all you have to say?
saggindaddy: Yeah, kind of... :)
Im>U: So like, where have you been, dude? I thought maybe you'd forgotten about me. Have you?

saggindaddy: Come on girl. Why u b bustin' on me like that? I mean, ain't like we b married or somethin'.

Im>U: Stop with the bullshit, Darryl. I know and you know that you can speak and write. Ok?

saggindaddy: Alright, alright. I hear you. Sorry to have disappeared like that on you. I've been like real busy lately.

Im>U: Busy? What kind of busy? What do you mean? Are you still working at the library?

saggindaddy: Yeah, yeah, I'm still there. S'all good.

Im>U: So, if it's all good, where you been?

saggindaddy: Uh oh, who's using substandard English now!

Im>U: LOL Yeah, I'm a regular illiterate. Now stop fooling around. I've been hearing things.

saggindaddy: Whoa, what have you been hearing?

Im>U: Okay, so it's going to be like that, huh?

saggindaddy: What?

Im>U: DARRYL!

saggindaddy: WHAT? :))

Im>U: I'm going to ask you a question. Promise me you're going to tell the truth.

saggindaddy: Well, that depends.

Im>U: Promise me, boy!

saggindaddy: Okay, I promise.

Im>U: You ready?

saggindaddy: Yes, I'm ready. Go ahead.

Im>U: Did you have a fight with Chucky that didn't turn out so good? FOR YOU?

saggindaddy: Wait, isn't he like, missing or something? What are you talking about?

Im>U: You promised, Darryl! Ok? Before he was missing or something, did you fight with him?

saggindaddy: No, I didn't fight with Chucky. Anyway if I had, I would've stomped that little chump. Why you asking me this? What happened?

Im>U: Are you sure?

saggindaddy: Yeah girl. I would know if I had a fight with somebody! So what's this about? Sheila? Are you still there?

Im>U: It's about a photo.

saggindaddy: Oh. A photo huh?

Im>U: Yeah, Saggin' Daddy. A certain photo that features you on the ground looking like you were NOT having a good time. Darryl?? What's this about?

saggindaddy: Tim found out that I was there when Maurice jumped him in the park.

Im>U: How? You didn't tell him, did you?

saggindaddy: Nah, I think he figured it out. He probably saw my glove that day, but didn't exactly remember seeing me since I was just standing on the side. He's been asking about it off and on for while.

Im>U: So, he just guessed?

saggindaddy: Yeah, I don't know. Maybe. One minute we were cool, the next he's slamming me against the wall, stepping on my chest and showing me a knife!

Im>U: A knife! What kind of knife?

saggindaddy: Who cares what kind of knife when it's pointed at your dick?

Im>U: Oh Shit! He did that?

saggindaddy: Yeah, cut my jeans too.

Im>U: Did he cut you?

saggindaddy: Nah, but for a minute, I thought he might.

Im>U: What then? He wanted you to confess or something?

saggindaddy: Yeah, I guess so because when I said he was right, he got up off me. Hey, why did you think it was Chucky anyway?

Im>U: Don't know. The dude disappeared. There's like, some serious mystery to it. You know?

saggindaddy: Yeah, it's blowing up on Twitter. When I told Tim that he probably did something to the punk, he got real mad and denied it of course. But I didn't believe him.

Im>U: DARRYL! Don't go around spreading no rumors about Timmy!

saggindaddy: Nah, baby. He's a good dude. Can't blame him for being mad at me. Deep down, I didn't really think he was going to cut me.

Im>U: HAAA! To me, you seemed a real believer in that photo!

saggindaddy: Aw man! HE showed you that? What was that about? He's going to put it on the net or what?

Im>U: I don't know, Darryl. Tim's been acting a little crazy lately. Don't think so though. I'll ask him. Hey, are you alright? When am I going to see you?

saggindaddy: Yeah, I hear that! Let me call you later. Something has got to be jumping off somewhere tonight.

Im>U: Cool. C U.

saggindaddy: Later.

FRAYING AT THE SEAMS

It had been a rough night at Les' place. Sleeping on a bench press after a workout and a six-pack had turned out to be a bad idea. But then bunking on the basement floor in a funky Boy Scout sleeping bag would've been an even worse choice. Tim had spotted three spiders before lights out.

But now…

How in hell had he ended up sitting on the floor in the middle of Sheila's room? Where the fuck had she gone to? Had he dozed off?

An upturned jewelry box lay next to his ankle, its contents strewn wide across the tan throw rug like abandoned homes of sea creatures on a beach. Sheila's favorite antique doll, lynched by a string of beads, swung from a clothes hanger protruding from a half-opened drawer. In the corner, an empty cola can, having found a depression in the cheap linoleum, made two last undulations before settling into a trough. His heart stopped as his finger touched something metal—his sister's beloved windup alarm clock. The large crack in its face rendered his memory perfect as he recalled throwing it against the wall, hearing the crunch-ding (*cring*?) of the impact and ducking out of the way of its rebound.

He brushed away earrings, hair clamps, pins, mascara, lipsticks and beads, making space to stretch out onto the floor. His head ached.

He told himself that he didn't understand why Sheila was so mad at him. But he knew that was a lie. When he'd arrived home from Les', she was chatting with somebody online. He'd paused at her doorway to say hi. Instead of waving him away as usual, she'd stopped writing, closed the laptop and started in on him about what'd happened at the music fest the day before.

She should've been grateful. Maurice had been fuckin' with them since the last week of school. Everybody there knew he had it coming.

Darryl was another matter. When out of the blue, she'd asked if he had seen *his tutor* lately, as she'd put it, Tim figured she had found Chucky's phone.

She must have lost her balance.

I just wanted the phone and to go the fuck to bed.

I told her that I would talk to her later, but no—she had to have answers right then and there.

I just wanted to go to my room and sleep.

She knows I can't stand somebody getting up in my face, talking shit.

She should've backed off like I told her.

They used to wrestle when they were little. Sheila was always on the big side and could take it like a lot of the boys.

Yeah man, that's it. She must have lost her balance.

A chill hit him as he remembered the way she held her hand to her face, sat cross-legged on the floor to watch him tear up her room, looking for Chucky's phone.

He didn't mean to slap her so fucking hard.

BERETTA F81

Tim hadn't seen Sheila for two days. Sometimes from his room, he would hear her fussing with their uncle or talking on the phone. Other times, like in the morning, when he would expect to see her, she would be strangely absent. Asking Gentrale about her was of no use. The old codger would raise his hands and say something like, "I think you just missed her. Please leave me out of this mess," before abandoning him to stew in his own juices.

A part of him, the shamed part, was grateful for the break, but by the second night, he could barely stand it. By Friday night, he had hoped a good workout would clear his mind. It was after closing time—he had the gym to himself.

As he performed curls, sweat poured off his body. It felt good. Finally the uneasy twinge in his arm had begun to subside—a constant reminder of the fall he'd taken while running from Chucky and his boys. As the discomfort faded, he could no longer pretend to himself that what had happened, didn't happen. Yes, he'd finally done it—gotten into trouble, real trouble this time. Or had he? Sure as he was that he hadn't dreamed the whole thing, he found it strange to not have heard a word about a body being found. *Shit*! *When I'm done here tonight, I'll get rid of Les somehow and then get my ass over to the park and fucking find Chucky—it—myself. Humph! Yeah—and then what?*

His arm began to ache again.

As Tim stowed away equipment in the dead quiet of the gym, shapes and sounds came and went with every turn of his head, scrape of his foot. The darkness of the joint didn't bother him. In a way he liked it. It suited his mood. Besides, the main light switch was all the way on the other side behind the juice bar.

It was getting to be about time to hit the showers. They had been running for a good ten minutes—working up a nice hot steam. He figured Les wasn't going to show up.

Something large and furry ran across his foot.

Damn! I left the door open for Les—hadn't planned on dealing with any other kind of wildlife. He laughed when he saw the opossum scurry into the shadows like a mangy bandit—until something else moved.

Fidel stepped through the door. His jacket had that new leather smell, his expression, strange—trouble with a smile veneer. Tim hated the snakelike deadness in his eyes. He didn't wait for the dude to speak.

"What the fuck are you do-doin' here?"

Fidel hunched his shoulders. Something black jutted from the inside pocket of his jacket. "Whoa–ho-ho, brother! I'm sorry. I really didn't mean to scare you. Hey, did I miss something? So, are you the owner of the joint now, the one who gets to say who comes and goes?"

"I ain't s-saying nothing, man. I'm asking you what the fuck you doing here?" Tim said, letting the dumbbell rest on the bench.

Fidel took a step further into the space. "Yo, I think you should check your tone of voice, my brother."

Tim walked to the exit and held the door open. "How's this for tone? I ain't *your brother.* Got it? Now you need to leave. I'm closing up tonight."

"Oh, so it is true? You do have some official role in here. Maybe—the manager? Or is it the janitor?" he said, flipping through workout schedule cards.

Tim glanced outside onto the street and slammed the door shut. Fidel smiled. "Are we expecting someone? Maybe your boy Les?" he said, still looking at the cards, chuckling to himself.

"Oh, so you *was* listening to us at the park the other day. Man, it's time for you to go now. I ain't got time right now and I gotta—" Tim choked on his words as he watched Fidel slowly remove one hand from a pocket. "So-so, like, what do you want, Fidel? As fa-far as I'm concerned, we ain't got no business."

"As fa-far as I'm concerned," Fidel mocked. "Oh, on the contrary Tim, we *have* business. Oh yeah."

Like what? You still going on about your ass-wipe cousin?" Tim shifted his weight from one foot to the other.

"Yeah, like where is my cousin?" Fidel sounded angry now. He paced back and forth in front of the entrance as he spoke. "And don't tell me you have no idea, *BITCH!*" he said, fixing Tim's eyes, pushing open his jacket. The black something was clearly a handle. Tim believed he knew what for.

"You the BITCH coming up in here like this, trying to scare som-somebody. I don't fucking know about your cousin. He-he's probably hiding out from those Weequahic boys. You know he's been toking up with them. I heard he owes money. Maybe they finally caught up with his ass."

Tim moved back towards the bench and picked up the dumbbell, removed the weights and held onto the bar. "I'm serious, Fidel. I don't know what you're talking about. But now, you gotta go. I'm serious."

They stared at each other without saying anything. The sound of open showerheads continued from the locker room.

Fidel shrugged again and tipped his head towards the noise. "Never mind what I have to do. Maybe you should, like a good janitor, save some water and turn that shit off."

Tim watched Fidel's body language, especially his hands. "Don't worry about that, yo! You be gone when I'm done," he said and turned towards the locker room. His body felt as if his blood had turned into glue. Even though the bar in his hand felt extra heavy, he couldn't put it down. In his ears, the ache in his forearm pulsated in sync with his heartbeat. He listened to Fidel as he walked away, the sound of the boy's voice receding with each step.

"Alright, Timmy boy. But I'm sure you had *something* to do with Chucky—word's on the street that you were with him the night before he disappeared—

Yeah…

I'm going to get the proof then I'm going to come for you—

Do you hear me, bitch?

I will come for your ass

it's not going to be a social call…

throw back a few brews and whatnot…

Hey! Did you hear what I said

motherfucker?"

Tim never heard when Fidel stopped talking. The white noise of the open showerheads covered almost everything.

Almost.

At the sound of footsteps running up behind him, Tim unlatched the first tall locker. Timing it just right, he turned and kicked open its door just as Fidel bolted through the doorway.

The blunt impact of Fidel's face crashing into the locker door reverberated from the shower tiles to the ceiling of the main room and back. The boy lurched backwards like a life-sized marionette whose strings had suddenly been cut. He hit the floor and skidded for about a foot back into the workout area and didn't move. Tim ran out to him, checked his breathing, pulled his jacket open and took the gun, a Beretta f81.

It was fucking beautiful.

Fidel spoke like a drunk. "Awww man, Tim. Shit, I think you broooke my noooose."

Tim yelled at the semiconscious boy on the floor. "I don't believe you. I told you to fucking leave. Why the fuck you had to come up on me like that?"

Fidel's whole body went limp. Tim *prayed* he was sleeping. *Shit, another scarecrow,* he thought. The Beretta was heavy. It wouldn't stay put in his waistband as he'd seen it done in countless movies. He had to put it in his back pocket and hold onto it with one hand as he sprinted across the gym to the juice bar where he'd last seen the duct tape. As he ran through the darkness, his eyes burned with fresh tears. *Les could show up at any minute. Then what?*

When he got back, Fidel lay where he'd left him on the floor, snoring. He dragged the boy inside the locker room and with the heavy tape, fastened his arms and legs to a metal chair that was bolted to the floor. Suddenly, someone started banging hard on the outside door and wouldn't stop. Tim pressed a strip of the tape across Fidel's mouth.

♪ *Chuck-keeee, Chuck-keee, pick-up swee-teee…* ♪

The thug's eyes popped open at the sound of the ringtone. So busy was Tim fumbling with his pockets, he hadn't yet realized that his secret was finally out. Chucky's phone had popped out of his pocket, hit the floor and slid through the door, back into the gym.

He dived after it.

Got it.

MISSED CALL: MOM

Tim sat on the floor staring at the text message until he finally heard it—Fidel's muted cries coming from the locker room. He wondered what the boy had seen, had heard. Then both the screams and knocking stopped at the same time.

The shower heads pushed on.

His own phone beeped. It was Les:

MEET ME AT THE CHICKEN SHACK IN 30

Still on the floor, Tim sat up and saw a long streak of blood leading back to the doorway. He hadn't known Fidel was bleeding.

"Fidel? You alright?" he hollered.

Nothing.

Tim held his stomach and sucked up mucus. His head ached. He yelled, "Quit fucking around, Fidel. I'm-I'm gonna let you go. Ju-just let me think for a minute. Ok?" he yelled.

Tim lay on the floor, listening to the *fisssh* sound of the open shower heads. He imagined the drains clogging up and water flooding the entire room. He saw Fidel, awake, waist deep in the drink, eyes gone buggy, straining against the nylon tape. He watched as the level rose to his neck, chin and mouth. Sans leather jacket and Beretta, he was simply a boy about to die.

In his mind, Tim saw the flood break through the doorway like a tidal wave to sweep him up with the rubber mats and everything else. Floating high, near the ceiling, he saw the backs of the great amber lamps suspended across the entire area. Finally the current pushed him into a corner against a huge skylight. A crow sitting on the other side of the glass seemed to be speaking to him. Hanging on, nose pressed against the window, determined to breathe the last available molecule of oxygen, Tim could finally make out the avian message. His body shook in such uncontrollable waves until it seemed that in the end, it would be the spasms, not the water that would kill him.

The crow said, *Fuck Fidel. Go find Chucky's body, deal with Maurice and settle with Jones.*

GOOD EVENING, OFFICER

In the late afternoon light, Gentrale looked peaceful as he smiled and stirred a giant pot of red beans slow cooking on the stove. It was going to be a good batch. The creamy texture had set in—you could barely see the tender morsels of salt pork.

Tim had entered through the back door and immediately sat down at the kitchen table. This time, a half-turn, a grunt and nod from his uncle served as a greeting. The slight smile and cool demeanor hadn't fooled him. Since his dad died, they had become pretty close. He could tell that his uncle was worried about him and struggled to keep his imagination at bay. He'd laughed real hard at Gentrale's latest: "*Boy*, you smell like a cloud of *dirty washrag* been following you around."

But the old dude could be cagey so he had to be careful.

Tim wondered what his uncle had been telling his mom. She would soon call again from Chicago, like she did every day, anxious for news. It had been only a few days since she'd gotten into that taxi for the airport, waving bye and blowing kisses at the three of them through the rear window as it sped off. You'd think it had been a year. Ever since that morning, Tim hadn't been sleeping at home or going to the library. *Had his uncle told her about that?* She had just started a new job and it was exactly the wrong time for her to get such news—especially about him.

Tim got up from the table.

"Where you goin', boy?" Gentrale said, turning from the stove, genuine surprise rising from his voice. His eyes gave Tim a good once-over from head to toe before he spoke again. "Uh, I need to talk to you about something. So don't you leave the house before I do."

"Alright, alright, Unk. I heard you! I gotta take a shower, I ain't going nowhere." He got up and made his way to the bathroom.

He knew Gentrale wanted to ask about his muddy sneakers by the way he'd looked at them.

After leaving Fidel at the gym, he had spent most of the night at the park, searching for the body. That's how he'd come to call it—*the body*. It seemed too much to call it by its former name, when it had a pulse, breathed air, got thirsty and chased down motherfuckers through the park. He'd looked everywhere, under all the bushes in the area as if *the body* could have acquired some kind of postmortem locomotion. Luckily, Les hadn't been too inquisitive when he'd tapped on his window at 4 am. Letting the surprise of the moment and his mumbled excuses slide by with a shrug, Les opened the door to the basement and went straight back to bed. There would be time to come up with a story.

Someone must have found it. But who? The police? Maybe that's why those two white guys in that big Ford with no trim and plain hubcaps were always hanging outside their door. Who were they supposed to be fooling?

"Hey, boy!" Gentrale barked, banging on the bathroom door. "Your beans are ready. Come to the kitchen!"

"Here I am, Unk. What's the rush?" Tim said, bounding through the doorway. But he was speaking to the back of his uncle, who had already turned towards the kitchen. With a wave of a hand he said, "No rush. It just doesn't seem right to let my best pot of beans get cold. You're going to like these something fierce! Don't fool around, come on and take a seat!"

Back at the table, Tim wanted to be cool and vague. Talking too much would open him up to too much scrutiny. However, the beans quickly eighty-sixed that plan. "Mmm—thanks, I needed some home cookin'—these beans are fierce, *Unk*. I always liked the way you say *somethin' fierce*. Ain't heard that one for a while."

"Well, you haven't been around! What have you been up to, boy?" Gentrale sat staring at his scruffy nephew.

"I told you, Uncle Gentrale, don't be calling me *boy* and stuff. I—
ain't no…"

Gentrale yawned and scratched his head. "Yes, yes, I know—you're
not anybody's boy," he mumbled in a tired kind of way. Then, holding
up a stiff index finger, he said, "*Except* to your mama! And don't you
forget it!" *Maybe with those beans in him, he'll loosen up some*, he thought.

Tim chuckled into his plate. "Yeah, yeah, I won't forget."

"So, what you been up to lately? I've been worried, son." Gentrale
watched Tim closely. "I don't think you've slept at home for the past
three or four nights. Before you had your shower, you didn't look so hot
to me, like you've been collecting dust for the most part."

"I-I been hanging with friends and stuff. I'm alright, I guess," Tim
said, before registering his uncle's quip. "Oh man—*collecting dust*! That's
funny," he said, as if in pain. His voice sounded as if it had been pushed
through a strainer. They laughed long and hard and for a moment,
everything was right. It felt to Tim that his dad had stepped in and
embraced them both.

After a few seconds, Tim couldn't be sure if they were laughing or
crying. His tears soothed him nevertheless. He certainly wasn't alone.
Gentrale had already made good use of the stack of napkins sitting on
the table. "Yo, Uncle Gentrale, on the s-subject of collecting…"

"Yeah?"

"You know those boxes of old records you let me have some time
ago?"

"Yeah. What about 'em?"

"I want to give them back to you," he said, playing with his food.

Gentrale grabbed another napkin, wiped his mouth. "What—why?
But they're yours now."

"Yeah, I know. But, ca-can you hold on to them for me? Will you
do th-that?" He looked his uncle square in the eyes now.

"What, you don't want to take them with you? Your mama says
there's plenty of room in the apartment and…"

At the sound of the hurt in his uncle's voice, he put his fork down.

"Uh—yeah, that's it. I don't want to take them. Well, at least not this first trip. They kind of heavy, and I got a lot of other stuff, you know?"

"You'll come for them later?" Gentrale asked, placing a hand on Tim's forearm.

Gentrale's touch surprised him. Looking down at his uncle's heavily veined hand, he said, "Ye-yeah, I'll come for them later. Cool?"

"Okay, Timmy. Yes, *cool*, as you say. I'll take care of them. But remember that they are yours! One day they will be worth some money, I think. Nothing but clean vinyl featuring Pops' to the Duke, from Bird to Miles."

"*Bird*?? Uh—okay, Unk. *Whatever* you say."

A loud bash of keys on wood at the front door made Gentrale jump in his seat. "Uh-oh, who's that coming in?"

Tim laughed. "It's only Sheila, Uncle Gentrale—you nervous or something?" He turned and yelled down the hall. "Hey Sheila—humph! Oh well, I think she went straight to her room—must not be hungry," he'd sort of sang nonchalantly. *Yeah, she's still pissed off with me.*

Ear cocked, Gentrale suddenly stood up. "Is that the doorbell? What's all this traffic all of a sudden? Wait a minute, Timmy," he said and then hollered. "Sheila. Are you going to get that? And when you're done, come in here and get a taste of these beans."

A minute later, the tone in Sheila's voice caught Tim's attention. She was being interrogated.

"Uh, yes, Tim lives here. Why?"

That was enough for Gentrale, who in a blink was up on his feet again and on his way down the hall towards the front of the apartment, cane thumping at a rapid clip.

Tim held his breath as he listened to his sister about to lie to the police. "What's this about, officer?"

While holding onto the screen to make a quiet exit through the back door, the gun in his backpack pitched heavily to one side—giving him pause. He listened to the hesitancy in his uncle's voice.

"Good evening officer, can I help you?"

WHERE IS HE?

"Sheila darlin', tomorrow's the first day of school, right? I think Timmy done forgot about his studies altogether and he's in a mess of trouble. Have you seen him? We've got to find your brother and keep an eye on him."

Sheila, half listening to her uncle, sat with him in front of the television and wondered what the crusty dude made of all the sexy soap opera action splashing across the screen. No matter how much rubbing and moaning went on, Gentrale for the most part, sat perfectly still on the edge of the couch. He hadn't even blinked once from what she could tell.

It had been three days since anyone had seen Tim. Before this latest disappearing act, the silly boy had the nerve to come to her room—yeah, just walked right in, tapping wood as he pushed in on the door. "Sheila, ca-can I come in?" It was perfect too—he'd caught her at the mirror, inspecting the dark spot on her face from when he'd slapped the shit out of her. She said nothing, simply turned and looked at him. She wanted to stare the shame out of him—pull it out into the open where it could do some damage to his stupid pride or whatever was pushing his skinny ass out of control. Tears had collected at the corners of his eyes. He was in trouble, she knew, but she had to be careful. She had to let him speak first. When he did, his voice broke. Like a Baptist minister, she wanted to forgive every sin he'd ever committed. Instead she held firm and listened. She wanted him to come forth with whatever it was, on his own. She didn't want to pull it out of him, make it easy as she'd always done, as their mom had always done. When he said that he was sorry, she asked, "About what exactly, Tim?"

"For slapping you so hard."

Something in her liked to see him squirm, but she wanted more. She wanted to ask about Chucky's phone and those strange photos, but fear of the answers made her hesitate. As kids, whenever they'd asked their mom why didn't she question Dad about his drinking and whereabouts, she'd always say, 'Never ask a question if you're not ready to hear the answer.' Anyway, she didn't need to ask about Darryl, although it did impress her that Tim could get the best of him. Something had gone bad in her brother. The light in his eyes had disappeared. He seemed done, used up. She wanted to help him so bad. *But how?*

"Oh, so you meant to slap me, just not so hard? What's going on, Tim? Before you try to put together a lie, let me tell you—I *know* about Darryl! *Yeah*—you heard me!" she said standing up now.

"Aw, She-Sheila, how do you know about that? What? He *told* you? What a pu…"

"He's no punk, no pussy—whatever you were going to say. He said you were like a madman, Tim. You had a knife?" she said, pushing him.

He stepped back and mumbled something like, "Hmm, uh."

"Timmy!" she yelled and watched a drop of her saliva land on his cheek.

Tim looked around at the door he'd left open. "It-it wasn't mine. It was…"

"Fool! I don't care *who* it belongs to!"

"Shh—Sheila! Damn! Talk softer, girl," he begged, waving a hand in front of his mouth.

"What were you doing with it? Is it here now?" She went to touch his pocket, but he batted her hands away. "Did you have it when you attacked me? You better hope Mom, let alone Uncle Gentrale, doesn't hear about this shit."

In the end, she'd accepted his apology but regretted it almost immediately. Not because he didn't mean it—it was clear that he did.

She regretted it because he'd used her acceptance as a means of getting out of the room before she could ask any more questions.

Gentrale finally shuffled out of the living room, no doubt down for the night. Switching channels to a late night comic, Sheila turned the volume down and stretched out on the couch. The air in the room was fresh. Her uncle had been cleaning the place a little bit each day from floor to ceiling. Home felt strange, the good kind, without the clutter and those stupid *ashtrays*—which, with Mom gone, were no longer necessary. Family photos, dusted and wiped, sat in neat rows starting from the early times to present day. A snapshot of Tim at his middle school graduation saddened her to think it was probably his last.

Her heart jumped at the squeak and click of her brother's bedroom door. He'd come home.

SWEET REVENGE

Sheila awakened early the next morning thinking of her uncle's words from the night before: *We have to keep an eye on your brother*. As usual, his words spoke to truth. This time, they had the effect of opening the floodgates—everything she'd been holding close over the summer burst out of her in tears and sobs: Tim getting beat down by Maurice, Darryl and the knife, how Tim had slapped her. When she thought of that goon Fidel, his cousin Chucky, the phone and those photos, she nearly choked on her own snot trying to mute the sound of her wails in the pillow.

Movement in Tim's room brought her out of her sloppy angst. The jangle of keys told her that he was about to leave the house. Getting dressed quickly, she followed him out onto the street. She felt bad to spy on her brother, but there were too many things going on. If she was going to help him, she had to know for sure what he was up to.

It was way too early for school. Her suspicions were proved correct when he didn't take the usual route. In fact, right away he turned in the opposite direction. Struggling to stay out of his line of sight, she kept on the opposite side of the street and ducked into doorways whenever he turned his head. Right after negotiating through an old junkyard, she was surprised to see her brother stop and stare up at the second floor windows of an abandoned brownstone. The building was the only thing standing for blocks—since there were no trees or anything to hide behind, she lingered at the junkyard exit behind a corrugated metal fence until Tim disappeared around the corner.

That's when the screaming began.

Blinded with panic, Sheila ran towards the house. Timmy couldn't be far—he was just there, in front of her. At the corner, her foot caught on a cinderblock leaving the rest of her to slam into a parked car. All she could do was to let her body slide to the ground. Fifty feet away, a crying Maurice Rice knelt on the ground. Mucus flowed from his nose as spit bubbles exploded from his mouth. The dude was nude except for a sock on his left foot and an oversized t-shirt that had ridden up over his ass. His sweaty junk had collected earth like breading on chicken parts. Six barechested homeboys, standing in the shadow of the house, smoked weed and watched in silence.

And there, over Maurice, stood Tim.

The only things that competed with the shiny black of his skin were Maurice's gold tooth and the surface of the Beretta f81. Pointing the piece at the boy's head, Tim listened closely to Maurice who had puked in the gutter. Yellow tank top clinging to newly minted neck and shoulder muscles, Tim bared his teeth like a street dog and yelled, "You shouldn't be surprised, motherfucker."

When Maurice held up his hand, it reminded Sheila of Darryl's photo in Chucky's phone.

She couldn't take any more. "Timmy! What the *fuck* are you doing?" she screamed.

Her first attempt to get up failed as all eyes turned towards the fat girl on the ground. "Tim. Stop this shit now. Wait, don't go—Timmy, don't *leave* me here," she pleaded, pushing up to her feet.

He did leave her, but not before hitting Maurice upside the head though. Not too hard—just enough to pull blood.

The thug screamed like a girl.

His boys laughed in the cool of the shade.

DAY OF RECKONING

Mind reeling, Tim ran straight to school after leaving that sniveling freak Maurice on the sidewalk. *Yeah, humph, that dude was lucky my sister showed up.* At the thought of Sheila having watched him point a gun at the punk, tears flowed down his cheeks. He couldn't figure how she could have followed him like she did, how he hadn't seen her. Tim slowed his run to a jog after spotting a police car parked in front of Barringer's main entrance. He could still get in through the gym doors and be on time for first period. Spank greeted him with a big grin and bro-hug.

"Yo, s'up, Tim? My man! Where you been?"

Tim struggled to control his breathing. "Nowhere in particular. You?"

Spank showed a lot of teeth as he spoke. But like a piranha, he wasn't exactly smiling. Tim felt the same vibe from Lucy. Things weren't right. Keeping things fluid, he managed to say hey to the rest of the gang in the stairwell without losing momentum. He had to escape before the questions started. When he reached the top of the stairs, someone yelled from behind, "Yo, Tim. Seen Fidel lately?"

At the mention of Fidel, the Beretta shifted again in his backpack as if it had recognized its owner's name.

From the taco truck parked in front of the gym entrance, Fidel watched Tim greet his homies. Chewing his fake Mexican breakfast, the jacketed-one recalled the last time he had seen the dude. It had taken him over two hours to get out of that damned chair at the gym. His wrists still ached from the tape.

His cousin Chucky hadn't come home yet. That boy Tim had to pay. But first, he had to get his piece back.

Jones was happy to be back at school. He didn't think anything could affect his mood—except for perhaps Tim, who had only fleetingly entered his mind the entire summer. Now, he genuinely wondered about the boy—if what had happened between them in June had gotten through—even a little bit.

The boy had it coming. He needed somebody to get in his case. He sure wasn't getting the message at home.

Opening the door to the music room, the entire encounter came flooding back to him as if it had just happened. Jones shook his head and sighed. *I doubt the boy heard me. Hope I get a chance to see his sorry ass today. Damn, I may have really blown it this time!*

When Tim sprinted off like he did, Sheila took a last look at the dirty tattooed boy Maurice, turned on her heel, and made haste back home for a quick shower and to think what to do next. By the time she arrived at school, it had been more than twenty minutes since the bell had sounded. The office attendant Ms. Morrison peered at Sheila over her glasses. "My, my, this is unusual for you, Miss Thornton—late on the first day? Sign here. Oh yes! Someone has been waiting for you, young lady." She pointed over her shoulder.

Legs crossed and leaning back in his chair, Gentrale beamed at her. "Close your mouth, girl. You gonna catch flies if you don't," he said dripping with affection.

Sheila raised her hands in surprise. "Wha-what are you doing here, Uncle Gentrale?"

"Well, I…" Gentrale leaned forward and reached into his shirt pocket.

"Shh, wait." She grabbed him by the arm. "Come over here—please don't tell me that something happened to Mom?"

"Don't worry, honey, all is well. I took a walk, that's all. Hey, have you seen your brother? They say he made it to homeroom this morning.

Here, take this—I think he came home last night—must've ran off and forgotten it."

Sheila stared blankly at Chucky's phone in her uncle's outstretched hand for a few seconds before she grabbed it. Without thinking, she pushed the front button. There hadn't been any calls and the ringer had been set on silent. *Good! He wouldn't have a clue how to access the photos anyway*, she thought.

Gentrale's smile disappeared. "You alright, child? What's the matter?" he said and squeezed her arm.

Sheila's fingers went limp at the surprise of Gentrale's touch. The phone bounced off the ceramic floor with a loud crack and broke apart. They watched the battery slide under a heavy cabinet.

"Oh shhh—oot!" Sheila said, immediately picking up the phone and leaving the battery to remain under the furniture. She took her uncle by the elbow and led him to an office attendant.

"Yeah, I-I'm fine, Uncle Gentrale. I'll get it to him. It's third period and I've got to get to class. This lady will show you out. See you later…" she said and before he could say anything, she had stepped in the corridor and disappeared into the crowd.

Timmy, where are you?

Tim sat in the same third-period English class he'd sat in last year. Having blown off the proficiency—what else could he expect? His entire schedule was the same except for calculus and something called humanities. A text beeped in from his sister:

> *Tim! Where are you? Come to the front entrance.*
> *That's where you'll find me.*
> *Come straight here. Don't do anything!*

The *don't do anything* part of her message prompted him to check for Chucky's phone. He'd left it at home! His heart raced so hard that he had to rest his head on his forearms. He ignored the inquiries from his classmates and breathed deeply to calm himself. He planned to keep his head down until the teacher approached his desk. In the end, he was left alone to his own thoughts. There would be no chance of getting the phone back this time. It didn't matter anyway. Soon he would have to deal with Fidel. He had no idea what that would look like. And besides, before anything else happened, he hoped to catch up with Jones.

At the bell, on the way to the cafeteria, he scooted down to the exit to check parking space 202. Jones' old Ford with the hanging hubcap sat as patiently as ever.

"Yo, s'up? Checking on your new ride? Haaa!" Spank held a cigarette in his mouth while balancing himself on the banister.

"I'm cool. S'up with you?" Tim said, trying to snatch the cigarette from his lips.

"Cool. Man, you be *cut*, dawg! What, you been like living at the gym?" Spank mumbled, still holding onto the butt.

"Nah, man, nothing like that, yo. Just doing what I have to. You know." Tim turned to leave the stairwell.

Spank jumped down from the banister. "Speakin' of the gym—you seen Fidel? I think he be looking for your ass." He said *ass* with a lusty smile.

"Well, I'm around, Spank-a-Lank. He don't have to look too hard."

Spank smiled that piranha grin again as he took a drag. "Says you got some property of his. Didn't say what. That true?"

Tim stopped short and turned around. "Tell him he can come and find me whenever he wants."

"I hear that! Yo, we gonna hook up later for some beer and splif. You in?" Spank snuffed out his cigarette, put what was left in his wallet.

"Le-lemme get back to you on that. Cool?" Tim said with a wave of the hand. He had to get out of there.

Spank watched Tim turn the corner. "Cool. Yeah-heh-heh...Tim! *My man!*"

"Yeah, yeah, Spank, whatever." Tim's words were lost in the noise of the halls.

248 *Donovan Mixon*

"Tim! Tim Thornton. You hear me talking to you, boy! Come over here. Do you know your sister been asking around for you?" It was Les calling from down the hall.

Tim turned around with his hand over his crotch. "Yo, I got your *boy* right here! Come and get it, ha! Damn, seems like she's always looking for me lately. I'll catch up with her sooner or…"

In a wink, Les had grabbed Tim by the arm and pulled him down the stairwell.

"Wa-wait a minute, dawg, what are you doing? Didn't you hear? That's the bell. Now I'm late," Tim said pulling away.

Les wasn't having it and wouldn't let go. "Yo, man, I don't wanna see you hanging around with that fool Spank. I told you what they're saying about you and Fidel's cousin. Do you hear me? He'll get your ass in tro…"

"*Ahgottahandleonit*, dawg. Now let go of my arm."

"What?" Les said, releasing him. He looked him up and down as if he couldn't believe what he was seeing/hearing. He was pissed too. "What the fuck does that mean? You *for real?*"

Tim held his hand up high. Les took it in his and they bumped shoulders. "Don't sweat it, homie, I'm not about to get involved with Spank and them. Good to know you always got my back."

Les pushed Tim back and gave him a hard look again. "Wha-what? You sick or something? *DID-YOU-SEE* the police out in front of the building? What's up with that? Are they still messing with you?"

"You seen Mr. Jones around?"

Les held up his hands. "Yeah, *okay—okay*, homie—if you wanna play it like that. He'll be in the cafeteria next period. I heard him talkin' to somebody. Uh-oh, look who's *comiiiing*. I'm outta here. Catch you later."

"Hey, Timmy!" Maria said, wearing a big smile and a pair of painted on jeans.

"Yo, I told you, people don't call me that no more. Okay?"

AHGOTTAHANDLEONIT 249

Maria folded her arms and pursed her lips as if she wasn't buying any of it. "Humph...*okay*, Tim. Hey—you got yourself some *new* muscles!" she said, laying a hand on his shoulder and letting it travel down to his bicep.

He took her hand away as delicately as he could. "Go on, girl, you don't want to mess with me, with your cute self—wha-what you looking at?"

Staring over his shoulder, Maria held both hands up to her mouth. "Turn around, Timmy."

"So, um like...whoa, wha-what's up?"

"TURN AROUND NOW!" she said, making a megaphone with her hands.

"Yo-ho-ho, Tim! You dim? Hee-hee. *Yeah*, motherfucker, I *am* talking to *you*, that's right, my *nigger*. S'up?"

"Fidel! You must be one crazy *negro*—still, in this heat, hanging with that leather jacket. Hey, it's summertime! Or didn't you notice?" Tim said, taking his backpack off one shoulder and unzipping it.

"Oh, so like you're all *concerned* about me now, huh? Hmm—since you have something of mine, you must think that you are in a position to punk me. I imagine you've been keeping it with you twenty-four-seven! Yeah, go ahead, I know what you're thinking to do, bitch. Do you think I didn't hear that click? Go on, pull your hand out of the backpack, *faggot*—if you got the balls."

"What did you say, *motherf*— ?" Tim reached deeper into the bag.

"*TIIIIMMY!*" screamed Maria.

"*WHAAAT?*" he screamed over his shoulder, not taking his eyes off of Fidel.

"A teacher is coming up the stairs! Hurry up and get the hell out of here! *Go, go, go!*"

He sprinted to the next stairwell, down to the lower level and then straight to the music room that was locked. Through the window in the door, he saw the primary witnesses to the shame: the old red, white & blue, hanging solemnly in its holder as the drum set and piano, ready to fill the space with sound at the slightest touch, sat silently under tarps. The trashcan, sitting on its side in the middle of the room reminded him of Jones' face when he'd kicked it against the wall. The memories brought the weight of the entire summer down upon him, starting with Jones to his pitiful father, weak mother, that chump Maurice, Darryl, dead Chucky, and finally this fool Fidel. Sitting on the floor now, he covered his face as Jones' words came to him: *What you do matters, Tim.* He wondered if Jones had thought about what he did? Had it crossed his mind even once over the whole damned summer? Even if he had meant good, he blew it when he tried to punk him. *Did the bitch motherfucker think about the possible consequences for jumping on me like that?*

The fifth period bell was about to ring. In the emptiness and quiet of the corridor, he reminded himself of the police hanging around. *Was it the lull before the storm?* Probably. He calmed himself by letting what he had to do take shape in his mind before what was surely to come.

Upstairs, the halls were electric with end of the summer energy. But Sheila moved in a daze as she searched for her brother. Even Rene, her rock, claimed she hadn't seen Tim since the music fest. His silly friends—Spank and Lucy—hung out at the west entrance like they were paid sentries. Yes, they'd seen him, but couldn't say where he'd gone.

"Me seems he was in a real hurry, *yo!*" Lucy told her. "You *know*, Fidel's been asking around for him—some shit's goin' down today."

Sheila didn't remember so many students last year. The halls seemed jammed packed with jabbering, laughing teenagers. She had to look twice at practically every other boy. Today they all looked like her brother. Then something that looked like a giant bandage in the shape of Maurice made its way towards her! However, when their eyes met, she had to laugh as the thug limped off in the opposite direction.

Her phone beeped with a text from Darryl:

Where are you going, girl? You trying to dis me?
Turn around.

The make-believe gang-banger had been in class all morning and didn't know anything—besides he would be one of the last people (after Maurice maybe) who would want to see Tim.

A voicemail from Gentrale chimed in:

Call me. The police are parked in front of the house again.

She returned to the main foyer of the building—two cruisers were now parked out front.

A familiar voice called out to her. "Yo, Sheila! Have you seen your brother yet?"

"No, Mr. Les, I'm still looking. When you see him, tell him, don't do anything! He needs to find me now!" she said, turning towards the exit.

"What you talking about? Do what?"

But Sheila hadn't heard. She had already left the building.

Jones, stewing in his own guilty juices, wolfed down his lunch: pizza, fruit salad, corn chips and Coke. He'd been watching the cafeteria door from a corner table for awhile and was having doubts. *Aw shit—he's not coming. It's strange that I haven't seen him all morning. I heard that he'd made it to homeroom. Maybe it's true what they're saying about him. Hmm…*

He had been hearing things—something about a kid named Chucky disappearing and Tim having something to do with it. From somewhere, he'd heard that Tim had gone off the deep end, was getting revenge for everything that happened over the summer.

Everything? Getting revenge for everything? he thought. *And who's this kid in a coat I'm hearing about?*

The air of the cafeteria, rank with the stink of processed foods, sat on top of them like a moist layer of imitation mozzarella. It was hot and crowded. Until the sixth period bell, students were allowed in, but not out. With their junk food lunches consumed and thirty minutes remaining in the period, spontaneous arm wrestling matches, rap competitions, card games, celebrity impersonations, and insult contests broke out willy-nilly. The security staff, knowing well who to keep an eye on, stood motionless at the exits, brandishing meaty forearms.

The noise, heat and stink had put Jones into a state of sensory overload. Though he had reached his limit, he couldn't move from his chair. Staring unseeing straight ahead, he sat with his elbows on the table. The idea that Tim was *getting revenge for everything that happened over the summer* repeated in his mind.

He never saw Tim walk up to the table.

"S'up, Mr. Jones?"

Tim's voice cut through the noise like a table saw. Taller, broader, blacker—he stood silently and waited. Jones hesitated, then banged his knee when he stood up and extended his hand. "Well, hello, Tim. How are you? How was your summer?"

Tim shook his hand. "Good—uh, interesting."

"Interesting? I like the sound of that. Hey, you've been working out!"

Tim snorted loudly, looked around to see if anyone was paying attention and muttered, "Humph, yeah, like *negro please.*"

"What did you say?" Jones asked, pretending to not have heard. But Tim saw a rash of anger flit over his teacher's face. It brought him back to their last meeting. He thought, *Oh! So now what, BITCH? Is this like round two?*

He took off his backpack.

Ten minutes before the end of the period bell, Fidel pushed into the cafeteria.

"I didn't say nothin'—*anything!*" Tim said as he reached into the backpack. "I-I wanted to say, uh —about last June…"

Jones had long stopped looking at Tim's face. Instead he stared at the backpack. "Maybe we shouldn't talk here, Tim."

"Nah, let me tell you here. *Now,*" he said, looking Jones dead in the eyes.

There was a jostling in the crowd of students behind Tim. Les had pushed through. "Psst, yo, dawg! You don't have to do this shit."

Tim kept his eyes on Jones. "Shut the hell up, Les. Mind your business and leave me alone."

Jones sat back down. Now, at eye level with Tim's concealed hand, he appeared to be speaking directly to it. "Uh, maybe you should listen to your friend."

Tim lowered his voice and stepped closer to the table. "You know, you had no right to jump on me like you did."

"Tim, uh—let's-not-do-this-here," Jones said with resignation. He wiped sweat from his brow with a handkerchief.

"What the fuck are you doing, man?" pleaded Les.

Tim shot Les a look and faced Jones again. "Nah-nah, Mr. Jones. We're *gonna to do this*. You know that you had no right to jump on me like you did? Right?"

Jones' lips quivered. "Okay—okay, yes. I shouldn't have jumped on you like I did."

Tim looked to his left for a moment, inhaled loudly before fixing Jones' eyes again. "Aw, so now you gonna to play me? Did you have the *right*, yo?"

Jones noticed that the crowd had quietly formed a circle around them, careful to not attract the attention of the security guards. None the wiser, they stood serenely at their posts glancing at their watches. There were still five minutes before the bell. "No, Tim. I had no right. Now let's get out of here and..." Jones went to stand up.

Half smiling, Tim held out his hand and gestured for his teacher to sit back down and was surprised when he did. "Yeah, what you do and say matters—and all that *shit*. Right, Mr. Jones?"

Jones' handkerchief was soaked completely through. So was the front of his shirt. He couldn't see the guards for the wall of students that surrounded his table. They were laughing, hi-fiving and shushing each other at the same time. His former student stood still as a statue, muscles bulging, his hand still in the bag. "Ti-Tim, it doesn't have to be like this."

"TIMMEEEE!" screamed Sheila from the hallway. Almost as if on cue, six huge cops dressed to kill burst through the cafeteria doors like bison. Tim turned around to see Fidel, grinning death as he tried to flip the switch on him—inducing death by cop.

"He's got a gun!" he screamed.

Everybody hit the floor.

CONTEMPLATION

Tim stretched out on his bunk and stared at the blank ceiling of his cell. He was thinking that the readings about astronomy that Darryl had turned him onto over the summer would come in handy now. Had he the chance and the supplies, instead of randomly throwing up star cutouts—as he'd done a couple years ago to his bedroom ceiling—he would arrange them so that Orion's belt would line up with the dog star Sirius. After that, placing the big and small dippers would be a breeze with Polaris positioned to appear as though everything rotated around it.

A single-piece stainless steel sink and toilet unit were bolted to the wall. Both he and his cellmate, Hernandez or *Hanz*, had taped up family photos on the wall at the foot of their bunks.

Light came from the harsh glare of florescent tubes recessed in the ceiling behind metal grates. Another grate at the top of the rear wall covered a tiny ventilation duct. A dirty beige color dominated just about every surface except the faucet and door handles. The door, as Hanz explained to him, was of triple-steel construction. It featured a single vertical 24" x 6" window that had wire running through it. Another rectangular opening underneath was used for putting on and taking off handcuffs when necessary.

The guards in the Juvenile Detention Center, armed with stun gun, pepper spray and clubs, were never more than ten to twenty feet away. He guessed that's why the place was so quiet, except for when somebody freaked out and got their ass kicked, which was daily.

He took stock of his stuff and wondered how he would fare as he waited for his detention hearing. Like every afternoon, the faces of the important people in his life—Sheila, Uncle Gentrale, his mom and dad, Les, Mr. Jones and Rene—came to him like a roll call of endearments. This time however, when his thoughts turned to Jones, he clicked on the recorder.

Hanz was in the infirmary. He was alone.

Dear Mr. Jones,

It's been about three weeks since the first day of school. I imagine you in study hall, sitting at that tiny desk, waiting like everybody else for the last bell of the day. You must miss me. No? Go ahead, admit it, it has to be boring without me.

Well, it's pretty boring here. As you probably heard, I've been in Juvie ever since my arrest that day.

You didn't see it, but after frog-walking me through the cafeteria exit, they had me on the floor face down, in the hall just outside of the doors. Dudes were standing on the backs of my legs as someone else handcuffed me behind my back. That shit hurt, man. Every time I tried to say something, the biggest dude would slap me on the back of the head and say *shut the fuck up*—or something like that. I kept trying to tell them that the gun in my backpack wasn't mine and it wasn't loaded. The dude only had to Tase me once, and I got the message. I thought that I would shake out of my skin. They all calmed down a little when they couldn't find a clip anywhere. They carried me out of the building like I was some kind of livestock, bumping me into the walls and doors along the way. My sister followed behind and kept yelling at me to stay quiet, that I would be okay. I wasn't convinced.

I was a relieved when I didn't see one of those police vans. You know what I mean? I'm really *scared* of those things. I didn't want to arrive at the police station all broken up like many dudes I've known. Instead, they put me in the back of a squad car sandwiched between two fat cops. When I started to speak, one of them slapped me hard in the face a couple times and warned me to stay quiet. I did.

They brought me to Juvie, took all my information. Someone who was acting like she was a lawyer told me that I would be there for a couple days, 'till I could have a detention hearing. I told them my mom was out of town, so they allowed my uncle to come there that day in her place. But she would have to come for the hearing. Man! Uncle Gentrale's eyes bore a hole right through me. Neither one of us could barely speak. I was blubbering and snotting all over myself and I still had the handcuffs on. Gentrale got my mom on the phone and I was a fucking mess. She was hysterical.

They put me in a cell with another dude named Hernandez. They call him Hanz. He's alright—kinda angry, but alright, I guess. I stay out of his way mostly.

Anyway, three days later at the hearing, the judge decided that I would have to stay in detention and wait for the pre-trial. I felt so bad, yo. My mom had just started this new job and now she had to take time off for my shit. On the outside, she didn't seem to mind. But I'm sure she was worried as shit about that too.

To make a long story short, after about ten days, at the pre-trial, I accepted the allegation of unintentional homicide of Chucky Black—or something like that. I was so fucked up, man, I couldn't focus on all the legal stuff. My lawyer was cool though. She had everything straight, or so it seemed. I let myself trust her. They sent me back here in detention—for how long, who knows—to wait for something called a disposition hearing. That's when I'll find out what the consequences will be.

Let me say here and now what I should've said last time I saw you, man. *Thank you for your help.* Or at least for trying to help me. Maybe you know it, maybe you don't, but for a while, I had hooked up with Darryl Campbell at the library every day, working for that proficiency until—well, you can imagine. Anyway, over the summer I found out it's true what you had been saying all along —what you say and do does matter. I guess that's how I ended up in here.

That day in the cafeteria, I wanted to say sorry for all the shit I put you through last year. I knew my problems weren't your fault even though often I acted like they were. Truth be told, I was embarrassed to be two years behind and was tired of seeing *loser* in the eyes of my teachers who, for the most part, had given up on my ass. Except for you, which on one hand was real cool. But at the same time, it pissed me off. Your fucking confidence made me see that all of this life-shit was mostly my own fault and scared the hell out of me. So, in the cafeteria, when I saw the fear in your eyes—instead of telling you how sorry I was and shit, I kept my hand in that backpack, just to see what would happen. Ha! You looked like you was about to run out of the joint screaming! By now, you, everybody knows that all I was holding onto in that bag was that old baton of yours. With everything else I wanted to say to you, I'd planned on asking you to keep it for me.

Kind of sappy, huh? Yeah, but the feel of that f18 (even if I *had* thrown the clip in a dumpster)—the feel of it on the back of my hand gave me the courage to hold out a while longer like that—watching you sweat. I would've stood there forever if it wasn't for my sister and her big mouth, bringing in the cops and shit. I mean, didn't she know they could've shot me? But then, maybe her scream was just the warning I needed—maybe it actually saved my ass. And then, there was that fool Fidel! Damn, that was some close shit! I never heard what happened with that dude. I wonder if they got him too, since it was his gun in my bag.

Anyway, you didn't deserve all that shit I know. I know. And I'm sorry.

And—I-I didn't mean for Chucky to die, Mr. Jones, really! I just got mad. And my lawyer thinks the judge believed me. She says I'll have to do time for sure, but she thinks it may not be as bad as it could be. The fact that I fessed up to the deed and that I didn't have a record helped a lot.

I also wanted to tell you that last term, the day before you jumped on me, I woke up in a sweat, wondering if life was even worth living.

I was having a hard time even imagining myself a grown man. I didn't see no point in it since everybody around me was so fucking miserable. You know the deal, stop and frisk, people being shot or getting fucked up on the street for standing on a corner, running a red light, talking shit to or looking cross-eyed at a cop, drugs everywhere, dudes coming up on you wanting to take your shit at gunpoint. Man, it was crazy!

Well, I can tell you, things are different now. I'm going to knock out that GED while I'm in here. Darryl keeps saying he's going to send me books and study materials even though I told him that I'm in school every day here and won't need them. My uncle Gentrale visits often just to check on me. My mom and Sheila call every couple days from Chicago—someplace called Skokie. While my mom will have to come for the hearing, whenever that happens, my sister promises to come see me at the first school break.

And Mr. Jones, I'll see you when I get out—*word* on that.

So, let me leave you this. I know it ain't perfect and all that, but I like it. At least it gets across the message that I got me some hope on.

Now *Old man*—try to give me a beat! LOL…

I wanna get old.
With the passage of time and living a true life,
    comes, wisdom, patience and the gift of hindsight.
I wanna get old.
My friends try to say
I'm afraid of the present,
    afraid of the times
    with all the murder, mayhem, injustice
    and crime.
The shit on the street
    Is enough to defeat
the will to live,
the will to fight
to survive another night – or day.
But to them, I say,
    In spite of all the mess,
Living is still about acceptance

doin' your best,
    taking your lumps, without excuses
and the rest.
    Yeah, I wanna get old,
    and so should we all.
To those who don't agree,
    It's you, not me
    who are the cowards.

Peace—Out,

TIMOTHY THORNTON

AUTHOR'S NOTE

One of the things that racism in America robs black men of
is the opportunity of being ordinary.

In *Ahgottahandleonit*, I wanted to show Tim—a black teen from
the inner city—as possessing a full life. He is trying to make sense
of, to learn his part and role in, what looks to be a dysfunctional and
discouraging world. I wanted the themes of this book to combat how
we too often see such black boys in the news media, literature and
film—as two-dimensional characters or 'super predators,' prone to
violence and crime. The proliferation of recently documented police
killings of unarmed black men and their immediate criminalization in
the media has contributed to this perception in the American psyche.

The reasons for this reality are many and deep. Since America has
yet to own up fully to its twin birth crimes of genocide and chattel
slavery, I suspect this crude depiction of black males will continue for
some time. However, the rapidly changing demographics of our country
give me hope.

In many ways, Tim is an average teenager. He has a father, mother,
sister, teachers, friends, aunts and uncles—and they care about him
deeply. Like the rest of us, he also has choices in his life and choices in
how he reacts to what happens to him from moment to moment.

His life over the summer manifests in a series of decisions that, to
his immature mind, appear to be rational, but in reality they are self-
destructive and related to the pathology of his social-economic status in
America. For many reasons way beyond his ability to fully comprehend,
he finds himself in the tragic circumstance of living in a state of crisis.

Sometimes, to quote a friend, making bad choices is how you find
your way.

I grew up in an environment much like Tim's. However, my folks worked hard for me to be one of the 'good boys' in the neighborhood (lucky me). I worked hard to walk that line of being down or cool and at the same time, studious. Later, I realized that my white counterparts I met in college were unconcerned with such things. They were free to be themselves, were socially and financially secure, had loads of positive models around them and didn't have to be an exception.

In *Ahgottahandleonit*, I try to show the ordinariness of Tim, a young black man born into a social history that has, through oppression, murder and exclusion shaped his and his family's perception of their lives. One of the things that racism in America robs black men of is the opportunity of being ordinary or average. We are either thugs or the exception. Tim is neither. He's a boy in a situation where kids think that exaggerated machismo will gird them against the systemic forces lined up against their lives, will define them as men. Without models and for as long as he lives in an oppressed environment, Tim has to put on the mask to survive.

So, yes, the jive talk and mannerisms are superficial—always have been. The story is in the hearts, decisions and circumstances of the characters.

—Donovan Mixon

ACKNOWLEDGMENTS

A heartfelt thank you to my wife Diana, my family and friends.
A special thank you to Lisa S. and the crew at Cinco Puntos Press:
Lee, Bobby, John, Jessica and Mary.
And to the Floating House crew: Craig, Sheila and Candace.
Much gratitude to my precious writing groups
in Istanbul, Turkey and Evanston, Illinois.